AURAS;
A Story of Love

BRIAN L. MURPHY

Code and Word Solutions, LLC
1603 Capitol Ave.,
Suite 310 A407, Cheyenne WY, 82001
www.codeandwordsolutions.com
Phone: 307–423-0688

© 2023 Brian L. Murphy. All rights reserved.

No part of this book may be reproduced, stored in a retrieval system, or transmitted by any means without the written permission of the author.

Published by Code and Word Solutions, LLC: 09/29/2023

ISBN: 979-8-9888698-2-5(sc)
ISBN: 979-8-9888698-3-2(e)

Because of the dynamic nature of the Internet, any web addresses or links contained in this book may have changed since publication and may no longer be valid. The views expressed in this work are solely those of the author and do not necessarily reflect the views of the publisher, and the publisher hereby disclaims any responsibility for them.

Contents

Chapter One 1
Chapter Two 7
Chapter Three 10
Chapter Four 20
Chapter Five 24
Chapter Six 32
Chapter Seven 34
Chapter Eight 38
Chapter Nine 44
Chapter Ten 51
Chapter Eleven 59
Chapter Twelve 62
Chapter Thirteen 80
Chapter Fourteen 90
Chapter Fifteen 96
Chapter Sixteen 101
Chapter Seventeen 111
Chapter Eighteen 120
Chapter Nineteen 124

Chapter Twenty 128
Chapter Twenty One 144
Chapter Twenty Two 151
Chapter Twenty Three 156
Chapter Twenty Four 165
Chapter Twenty Five 173
Chapter Twenty Six 187
Chapter Twenty Seven 192
Chapter Twenty Eight 200
Chapter Twenty Nine 205
Chapter Thirty One: Epilogue 220

Chapter One

THE COMMITTEE HAD BEEN FORMED decades ago, by well-intentioned men, determined to use their wealth and experience to affect changes for good in the world. Tonight, July 23rd 1976, however, what one faction called a solution could be described as mass murder.

In the rented conference room overlooking the San Francisco Bay, the florescent lights hummed and flickered on, as the diagram of a human form disappeared from the overhead screen. Standing there as his eyes adjusted, Doctor Richard Coleman put down his pointer and concluded his presentation.

"It's been a hard grind coming up with it, gentlemen," he told the two men seated, still watching the screen. "What we have is an encapsulated toxin, the coating of which behaves very much like that of a cold remedy you might buy over the counter. But, when heated and injected, the active ingredients will be carried to all of the major organs, becoming especially concentrated in the liver and kidneys. Once in position, the 'tiny time pill' effect will release toxins. If there has been only a small amount injected, the effect will be painful, yet minimal, and the subject will live. If, however, a large amount is present, as would collect in a short time if the subject were a heavy user, the effect will be a general shutdown of all filtering systems of the body and the subject will die, and die fairly quickly. We know it works on rats, and it should work equally well on your subjects. Of course, we'll only be certain when it's been field tested."

As the lights flickered on, and as Coleman finished his remarks, the stabbing pain just behind the younger man's eyes spiked. Pursing his lips, and closing his eyes, he breathed deeply. The older man, pausing for a moment, reached over to squeeze his forearm, whispering, "Concentrate. "The younger man began counting back from ten. By Seven, the pain had ebbed. By three it had gone.

As in their previous meetings, John Ferrel and Arthur Gorman were alone at the briefing, and they remained seated in the conference room as the doctor packed his case and left the room. He would be called later and given further instructions. Having collected himself, Ferrel turned his attention to Arthur and noticed a slight tremor in the older man's hand and in his voice. He sat respectfully quiet, wondering if he had actually noticed them before.

The previous January, Dr. Coleman, a biological chemist, had been contacted by Ferrel and offered funding to identify or develop a substance, that when mixed with heroin would build up in the human body over a suitable number of usages, yet had the possibility of going undetected using normal laboratory procedures. The final requirement, and the ultimate point of the project itself, was that, after the final injection, and assuming the quantity in the user's system was sufficient, the material had to be adequately toxic to cause the user's death.

Still staring at the blank screen, Arthur exhaled slowly, explaining again. "As we sit here, drug use is sapping our economy's strength, and the strength and vitality of economies around the world, costing all of us billions of dollars every year. It's simply got to be stopped. If we're successful, we can eliminate large numbers of hard-core users and convince anyone else who might consider using drugs to abstain. Only then, when the demand is eliminated, and ending the growing demand has always been the key, will there cease to be a drug problem. Try to imagine the positive effect a success here would have on the world." Ferrel, still struck by the coldness of it, spoke softly. "Arthur, this is wrong." His eyes locked on the older man. "Thousands of people are going to die."

"Wrong? Nonsense," the older man responded, clapping his hands together to emphasize his words. "Those people are dead already. And please," he said glaring into his companion's eyes, "spare me the sentimentality. No one forced a needle into their arms. Our efforts simply eliminate their personal addiction, now that it's become a drain on the rest of us."

The room was silent for five seconds, then ten, as Arthur closed his eyes briefly and regained control. Then he continued with a new calmness. "By holding the price low, below the street price of the drug, we can move however much laced heroin as we can make through known distribution channels beginning in Miami. Then, market forces will carry the product to those we're trying to reach, which again are only the heaviest users of hard-core drugs. The casual user will scarcely be affected. Once the addicts have consumed enough of the altered drug, large numbers of them will begin to die, leaving the doctors and other social workers perplexed and with no time to react. Before the gears of the medical machine can begin to mesh, our material will have had its effect. The job will be finished." Arthur was sure he saw fear in his young friend's eyes, but pressed on.

"Meanwhile, unless I've completely misread human nature," he continued, "local citizens, as well as politicians, will notice that the economic drains on their city and state government services are trending downward as the number of 'former users' rises. Of course, the pillars of their communities won't be able to say so publicly, but they'll appreciate the outcome. And the long-term effect on the finances of their cities and states will allow them to invest more time and money in searching for answers to other problems. We'll begin on the east coast, and then spread out from there."

Ferrel's faith in the older man, and his sense of their shared mission rekindled, he nodded. The most gruesome effect of their project could only be marginally worse than the current situation in many large cities around the world. Even given a larger number of bodies on the streets in the short-term, over the long-term, the numbers would dwindle to nearly zero as the majority of users would realize what was happening around them and begin to fear taking any drug. Arthur rose from his seat and picked up his attaché case from where he had laid it on the floor. Knowing young John Ferrel wanted to believe, he patted him on his shoulder and said, "At any rate, it's a job that somebody has to do, and why else did we form the Committee? You and I have followed the bylaws and procedures to the letter. The good doctor thinks his funding is coming from somewhere in Washington, and he wonders if it's CIA, DEA, or Army Intelligence. On the other hand, we may help lift a terrible financial burden from decent people and set the stage for the economic advancement that most of the civilized world is waiting for. For now, though we'll keep things under wraps. When the test results are in, we'll unveil the project as a whole for the rest of the members." The reaction of the other Committee members to what they were trying to accomplish was sure to be mixed, but Arthur knew his friends and he knew that they too would appreciate the results. But Dr. Coleman was less predictable. So far, he had said all the right things but Arthur Gorman was not a man who trusted easily.

As for the next phase of the project, the doctor had been very clear from his earliest discussions with Ferrel that he would not take part in anything that had to do with human test subjects. "How you do that is your own affair". By working strictly with the resultant figures from the tests, Doctor Coleman rationalized that he could both maintain his objectivity and add a sense of sterility to the work he had agreed to do. He also had no intention of waking up at night and seeing death in the eyes of young men and women.

Keeping the doctor ignorant about parts of the project he was not directly involved in, had been a part of the plan from the beginning. Even the actual names of the two men he reported to had been kept secret from him. He referred to them only as Sam and Sam Junior, reflecting their age differences. "Junior" phoned at least once a week for progress reports and "came to visit" at least once per month. Neither party wanted any more contact. The outcome of the tests would determine what would happen next.

The testing plan was to collect observations, and when the last subject had been dealt with, specific details such as their ages, weights, and their "toxicity dosage" would be relayed to Dr. Coleman, who would then proceed to adjust his formulation and then produce the initial large batch of material. At that point, they would know what the dilution factor should be.

Should the test prove disappointing, and the material fails to meet one or more of the project's criteria, Coleman would not be given a second chance. His funding would simply stop, and his benefactors would disappear.

But, information about a breakdown in Committee protocol had leaked on June 23rd, in a phone call made by Sherry Minton, a supervisor in Arthur Gorman's finance department, to Ron Patterson, another founding member of the Committee. She left the message that she needed to talk to him about something that "just wasn't right."

Arriving first at the restaurant they had agreed to, Sherry shifted in her seat, while waiting and watching the door. When Patterson arrived, she waved to him and he smiled. As he sat down, she shuffled some papers she had brought with her, but Ron paused, looked at her, then reached out to touch her hand. "How are you Sherr?" he asked. "It's been a while."

Patterson could see the woman was upset, and unsure, as to whether what she was doing was the right thing, or being disloyal. But, as he held her hand with the boyish grin she remembered, she began to feel calmer and more confident. For Sherry, being with Ron had always felt that way. It was the thing she had noticed most about him when they'd first met. It was 1961. He was tall and brash. She was thinner. He said she was beautiful. She was married. It was during a trip she had taken for training. It was his company. When he held her in his arms and made love to her that night, just his touch thrilled her, and made her feel as if she was the universe for him, at least for that night. They had returned to their own worlds, neither mentioning, nor forgetting what they had shared. The bond between them had formed. This morning she had called him.

"It's probably nothing," she began. "But it's not like Arthur to bend the rules." Looking around the room, she drew three stapled sets of documents from her purse. Looking up at Patterson, she continued "These began to come in last February." Sherry looked up to see Ron's puzzled face. "Working for Arthur," she continued. "I've processed dozens of these Request and Approval forms, where one Committee member draws out money for a project and Arthur approves it." Sensing that Ron was still not understanding, Sherry pointed to the name under 'requested by'. "The first signature is John Ferrel. Arthur is approving money for his own department, and no one else is countersigning."

Patterson examined the request forms, and the signatures. Arthur was an old friend, and he knew his signature. However, what Sherry said rang true. Arthur was a major pain in the neck about following procedures, and he had made Ron jump through hoops from time to time. The requests were for lab equipment and construction costs, and there was nothing ominous in that. If someone else had co-signed, Ron wouldn't have given it a second thought. But this was Arthur, and it did seem odd.

"Can I keep these papers?" asked Ron.

"They're copies that I made for you," Sherry said.

"It's probably just an oversight, just Arthur getting old." He smiled. He looked at her, and knew he missed her. Once again, Ron had made her feel like she had done the right thing. Just before he released her hand, he said, "Are you ok, Sherr?" She smiled, and nodded.

He could see the change in her and smiled to himself as he watched her walk out the door. "She is beautiful" he said to himself. Then, quickly glancing over the documents, he shook his head slightly, folded them, and slipped them into his jacket pocket. "Maybe Arthur is getting too old for this game," he said, then chuckled.

Chapter Two

In Longstown, New York, Saturday, July 23 brought an odd mixture of sadness and joy. The cab to the airport was later than Tim Conolly had asked for, but the delay allowed him an extra few minutes to spend with his mother. Standing in the hallway of the house he had grown up in, and looking at her while they each tried to create a conversation, Tim suddenly felt terribly alone. Today was a turning point in his life, and he knew it. Just as the taxi arrived, his father and his brother Patrick came down the stairs. Da took his son in his arms and gave him a healthy squeeze. "Call when you get there, son," he said "or your mother will worry. And don't forget to write to her whenever you can." Mike Conolly fished for other words, and later he would think of hundreds of things that he wished he had said to his son. But, in a strange way, the situation was better as it was. Tim knew that his parents loved him, and, he also knew that he had to leave. They had done their job of parenting, and he was prepared, both mentally and emotionally, to move ahead. But there were tears forming in his eyes that he had meant to hide.

Patrick helped lighten the situation by calling his younger brother a knucklehead and making Tim swear to check out the "California Girls" once he got there. Tim smiled and promised that he would. "And don't forget," Patrick laughed and went on "you're coming back for Christmas, and girls make great stocking stuffers."

When the cab sounded its horn, Da and Patrick carried Tim's bags out, once again leaving Ma alone with him. "Tim Conolly," she began "you take the pride of your family with you to California, just as Casey did when he left home for the Navy. Be yourself, and never, never let anything prevent you from living your own life. Learn to enjoy all the newness around you and make it part of what you can become."

The speech was vintage Ma, but it helped fill the silence, and no more than that was necessary. The cab driver sounded his horn again and Da came back inside to get him. "Come on you two," he said. "Or you'll both start blubbering and this whole thing will get messy. Kiss your mother, boy. And promise her you'll write."

Tim kissed her and promised again that he'd write as often as he could, then his father led him to the cab. He pressed a twenty-dollar bill into his son's hand, and said, "Have a drink on the plane and buy something to read." Inside the cab, Tim watched his family wave goodbye and he idealized what he saw as the final scene in an overly-produced movie. In it, he would shout "Stop the cab" and run back into their waiting arms as the credits began to roll. And he did almost hold the tears back. But, this was the way he had asked them to let him go. Not in public, at the airport, but at home, the place where he had been born and where he was brought up.

The house where he had lived, like most others in this area outside Longstown, was joined to its neighbor by a common wall and a shared front porch. Today, even to Tim, it seemed rather small, consisting of only three small bedrooms upstairs and a kitchen and a living area downstairs. But, as a refuge filled with warmth and good times, it had always been more than enough. As the cab pulled away, the thought occurred to him that this could be the last time he'd ever be at home here. Worse yet, this could be the last time he saw his mom or anyone else in his family. Then he chided himself for being overly dramatic.

Tim Conolly had been just above average as a student in high school, but he had seen enough manual labor being performed around him to know that, though it was honorable and was needed by society as a whole, he didn't want to spend his life doing it. And the only way for Tim to avoid doing solid, honest labor, and probably following Da and Patrick into the Carpenters Union, was to go to college and get a degree. And the union helped him. In fact, Da was able to get him what they called a Three-Quarters Scholarship. As his father's dependent, the union would fund three-quarters of his fees and books if he was able to come up with the rest. Hard work was in his blood. Tim had followed in his father's footsteps, in that way, by working hard, every weekend and all of his summer breaks, doing any job that would pay a day's wage.

On May 21, 1976, Timothy Michael Conolly became the first of his family to graduate from college. He received a bachelor's degree in business administration from the School of Business, Kennedy State University. Da had said something profound like he was now the "captain of his own destiny", but what Tim remembered most about the graduation ceremony was how Ma smiled all through it, and that she beamed, rather than cried.

Chapter Three

After all the fanfare of graduation, though, what Tim needed most was a job. He was twenty-four years old, and it was time that he began to make his own way. As a student, he had used the college placement agency to brush up on his resume, and he had sent out a large number of copies to anyone he thought might be interested. In addition, the agency offered role-play practice sessions that helped students prepare for their first meeting with employers. But Tim had never been out of Longstown, and the blue-collar jobs he had done did not weigh heavily in his favor on a resume. Furthermore, he had a hidden concern that the school counselors and other academics, who were supposedly helping him and his fellow students prepare to enter the work-force, had never themselves been out of the classroom. To make things more difficult, he also possessed enough imagination to dream up terrifying scenarios about what was awaiting him when he went to a real interview.

On the other hand, there were thousands of other new graduates out there who were finding jobs, and Tim knew that he was not any less qualified than they were. Contrary to what he had read in textbooks, in the final analysis, finding a career looked to be nothing more than a shot in the dark where one just hoped to get lucky. And he had always been lucky.

Three weeks later, though, with no hot prospects in sight, Tim began to think seriously about giving up and joining the Navy. His brother Casey had become a supply officer aboard a small cruiser, stationed out of Hawaii. And he enjoyed life. In fact, the stories his brother told about traveling and the people he met, namely the women from all the countries that his ship visited, began to make the Navy sound like a far less dreadful alternative.

However, when Tim drove downtown to talk about enlisting, fresh diploma in hand, the recruiter, a chief petty officer with a bad attitude, sat him down and explained a few of what he called the "realities of historic fact". The main "fact" was that the war in Vietnam was over. And, though the chief said he would help him fill out the necessary papers if he wanted to, the Navy really didn't have a need for any more bright young men to trade their diplomas for "ninety-day wonder" Ensign shoulder bars. The chief couldn't tell him not to apply, but he told Tim, "When we needed you were a few years ago."

Once again dejected, Tim began to reconsider the advantages of becoming a carpenter. The phone call that made that choice unnecessary came on June 21, from Mr. Ron Patterson of a company called RDG. "Mrs. Conolly?" the voice asked. The voice was that of an older man, possibly the age one thinks about as grandfatherly. "May I speak to Timothy Conolly from Kennedy State University?"

Tim had been outside on the porch, attempting once again to revise his resume into something that would work a little better, and, he was not having much success. But, he took the phone from his mother, trying to sound more confident than he felt. Actually, though it never showed up on any transcript or resume, remaining outwardly calm during critical times was one thing that Tim had always been good at. Da had said that he was a lot like a duck that way, "smooth as anybody's business on the surface but paddling like crazy under the waterline."

"Yes, this is Tim Conolly," he began. "Can I help you?"

"Can I help you?" he thought to himself.

"That's the lamest thing in the world to say to someone. Why not just say "Stupid here. I'm desperate for any job I can get." But the caller wouldn't know his composure had slipped.

"Mr. Conolly, my name is Patterson. I have received a copy of your resume and your college transcripts and they contain a number of qualities that I'm looking for to fill a position in my firm."

Having received lots of so-called advice from his friends at school, Tim had come to a conclusion that handling a potential employer was a lot like bringing in a large fish. If you were too quick to agree, it could mean that less compensation would be offered for your services. On the other hand, if you didn't seem willing enough, the opportunity might go elsewhere.

The older man continued: "And, if you are not yet decided on another position, I would like to meet with you to discuss the future."

"When did you have in mind, Mr. Patterson? I have some openings on my calendar."

Where did those words come from? But this was Tim at his best and Patterson did not seem to be offended.

"Does your schedule," he said, pausing, "have an opening for around two o'clock tomorrow?"

Tim didn't have anything more than going to the store with Ma scheduled for tomorrow or any day, for that matter.

"Mr. Patterson" Tim replied. "Earlier tomorrow would be better for me. Perhaps we could meet sometime before noon."

Experiencing a thousand deaths in the flash of an eye, Tim waited through the silence on the other end of the line. But then Mr. Patterson came back and he sounded as though he found the conversation amusing.

"All right, young man," he said. "Suppose we meet tomorrow morning at eleven. I'm staying at the Columbia Hotel and I'm told that they have a dining area where we can talk and hear each other. Suppose we meet there for an early lunch."

Tim had played the coy prospect card as far as he dared. After all, the idea here was to get a job, not to tell the story about how cool he had been while remaining unemployed.

"That sounds fabulous, Mr. Patterson." He said. "Eleven o'clock at the Columbia, it is. I'm looking forward to meeting with you."

Perhaps fabulous was overdoing it a bit, but Tim wanted Patterson to know that he really was interested. He mentally kicked himself anyway for using it.

"Fine, Mr. Conolly," said the voice, signing off. "We'll meet then. Good-bye for now."

Tim stood there with the phone in his hand and wondered what had just happened. An older man, from a company he had never heard of, had sought him out from among the hundreds of Kennedy University's new graduates, and had then asked him to lunch in the restaurant of the most expensive hotel he had ever been near. And what had he done? He haggled over the time of the meeting.

From the look on her face, Ma clearly had reservations about the phone call being too good to be true, but she kept them to herself. Tim, however, decided that he didn't know enough about what was normal outside of Longstown to make a judgment. "Besides," he said. "I'll be in a public restaurant. If anything sounds fishy, I'll simply get up and leave."

"Well, kid," said Patrick. "You're the college boy in the family. Maybe it'll work out. Either way though, order yourself something expensive from the menu and just hope the old guy means to pick up the tab."

Even Tim had to laugh. Maybe the situation was not what he expected, but maybe that was okay. Perhaps this company, RDG, did things differently from other companies. That's not illegal. Maybe this was Da's "luck o' the Irish", and the world was about to be laid at his feet. Maybe not. Either way though, at least he had his first real interview set up. And maybe it would work out. It certainly wasn't going to cost him anything, except emotional trauma, to find out.

According to all the textbooks, the best thing a man can wear to a job interview is a dark jacket, a white shirt, and a matching, yet slightly subdued tie. This is called "business attire". The advanced editions of the advice books say to also get a quality briefcase to carry your resumes in. This looks very professional at a time when looking very professional is the point of the exercise.

Tim had gone out weeks before graduation and bought just such an ensemble, including a dark brown, genuine leather case. It had cost him more than he could afford, but now he would at least have a chance to use it. And there were other customary rules for interviews. First, one should arrive at the location of the interview exactly three minutes early. Not five, and never show up late. Three minutes early. And one should always bring one more copy of their resume than there were likely to be people involved in the interview. Being prepared for this kind of surprise looks very, very good. And whatever else one does, no matter that this single meeting could turn out to be the single most crucial moment in your entire life, remain calm and composed. Don't sweat. And don't fidget. Have a firm handshake and look the interviewer straight in the eye when you talk to them. Also, speak firmly and clearly. And don't let yourself seem confused or unsure about any answer you give to a question.

"And have a good time." He chuckled to himself.

It was a stupid situation for a worker to have to go through in order to spend years in the service of someone else, but then again, he had very few choices.

The following morning, the whole family was up at six and Tim mentally began to prepare for his eleven o' clock skirmish with Mr. Patterson. If Patterson asked about "this", he would have "that" to say about it. Reviewing what he thought were his strong points, he practiced different phrasings to make them seem even stronger. Weak points were harder to cover, but Tim was good enough at the verbal tap-dance, or what Da called Blarney, to be wary but not terribly concerned. What he was concerned about could neatly be packaged as the "unknown". However, even after hours of mental preparation, an interview did boil down to a meeting between two sensible people and a conversation about a job.

"Yeah, right." Tim had to laugh again at the silliness of the whole situation. "Hey," he said to himself. "I don't have a job now. And if I don't get this one, I'll be no worse off. They can't take away my birthday." Then, as he knew he would, Tim began anew the whole mental drill of "if he says this, then I'll say that". In the end, the one thing he was most delighted about was that he had asked to have the meeting earlier, just to get it over with.

At seven thirty, Tim drove Da's Chevrolet Impala over to the Columbia twice, just to time how long the drive would take. Both times it took only thirteen minutes, and that was if he hit every red light along the way. Then, back at the house, by nine-thirty Tim was showered, shaved, and standing in front of Ma's full-length mirror, wearing his navy-blue jacket. Ma told him how handsome he looked and Da pressed a crisp ten-dollar bill into his palm. "Don't worry about a thing." he said. "If this Patterson is a cheap bastard, and he doesn't foot the tab, I'll cover you."

By ten thirty-five, Tim was back inside the Impala and enduring the thirteen-minute drive to the Columbia. Again, he drove as slowly as he legally could, and he even stopped at the grocery store to buy extra breath mints. Still, it was nine minutes before eleven when he parked the car in the hotel parking lot. And now the Columbia Hotel's parking lot seemed smaller and quicker to cross than he had remembered. Tim looked at his watch as he entered the front door and saw that it was six minutes until eleven.

Glancing around quickly, he found the sign that read "Gentlemen" and went inside the bathroom, check out how he looked one last time, and more importantly, kill three minutes. At exactly three minutes until eleven, a very cool and composed Tim Conolly approached the hostess in the restaurant and asked if Mr. Patterson had arrived yet. He had not. "Would you like to be seated now?" she asked him. "Or would you rather have a drink in the lounge?"

Another rule. Don't drink alcoholic drinks while interviewing. It just looked bad.

"I would like to be seated, please." he said. "My name is Conolly and I'm meeting a Mr. Patterson for lunch."

"Yes, Mr. Conolly. We expect Mr. Patterson down shortly." The hostess replied. "Can I get you a soft drink while you wait?"

"No, thank you." Tim said, primarily because the only money he had brought was Da's ten, and he thought he still might need that to pay for lunch. "But could I get a glass of water, please?"

It helped his nerves that the restaurant was busy. But, as time passed, Tim began to get irritated by the fact that Patterson had not arrived, yet. After all, Patterson was staying here in the hotel. He had to drive across town. The least the man could do is be on time.

Tim had never been good at waiting. Now, the minutes seemed to crawl by. There were two hostesses covering the entry and three waitresses, each covering a given section of the room. From where he was seated, Tim watched the door and he began to wonder if he had misheard Mr. Patterson when the time was agreed on. "No." he said to himself. "We both agreed to meet at eleven and now it's", he looked again at his watch, "quarter past."

As he continued to watch the doorway, an older man entered the restaurant and at once Tim inexplicably knew he was Patterson.

"This old man is the guy who called me out of nowhere and is going to start my career?" he thought to himself.

Patterson walked slowly with the help of one of the waitresses. When they arrived at Tim's table, the old man nodded an acknowledgment to Tim and he sat down with a softened thud. The waitress tried to regain his arm but Patterson smiled at her and thanked her, and she departed.

"Well Tim," Patterson said, nodding in the direction of the retreating young woman, "What did you think of the legs on that one?" He laughed, and smiled at Tim, held out his hand and introduced himself as Ron Patterson.

Tim took his hand and replied: "Tim Conolly, sir. Pleased to meet you."

Prepared for what he expected as "usual" at the initiation of an interview situation, Tim immediately reached for his briefcase and pulled out a perfectly spaced, crisp copy of his resume. It was apparent from his entrance that Patterson hadn't brought a copy for himself, and Tim was thanking the rules for preparing him for this eventuality. "Oh, put that thing away," said Patterson. "I've read it and it's a good representation of an above-average student who has worked his way through college, with some financial help from his parents. I didn't need to meet with you to understand that."

Tim stared at the man, and felt off balance, realizing that the hours he had spent going through his preparations had probably been wasted.

"What I really want to hear," Patterson continued, "is what your belief structure is. Or even if you have one, that you're aware of."

Belief structure? Tim thought about the question for a minute and he looked at Patterson. Was that a legitimate question to be asked at an interview? What kind of "learned" answer could a young man give? The truth? Okay, he could roll with the punches. Tim had taken psychology classes as part of his major and he had taken an Aristotelian Logic class as a freshman, but most of his basic ideals had come directly from Ma.

"Well, Mr. Patterson," he replied. As he began to answer the question Tim mentally decided that this interview would go nowhere and that he should leave. On the other hand, when you are twenty-four-years-old, how many times does someone ask you to state your beliefs and actually, sits quietly to hear them?

"What I believe" he began. "Is that there are only two facts in the universe that can be proven logically. You can prove your own existence, 'I think. Therefore I am.' And, you can also prove the existence of God, or the 'prime mover'. Everything else might be an illusion." Tim thought he remembered the first being proved by either Euclid or Aristotle, and the second by Thomas Aquinas but he wasn't at all sure of any of it at the moment, so he didn't cite them. The old man was silently listening and nodding his understanding, so Tim finished: "What that means" he said. "Is that there are only two "knowns" in the entire universe, God and me. And it also means that there is nothing as important in all the universe as the relationship between those two points."

Patterson remained quiet, but it seemed that Tim had touched a solid chord. And then Tim said something that he couldn't remember saying before. "And for some unknown reason, God loves me."

Patterson-watched the young man's eyes and Tim braced for an expected rebuttal. But the old man just smiled. After a thoughtful pause, Patterson reached into the inner pocket of his suit jacket and handed the younger man a folded sheet of paper that appeared to be a copy of a help-wanted ad, and an unsealed envelope.

"Tim," he began. "Beginning Monday and running through Wednesday, this ad will appear in a major local newspaper in San Jose, California. What you have in the envelope is a revised version of the resume that you've been circulating. I've altered the presentation of the resume to suit what the ad calls for and what I know the company is looking for. I didn't alter any of the facts, just the way they were stated."

Tim's mind was awash with all the likely questions. "Why me?" "Who is this guy?" "California?"

Looking at the copy of the new resume Tim immediately surmised that the changes Patterson had made did make his resume look far better than the one he had sent out. And he tried to make some mental notes of things that were different from his original. But for now, enough was enough. Returning the resume to its envelope and then handing both back to a somewhat surprised Mr. Patterson, Tim folded his hands together and looked his table partner in the eye. "Okay, Mr. Patterson," he began. "Nobody comes out of the blue to Longstown, New York and hands a just graduated student a job in California. And if they did, I don't think it would be done like this. What I want to know is, who are you and why was I selected for this? And you should know in advance that I'm not going to be part of anything that's underhanded."

"Tim," replied Patterson, calmly. "If you'll work with me, I'm prepared to open a door to you that will give you the power to affect your own history, and perhaps that of a great many other people. You'll just have to trust me."

Chapter Four

In February of 1976, on the outskirts of Monte-Cristi, a port city in northern Haiti, a laboratory allegedly built for research on pesticides and other agricultural chemicals had been constructed and fitted with the latest machinery and equipment in the name of, and under the watchful eye, of Dr. Richard Coleman. Though the source of the doctor's funds remained a secret, whatever tool or piece of equipment he requested for the lab had been paid for in cash, brought to the island and delivered or installed.

The size of the building itself, its inner wall locations, the ventilation scheme, the location of housing for experimental animals, as well as the design of the drainage system beneath the flooring had been done according to the doctor's own specifications. And, as an added incentive, when his current project reached completion, regardless of the outcome, Sam Junior had agreed to reship the contents of the lab to anywhere the doctor specified, and it would all remain his property. During moments of insecurity Coleman wondered how the U.S. Tax payers might react if they knew how much he was spending, but he continued to ask, and his benefactors continued to provide what he asked for, until the size of the building itself became a limitation.

Initially, progress had been good. The lab was completed, the doctor had tested each element on a list of known toxic substances that would build up in the human system over time, and he had monitored how each had reacted when blended with various strengths of heroin and injected into a test animal. When Junior arrived for his April visit, however, the doctor was frustrated and work on the project had stopped.

"I have two or three known substances that are strong enough in tiny doses to kill a bull for standing too close. The problem," he said, "is that, although I can titrate any of them down and mix them with the narcotic, controlling the release is a problem and any kid with a chemistry set will be able to find and identify them. And there's nothing I can do to prevent that."

For the following three hours Ferrel asked Doctor Coleman to explain the details of each method he had tried, attempting to chemically control and disguise the toxin. After talking through each detail and then having to explain each step in layman's term to Junior, it was Coleman himself who hit upon the answer. "We don't have to change anything. We just have to coat it with something."

The change in the plan's focus was accompanied by additional requests for equipment from Doctor Coleman, and once again, everything he asked for was delivered. Three months later, in July, the doctor requested a meeting with Ferrel and his superiors, prepared to display what he had accomplished and to make his recommendations. It was time to test.

Beginning two days after the July 23rd San Francisco meeting, a small sample group of young addicts in Amsterdam were given free doses of the altered heroin and their reactions monitored. John Ferrel had been recruited for the Committee following his premed days at the University of California at Davis. He never went on to med school, choosing instead to follow a strange older man, Arthur Gorman, into what Arthur had promised to be a life different from the "humdrum" that other young men were living. Using the precaution of traveling under another name and false identity papers, when he stepped off the ferry boat that traveled between England and Amsterdam, Ferrel was approached by a young blonde man, wearing a wrinkled, dirty, and stained brown US army coat, who had spotted him as a fellow American. "Hey, man," he said, as if he had recognized Ferrel as a former college roommate. "I'm an American, from New Port Road Island. They call me Pauly," offering his hand, which Ferrel did not take. "Can you maybe spare some change?" Looking into the vacancy of the man's eyes, Ferrel didn't feel the need to check his arms for track marks.

"Sure, man, Pauly, is it?" he replied, noticing and trying to avoid the body odor rising from him. "But maybe you could do something for me, and maybe we can help each other." For the next few hours, with the help of his new friend, Ferrel unloaded his shipment of medical supplies from the ferry and moved them to a prearranged house on the outskirts of the city. Most closely guarded was a brown case that contained dosages of the heroin and the toxin he would mix. Ferrel carried the case himself, and constantly felt under his coat for the 38 caliber pistol he carried. Pauly, after a required bath and new clothes, would serve as one subject, and with his help, his knowledge of other addicts, six other subjects were lined up, each told that they would be given heroin, if they would be injected under Ferrel's observation, and answer rudimentary questions. Three of the recruited subjects were women, according to Coleman's protocol, one white, one black, and Tina Wendal, a small blonde in her twenties, who had come to Amsterdam at eighteen from a troubled family in Northern California. She had been arrested as a child for petty crimes and burglary, been suspended and eventually expelled from high school, and came to Amsterdam on the arm of an older boyfriend who told her they could live free there, without the drag of her parents. Within a year, she had become addicted to heroin, and then turned to legal prostitution to meet their needs. When another girl caught his attention, the boyfriend deserted her, and Tina, now looking like a small animal with stringy hair, did what she needed to, to survive.

For the next week, each of the subjects was injected with a low enough dose of heroin, without the toxin, to bring them down to a baseline according to their body weight. The subjects complained, wanting more of the drug, but Ferrel explained to them that they would build up their dosages, and that the low point was necessary for the test. Unhappily, the subjects went along. After another week, with charts containing information on each subject's body mass and baseline consumption, Ferrel called them all together for their "reward" dosage. After they had all taken their seats, he placed the needles and the rubber tie-offs at their tables and instructed them to inject. Premixed and prepared for them, the addicts tied off their arms inserted the needles and felt the drug as they pressed down on the syringe. John Ferrel watched from behind them, as they slumped down on their chairs. Knowing which syringe had which strength of the toxin, there were no surprises as he watched them over the next hours, simply stop breathing, turn mildly blue, and die. Tina Wendal, and one of the other men, had been given the lightest dosages, and therefore would not die of the overdose. But, their data collected, they could not be allowed to tell authorities what had gone on there. Days after Ferrel had disposed of whatever evidence he could, he rented a car to drive to Berlin, where he changed to still another identity, and he flew to Mexico. From there he would return to Haiti and Dr, Coleman, with his results. Amsterdam officials would report the deaths of seven addicts, found in a single room. Five had died of overdoses. Two had died of 38 caliber bullets to their heads.

Chapter Five

The call from RDG's personnel department, asking Tim to come to California, came two weeks later on Monday July 11th, followed by an interview which took place one week after that, on Monday July 18. "What we're looking for," Jack Abrams said, trying hard to be aloof. "Is a bright young person to help us develop a product planning function for our new manufacturing unit."

Tim had only taken one course at Kennedy State that had anything to do with production control. And the class had only been a computer simulation, with a limited number of variables, that had been loaded into it by an instructor who had never worked in industry. That was possible problem number one. Possible problem number two was the fact that he had not been terribly interested in the subject and had done only marginally well in the class. But this was not the time to bring these facts into the conversation. "Well, Mister Abrams," Tim said. "The basics of any control function are pretty straightforward, but each application has its own set of problems. Handling those problems is what makes the job interesting."

Tim had put on his tap shoes and now Abrams was going to see the dance. Abrams had referred to a "new manufacturing unit" and

Tim hoped that Abrams, as the new manager of the department, knew less about control systems than he did.

"What kind of system are you using today?" Tim asked. "If you're in business now, you must have either developed a system and put it in place, or just let one evolve around what was necessary to getting the job done. Either way, systems that evolve like that are usually pretty good for the businesses they're intended for, especially if the business is fairly small and new."

Momentarily Abrams's demeanor softened. Maybe this "college kid" was not going to be the "pain in the ass from upstairs" that he had been concerned about. Maybe the kid could actually add some value. "Well Tim," Abrams said. "As you probably know, RDG has been a research and development company, chiefly funded by the army. We developed a range of medical tests for the guys coming back from Vietnam, primarily screening soldiers for use of illegal drugs. The army had agreements with several companies across the country, and a few 'across the pond' in England. But the founders of RDG thought that their technologies were at least as good as the competition. Once the war began to wind down, they decided to broaden the spectrum of identifiable agents, and to offer these same kinds of technologies to the general public. If we can develop a few more uses for what we have and then position the resultant products well enough in the market, the company founders feel we stand a good chance to establish ourselves as the leading technology in the industry. And as a result, the initial investors believe they can make a tremendous amount of money. That's why we're about to go into a hiring frenzy."

Even if Tim knew nothing more than what Abrams had just said to him, he would have found what he had just heard exciting.

"As to how we're handling the function now," Abrams continued. "One of the women that had been doing contract billing, was bored with that and she offered to handle the planning function until we found out if the new venture was going to work out. Now, because it looks like it's going to grow like a weed, she needs some help."

"Mr. Abrams," Tim began. "Clarify for me what my professional relationship would be with the woman from Contracts. Do I report to her? Does she report to me? Or do we both report to someone else?"

The question clearly made Abrams uncomfortable and he began to fish, in his mind, for the correct wording of the answer. Tim noticed and began to wonder why the man wasn't more clear about his own organization. "Let me explain it to you this way," he said. "Mary, the woman from Contracts, is not seen by the 'powers that be' to have the necessary talents nor the drive to lead the planning function into the future. Frankly, I disagree. I think she's done a fine job and that she'll continue to do so."

Though puzzled as to why he had been told such intimate information about another employee, the explanation only skirted the issue. "Mr. Abrams?" he asked. "How do I fit in, if I join your planning group?"

In response, Abrams fished silently through the center drawer of his desk, giving Tim more time to think. After his strange introduction to Patterson, and Abrams' lack of confidence, Tim determined that, in spite of the possibilities for growth, this was probably not the job he should accept.

Abrams finally pulled out a crumpled organization chart, and generally described the roles of each of his seven direct reports and their staffs. As Tim studied the chart, and considered what he now knew about Abrams, it was clear that even though each of Abrams' direct reports appeared to be equals on paper, it was far more likely that he ran the department, heavily influenced or even manipulated by his favorites. And those favorites would be Abrams' old friends. In short, the "college boy" wouldn't have a chance. When he was offered the job, Tim was prepared to shake hands with Abrams and decline.

To Tim's surprise, though, Abrams made no job offer that day. And when the interview was over, he just said that they "would be in touch". Maybe that was just as well.

Just after two o'clock, Tim left RDG and walked across the parking lot to where he had left the rental car. He realized that he hadn't eaten anything that whole day and, now that the interview was over, he was hungry. It also occurred to him that Abrams hadn't even offered him a cup of coffee. But that was probably okay, too. He was dead tired, and the time change between the coasts had made it impossible for him to sleep the night before. When he got back to his hotel, he would call for room service, and then take a nap.

The Driftwood Hotel kitchen did a fine job with the beef over noodles that Tim ordered from room service, and his exhaustion would have made any bed a wonderful experience. Twenty minutes after the food arrived, around three-thirty, he had hung up his jacket and pants, draped his shirt over the only chair in the room, and was fast asleep with a muted local talk show on the television. Tomorrow he would fly home, and then he would have to explain to Da and Patrick why the trip hadn't worked out the way he had planned. Ma would see in his eyes that he was disappointed and she would say something to make him feel better. She always did. And it always helped. But explanations would wait. And, though it was quite early according to local time, Tim wanted to sleep until tomorrow morning. He had turned the television set on, with the sound very low, so that he didn't feel so all together lonely.

At roughly five thirty, two hours into a deep sleep, the phone in Tim's room sounded loudly and persistently. Though he wasn't expecting to hear from anyone, he had given Ma the number of the hotel, just in case something happened and she needed to get in touch with him. It might be her, calling just to make sure that he knew they were thinking about him. However, what he got was a surprise. The call was from Patterson. "So, Tim," he began. "How did it go? Are you as excited about coming to RDG as we are about having you aboard?"

Tim was always a little grumpy when he first woke up, and after spending his morning with Abrams, the last thing he wanted to talk about was RDG. After Patterson's happy opening question, though, Tim let the line go quiet as he tried to collect his thoughts. "Mr. Patterson," he finally replied. "I don't know how much direct knowledge you have about Abrams' department, but I think what you have there is a 'go nowhere' trap that doesn't offer whoever takes it much of a chance at a future. You know how much I appreciate being considered, and I need a job, but I would be coming a long way for not much. Besides, Abrams didn't offer me the job."

Patterson had expected some response, but this was not it. Concerned, but not wanting to continue on the phone, the older man asked Tim if he had made any plans for dinner. Tim hadn't meant to be awake for dinner, so he replied that he had not. Patterson asked that he be "allowed to buy you a meal, before you go home. And Tim," he added. "Don't make up your mind about our arrangement until I see you for dinner. Okay?"

Tim agreed. When Patterson asked if seven o'clock in his hotel restaurant was okay with him, he agreed again, and they both hung up.

Sitting on the edge of the bed, looking around his room, Tim began to reevaluate how the meeting with Abrams had actually gone. Patterson was obviously surprised when he was told that the interview had gone badly. He must have either assumed that the session would go well, or someone at RDG must have told him it had. Immediately, Tim began to wonder if he had overreacted. Or maybe he had misread what was going on. Again, and again he went over the entire morning, in his mind. And again, he felt he had gotten a true and accurate picture. "I didn't have to get through college, and then move all the way to California, to be some body's lackey." he said to himself.

Watching the clock in his room, at five minutes after seven, Tim got up from his bed. He had already dressed, except for putting on his shoes. Looking into one of the mirrors on the walls to check his hair, he saw the reflection of the clock again. As he went out the door, he smiled. He was now a full seven minutes late for his appointment.

The elevator stopped immediately outside the entrance to the restaurant and when the hostess asked him: "How many in your party?" Tim smiled.

"I'm meeting a Mr. Patterson, for dinner." he said. "Has he arrived yet?"

Just then Tim spied the older man sitting at one of the tables in the back of the room. Patterson looked up, smiled, and waved. "Never mind," Tim said to the young woman. "He's right over there."

As he sat down at the table and once again shook the old man's hand, Tim was prepared to let Patterson try to convince him to take the job. But it would be a hard sell.

"Well, boy." Patterson said. "So, what's your problem?"

Immediately, instead of his being in the strong position of being the one to be convinced to stay, with that one question Patterson had taken control of the conversation. And Tim was left in the completely childish position of trying to explain why he was unhappy. The old man was very good. However, far from getting upset, Tim found himself appreciating how well the old man had turned the tables on him. But he held the trump card. "Mr. Patterson," he said, looking the old man in the eye. "I have a return ticket for a flight in the morning, and I expect to be on that plane. If there is any reason for me to come back here, now is the time for me to hear it. Like I told you on the phone, the situation that Abrams has going is hopeless. And, though you and I have agreed about a number of things, I'm not excited about spending a lot of time in a hopeless situation. The minute I agree to work for him, I become a flunky to a Contracts Billings person. And years later, I'll be no better off."

The old man had folded his hands in front of him and was again listening carefully to what his companion was saying. Oddly, Tim began to feel calmer, somehow stronger, and more assured about himself as the old man looked into his eyes. "Tell me." Patterson replied, as he picked up a piece of bread and began to butter it. "Did you think you were going to be made king, the first day?"

The question, again, was not the one Tim expected. Patterson put the piece of bread down on his plate and continued: "Of course you have to be brought in at a beginner level. Good gracious, son. You are a beginner.

You don't know anything about how a business really works. I'm impressed though, that you picked up on Abrams's situation. Actually, you're quite correct. Abrams is a good man, but he may not be the type of leader we will need in his position. Fairly soon, say in the next year or so if things don't change for the better, he may have to be replaced. But for now, to get us off the ground, he'll do fine."

Just then a waitress appeared and asked the two men if they had time to decide on what they were going to order. Patterson said that he had. And then he smiled and winked knowingly at Tim. "I had a little more time, this time."

They ordered, the waitress left, and Patterson continued: "Tim," the old man began. "Today you formed an opinion and you made up your mind, impulsively. And at your age, some of that is to be expected. But you've got to try to see things from a much larger perspective. Back in Longstown, when we first met, I offered you an experience that would open your eyes to a whole new world and to a whole new way of thinking. You're going to have to trust me to do right by you, or we're both headed for frustration."

Tim had nothing to say and, in fact he now wished that he had said nothing to begin with. Patterson seamed to understand how he felt and both men knew that the incident was only part of a learning situation. But Patterson reassured him about the situation at RDG. "In some ways, I guess I did bring you out to California to be Mary's flunky. For her, this new position is as far as she is going to go. And that's okay. It's as far as she wants to go. But for you, it's a great opportunity to break into a new situation and to begin to understand the people around you. That's the key."

The waitress returned with their meals, and Patterson watched her as she walked away.

Patterson continued while picking up his fork. "You're a big blank slate now, son. And, over the next year or so, you're going to be exposed to a great things that will be new to you. You should enjoy this time for what it is, but never forget that it's all a necessary preparation."

Tim listened, quietly. There had always been a great deal about what Patterson had referred to as an opening of his eyes that he had taken purely on faith. In fact, he still didn't even know exactly what the phrase meant. However, back in Longstown, Patterson had asked for trust while he proved himself trustworthy. And, primarily because he had no other offers, Tim had agreed. And, in fact, the old man had thus far done everything that he had said he would. As a result of having faith Tim was now sitting in California, on the verge of being offered an opportunity to break into a company that was set to grow by leaps and bounds. And, he was being offered a position that he could learn about and grow into. As they spoke, it was even clear that Tim's situation with Abrams and his cronies had been well thought through.

"And Tim," the old man continued. "Don't be so fast to count Abrams and the others out. Some of them are really fine people. Some of them are better people, in some ways, than you and I are. Just learn as much as you can about what they can teach you and about the kinds of people they are. Trust me." This time he chuckled to himself as he spoke the words that summed up their entire history. "You'll be glad you did."

The two men continued sharing stories about Tim's family and about Patterson's ill spent youth until nearly midnight. The next morning's sunshine found Tim Conolly in bright Irish spirits and humming a tune that he remembered Da humming when he was a child. Over the years the words had been jumbled in his mind, but he remembered the tune, and it brought back warm memories. Inside him, there was a new sense of balance. Even the flights back to Chicago and then through to New York seemed a bit shorter than he remembered just two days before. In fact, after his initial fear during takeoff, Tim actually began to relax. This process, however, was quickly halted when the airplane went through a small area of turbulence over the Rocky Mountains and Tim began to pray. Thursday, at twelve noon Longstown time, Jack Abrams phoned and offered him the planner position at slightly more money than even Tim expected. He accepted.

Chapter Six

His position at RDG arranged only two days before, Saturday morning Tim was leaving home. His taxi arrived at the airport fifty-five minutes before his flight, leaving him plenty of time to check his two suitcases and to find a book in the gift store.

That morning's excursion would be Tim's third fight in an airplane. The prior Sunday, just one week before, he had flown out to California to interview with Mr. Jack Abrams at RDG. His second flight was the return trip last Tuesday, And this Saturday morning, his third. What Tim knew about flying was that it frightened him in a way that nothing else in life did. Casey said it was ridiculous and had called him a "white knuckled flyer". But every time the plane he was on went through an air pocket or encountered turbulence, Tim's whole body would tense, sure that he was falling to his death. And it was almost worse on his nerves when nothing bad happened.

It was crazy to do something that scared him so much. But, there was no other way to get between New York and California as quickly as he needed to. Tim decided, however, to convert his fear into a positive thought. He would pray during takeoff, and he would pray during landings. And he would pray frantically during turbulence.

Not totally convinced that his fears were unjustified, Tim had told Da after his return trip: "If I'm on my way to meet my maker, I want to have talked to Him recently." Da laughed.

After a fifty-seven-minute stopover in Chicago, painfully requiring an additional landing and another take-off, and a continuing flight of nearly five hours, Tim Conolly landed at San Jose Municipal Airport in San Jose, California. The outside temperature had been announced by the Captain as being eighty-four degrees, but because the air lacked the wetness of the air on the east coast, it felt much cooler. In fact, he thought it felt great. The weather in what was called the San Francisco Bay Area had actually been one of the factors that he later told people, had helped him decide to join RDG. The money the company offered him was very good, but, for reasons that were now clear to him, Tim had been instructed not to tell anyone at RDG about his conversations with Patterson, either about the job itself or about the other experiences that lay in store for him. He would, though, enjoy this weather.

Since RDG, or rather his new boss Jack Abrams, had insisted that Tim start immediately, it was made a condition of their agreement that he was to have the use of a rental car for four weeks, while looking for his own transportation. RDG had also made reservations, and agreed to pay for a maximum of four weeks at the Driftwood. Once he landed and retrieved his luggage, all Tim had to do was get to the car rental agency and to his hotel.

Chapter Seven

THE RENTED GRANADA ACCELERATED EASILY out of the airport parking lot, and then merged flawlessly onto the freeway. Truly, there was a tangible feeling of power, while sitting behind the wheel of a car, that probably helped to explain the California obsession with the automobile. As far as he was concerned, this Granada was a new car and his lack of familiarity with it gave operating the vehicle a sense of danger, which Tim found that he liked. In Longstown, while he was in school, there had never been a need for him to own a car. And when he did need to drive somewhere, there had always been the Impala. In addition, as a student, he could never have afforded the price of insurance and other upkeep that came with owning a car, even if he could have come up with the purchase price.

Having returned, hopefully for a while, to California, Tim now began to feel the ticking of an internal clock. First, he had to get a car of his own and then he had to find a permanent place to live. Or maybe the order should be reversed. Either way, both chores had to be taken care of, and fairly quickly. Another item on his agenda, one he could handle tomorrow if the stores were open, was to get out and buy more clothes to wear to work. The two bags that he had brought with him from home contained his dark jacket, some dress shirts, and a few pairs of pants, which he could match up and wear for his first couple of days at RDG. But he had kept his eyes open during his interview with Abrams, watching how the other people at the company were dressed, and he would clearly need a larger wardrobe. Now, though, he just wanted to get to the hotel again and find his room. Tomorrow he would go clothes shopping, but his top priority for this weekend, and the reason he did not wait until Sunday to arrive in California, was that he wanted to relax and to be at his best for his first day on the job. "First impressions," he said to himself. "In the long run they might not make much difference, but in the short run they can probably either hurt or help a lot."

Monday morning at six o'clock, the wake-up call from the front desk found Tim wide awake. As for a starting time Monday morning, Abrams had not said anything, but Tim expected that, as the head man of a new and growing department, Abrams would very likely arrive at work by eight o'clock in the morning. And, knowing that he had a new man starting that morning, Abrams might even arrange to be there a bit early. If that was true, Tim did not want to arrive even a minute later than eight. And, it probably wouldn't hurt if he, too, were just a bit early.

As he pulled the Granada into the parking lot at RDG, Tim checked his watch. Surprisingly, it was seven minutes before eight and there were only three other cars in the entire lot. One of the cars, an old Rambler American, caught his eye because it had a faded bumper sticker that read "BIO IS MY BAG". Skipping a space but parked near the Rambler, was a brand new, gold colored Camaro. Tim decided to skip another space and park on the other side of the Rambler. The third car in the lot was a Volvo, but one that looked to be about ten years old. It was parked, alone, on the opposite side of the lot.

Taking a final check to make sure there wasn't anything sticking between his teeth, and that his tie was straight, Tim got out of his car and proceeded with unfelt confidence to the front entrance of

RDG. When he entered the lobby, he learned to whom two of the cars outside belonged. Seated in one of the four available chairs in the lobby, and wearing a dress that was "overly formal" to about the same degree as was his own dark jacket, was a young lady, who surely only weeks before had been a student, herself. She was also one of the cutest girls he had ever laid eyes on. Sure, she was attractive, standing only about five foot three and wearing her blonde hair in a pony tail. But what struck Tim was an undeniable quality that somehow said that "this girl would be fun to get to know".

The other woman in the lobby was seated at the receptionist's desk and it was she that Tim attempted to introduce himself to. She wore an RDG badge that had a six-digit number on it, and then spelled out her name, "Hartcourt, Alice".

"And who are you here to see?" she snapped at him before he could utter a word.

"My name is Tim Conolly. And I'm here to see Mr. Abrams."

"Well, have a seat," she said, pointing to a chair by the door. "Abrams isn't here yet, either."

Alice Hartcourt stood approximately five foot nine, had a lovely mane of flowing blonde hair and was knock out beautiful. This morning, and every morning thereafter that Tim noticed, she wore a tight fitting, short skirt that truly accentuated a figure that, even at this time in the morning and under these circumstances, had to turn a young man's thoughts to things other than work. She was lovely. As it turned out, though, it was only when she opened her mouth that it became apparent that Alice Hartcourt's nature was somewhat different. "Excuse me," she said to Tim. "What's your name again?"

Tim was taken back by her tone. Surely, he hadn't been inside the building long enough to offend her, or anyone else. "Conolly, Tim Conolly." he replied.

With that, Alice Hartcourt pushed a button on the intercom that sat on the receptionist's desk, and alerted someone on the other end: "He's here. Better come get him." she said.

Still on the phone, as she prepared a Temporary badge for Tim, she paused, then she answered the other person on the phone: "They say he is, but not to me. Come get him." Then she hung up.

For roughly ten minutes, Tim remained sitting in the lobby. Then, an older woman, about forty, walked out of a nearby door and introduced herself. "Good morning. You must be Tim." she said as she extended her hand. "I'm Mary Rose. Mr. Abrams asked me to keep an eye out for you. He'll be in later. Why don't we go back and get you settled in?"

Tim shook Mary's hand and smiled. "So, this is Mary," he thought to himself. But what he said was: "Pleased to meet you."

Chapter Eight

Silently, Mary Rose lead the way down a long-walled passage, toward the interior of the building until she came to a solid wooden door, with a large blue sign with white lettering that read "Materials Department". The part of the building that he was now looking at was definitely not the same one that Tim had been shown during his interview with Abrams. This new area was strewn with packing boxes and file drawers that indicated that it might have only become the "Materials Department" that morning. He followed Mary inside.

"So, this is it," he thought, slightly disappointed, but nonetheless ready to get started.

The remaining members of the Materials Department, including Abrams and two schedulers, Al and Dave, arrived between eight thirty and nine that initial morning to sort through the mess that was their offices. The Purchasing Supervisor, Roberta North, a thin yet very attractive woman, arrived, looked around at what had been her collection of well-organized files, laughed a little and grimaced. Then she and her data entry clerk Jill went right to work returning the files to the order in which she was determined that they would be kept. Judging by their jovial entrance and banter about their weekend activities, Tim decided he might enjoy this new place, after all.

After determining where Tim's desk would be, and exchanging a few pleasantries and introductions, Abrams and Mary decided that a good introduction to the company, and to what the company was involved in, would be to have Tim attend a "mini-seminar" that was being given over in the Research Department. "Then maybe I can get some of my work done." she said to Abrams. "I got in here around six this morning and I've only just now got my files back in order."

Mary took Tim out through the back door of their building and across to a nearby building that also sported the initials RDG over the doorway. The interior of this building was dedicated to laboratory space and it smelled a bit like burning sulfur. Over the door of one large room was a sign that read "Research Conference Room A". A number of people were milling around, both inside and outside of the room, and Mary indicated that this was their destination. She told him: "These things take about two hours, and it will be good for you to hear about what the Post Docs are working on. When it's over, come back to our area."

Tim was told later that a Post Doc was someone who had earned a Doctorate in his field but was working for a private business under a contract between the company and the University. However, since he had earned his bachelor's degree, and was now determined to avoid any more higher education, the idea of staying in the educational system long enough to get a doctorate degree seemed absurd. "But, it takes all kinds."

Tim stood outside the conference room door, all dressed up in a strange place, and not knowing a soul. Plus, as opposed to his dark jacket ensemble, most of the people entering or leaving the conference room were wearing white lab coats, blue jeans, and tennis shoes. The meeting room itself looked to be about the same size as the one that he and Mary would share in the other building. Instead of being empty, though, this room's walls were lined with folding chairs. There were also ten rows of chairs that had been set up in the center. Tim, knowing very well that he had been sent there to kill time and yet hoping that he might learn something, sat down in an unoccupied chair along the wall opposite the door, and toward the front of the room. As a large number of people kept arriving, though, it became fairly obvious that there was not going to be enough seats to hold everyone who wanted to be there. Already, people were beginning to sit on the floor.

Apparently, though, sitting on the floor at one of these "mini-seminars" was a common practice at RDG and most people thought nothing of it. As he sat there in his chair, Tim began to be engaged in short but welcomed conversations with some of the people sitting around him. There was a woman on his left who he guessed might be Chinese, who asked him in heavily accented English who he was and what department he worked for. When he replied that this was his first day at RDG and that he would be working in the Materials group for Mr. Abrams, she smiled broadly and extended her hand. "Welcome to RDG," she said. "My name is May Fong and I work in Biological Research."

Tim shook her hand and returned her smile. Then, an older man on his other side also offered his hand and introduced himself. "Welcome aboard," he said.

"I'm Rich Barlow."

He couldn't remember if Barlow had said what he did at RDG or not, but looking at him, Tim hoped that Rich did something which allowed him to wear his lab coat most of the time. As the older man sat there, his tie was both wrinkled and badly tied. It looked as though the man's shirt, a cheap green throwback, had been stained by remnants of this mornings' breakfast. But Tim had heard about lab scientists being a strange lot, and he wondered what he would dress like after having been closed up in a lab for a few years. After a few minutes of small talk with Barlow and with some of the other people around his chair, Tim found that he actually liked these people quite a lot. At least they were not all like this mornings' receptionist.

For the following two hours, Tim sat among the scientific minds of RDG and tried valiantly to follow the subject matter they were discussing. The "mini-seminar" appeared to be an "update" session about a series of new products that RDG might be able to provide to the market in the future. But these folks were not the sales people of the company, nor were they the accountants. Instead of worrying about market conditions and cost estimates, like Tim or any other business school graduate, these people were interested in discussing how the various cells that they were observing, formed and interacted, as well as what common properties these new cell growths exhibited during their various levels of mutation. At least that's what he thought they were talking about.

In a nutshell, as Tim would try to explain to Da later that night, RDG sold "test kits" to medical labs, that would react in a predetermined way to the presence of whatever chemical, they were looking for. And, the technology was precise enough to cause different reactions, based on the concentration of the chemical. "What that means," he would tell his father, "is that if you had to maintain a certain amount of heart medicine, or any other kind of monitored medication, in your blood stream, this test could tell if you were within what they call the therapeutic range where there would be enough of the medication in your bloodstream to be doing you some good. The test could also tell you if you were above what they call the toxic level, where there was too much of it in your blood and that it might be hurting you to take it."

Da interpreted what Tim told him to mean that RDG had come all the way to New York to ask his son to come to Sunny California because they needed him to keep their "lab doctors" in line. Tim tried to explain further, but sometimes Da only listened until he heard something he wanted to hear.

After the lecture, he left the research building and made his way back to the door of the Materials Department. As he entered the open area between the offices, Tim could see that things had begun to take shape. Alice Hartcourt, the receptionist, had set up a desk and some files outside of a door that now had a sign on it that read

"Materials Manager". As he walked by Tim could see that Abrams was talking on the phone, with his back to the door.

There were two new signs that had been put up. One, attached to the small office furthest from the conference room, read "Purchasing Supervisor". The remaining office's sign that read: "Data Entry". As Tim entered the open area, on his way to his desk, it was clear that Alice had seen him come in, but having made eye contact, she ignored him as he said "Hi, again." and passed by.

When he entered the conference room, Dave, one of the schedulers he'd met earlier, looked up from where he was seated, smiled and said: "Hey, so they let you out."

"Yeah," Tim replied. "I guess they filled my brain with as much as it would take, and then sent me back. I met some nice people though."

On the wall, over Dave desk, the facilities people had mounted a large scheduling board. Across the top were written "week ending" dates. And down the left side were places for what they called "product cards"." Show me how you guys use this thing." Tim asked Dave.

The existence and design of the scheduling board had been chiefly an idea that Dave had brought with him out of the Navy. Al was his supervisor, and he had added a few ideas, but the board was generally known to be "Dave's baby". Almost visibly puffing up his chest, Dave described the operation. "What the board does, is let anybody who wants to see what's going on, look at the status of each product and tell if all the parts are coming together." It avoids the need for a lot of questions, and avoids uncertainty."

Tim had seen and heard enough that morning, and during his interview with Abrams, to know that he and Mary, as the "planners", were responsible to initiate and monitor the production of each phase of the respective products. But what he didn't know yet was the mechanism for doing that.

Dave picked up one stack of blue, eight and a half by eleven inch, cards and handed it to Tim. "You just fill in the blanks, and we'll get it done for you." Dave added this last with an evident pride of the work that he and Al had been known to do.

Mary had been working with her head down during their conversation, but now she looked up and asked Tim if he "finally wanted to go over the procedures." Tim nodded and said that he did. Then he wheeled the chair from his desk over to Mary's desk and sat down next to her. "Before we get started," he said to her. "I want you to know that I appreciate you taking the time to go over this stuff with me. I can see how busy you are, but hopefully I can help take some of the pressure off you. In the meantime, I just wanted to say thanks."

Mary's reply was a short "Well, there's a lot to do, and they're bringing more new products on line, all the time." But, for the briefest of moments, Tim somehow sensed that these few words of his might have been the first sign of appreciation that she had heard in a very long time. Somehow, he felt a sadness in her that she masked by being abrupt and rude. The problem was that she masked it very well.

Chapter Nine

WHILE TIM WAS GETTING ACCUSTOMED to the RDG routine that first week, by Wednesday night, another meeting was being held in San Francisco. As Ron Patterson entered the mahogany trimmed room, and took his place at the single round table that all but filled it, he looked around and recognized the other eleven members of the twelve person "Committee". To his immediate left sat Rich Barlow, the current president of RDG, and next to him, Rich's assistant and a member herself, May Fong. They both greeted Ron with a warm handshake and a smile. And they each offered their appraisal, having met Patterson's new "protégé".

"All the young girls think he's very nice looking." said May.

Barlow added that he had only met Tim at a lecture given by one of the Post Docs, but from what he was able to see, "the young man certainly has as much going for him as I did at that age."

"And he's a very nice young man, Ron." May added. "How did you find him?"

"Actually, I just blundered onto him." said Patterson. "I've been going through hundreds of resumes from hundreds of bright kids, from across the country, trying to find any of them that might fit the profile. But with this one, the minute I met him, I knew. He has it in his eyes."

"That he does," agreed Barlow. "I just hope it's tempered with some self-control."

As the seats at the table filled, and the doors to the room were closed, another man of about Ron Patterson's same age stood up and greeted them all.

"Thank you all for coming tonight." the man began. "As I've spoken with each of you individually, you know that our work over the past year has continued successfully, and our total assets have increased by roughly eighteen percent. And, as usual, at this time I would personally like to thank each one of you who operate the companies, which have done so well, and have allowed our work here to grow."

Arthur Gorman smiled broadly as he spoke to them. Decades earlier, Arthur, Ron Patterson, and ten other "do gooders", as the younger members of the Committee described their organizational forefathers, had joined together to search for ways to make use of their considerable wealth and combined talents to make a positive contribution to the country and perhaps to the world. As individuals, each man had built a personal fortune and had earned millions of dollars through hard work and risk taking. However, having accomplished becoming wealthy, each of them had also arrived at the place in his life where the challenge was no longer there. In short, they had each become frightfully bored. Then as now, Arthur Gorman had been the instigator. It was he who had sounded out and invited Ron Patterson to the first meeting of what would eventually become the Committee.

The twelve "originals" had come from all industries and all levels of society. Ron had grown up fairly poor, in a steel town in Pennsylvania. Arthur and some of the others had begun life nearer the upper class. Now they were each quite rich and willing to invest some of their holdings in a common venture. At that initial meeting they formulated a series of working agreements that the current Committee still closely adhered to.

Their first agreement was that the group's existence and the identities of its members was to remain a secret from outsiders. Anonymity would give them the freedom to act out of choice, not obligation. It would also help them to avoid the prying eye of government.

Their second agreement was that, whatever course of action the group decided on, the Committee would act strictly alone. Not even the people or organizations that actually received their help would be allowed to know anything about their benefactors. Theirs would be that unexpected contribution that would enable a chosen cause or a crusade to go forward. Anonymity would be their hallmark.

Over the decades that followed, the original members of the committee also decided that they wanted the work they had begun to outlive the twelve of them. At first, each member was charged to find their own replacement, and to develop them. But mistakes had been made. And finding and developing suitable young people had proven far from easy. Whether because the mentors were better at achieving than at teaching, or for a host of other reasons, it proved far more "normal" that a candidate would accept a given amount of tutoring and then elect to quit. As members died over the years, some had been successful with their students however many had not. Ten years ago, Patterson had volunteered for, and after some argument from Arthur, had been assigned the responsibility of finding and, with the total Committees approval, developing all new candidates. He loved the job. These young people, after all, would be their legacy. Tonight, he would try to concentrate, but something was on his mind, troubling him.

To qualify as a candidate, a young man or woman was first required to be what Ron romantically called "pure of heart and steady of hand". This sounded lofty, but it meant that he wanted to find young people who had been raised with the same bedrock values of independent self-reliance that had been characteristic of the original members. He also felt that it was important to the future of the group that each candidate had shown "the gumption to get off their butts and do something that was uncomfortable or personally challenging." Attitudes though, were merely the beginning.

Ron Patterson, Arthur Gorman, and three others, were the last of the original twelve. May Fong had been the last new member successfully added, and that had been seven years ago.

Primarily to continue the funding of their humanitarian activities, but also to allow for a semi-controlled environment in which to develop candidates, the Committee agreed to set aside a portion of their assets to create and develop new companies. Using only the latest of technologies, each embryonic organization would grow and, hopefully, develop into an industry leader in its respective field. In time, as the new technology played out and the company itself became less lucrative, it would be sold off and new training situations would be established. As for the original twelve, building up the new companies and helping to oversee the upcoming generation would have the pleasant side effect of helping them feel invigorated and young.

That night there were three reports to be given by various subcommittees seated around the table. One had to do with a group of South American farmers who were beginning to experiment with an insect larva, closely related to the southern boll weevil, which when introduced into an area would seek and devour the specific strain of coca plants required to produce cocaine. After the United States Drug Enforcement Agency, had been forced to eliminate its funding of the operation, an anonymous donor had contributed several million dollars (in German mark denominations) allowing the project to continue. The general understanding of those involved was that the money came directly from the American CIA, a notion the Committee was comfortable with.

Patterson sat up and listened intently to every word of the second report, on the overall growth in the total financial holdings of the Committee. Arthur had already given the number as eighteen percent. And, given the overall slow pace of the world economy, Ron knew that this level of growth was more than exceptional. But Arthur now laid out the details. Profit and loss numbers for each business unit and its net value were displayed on an overhead projection, as part of its industrial grouping. Then the numbers for each grouping were rolled up into a total. The total holdings of the Committee, consisting of separate legal entities for all purposes beyond this report, stood at nearly one billion dollars. Ron looked across the table to find Arthur looking back to him. Then the two old men smiled and shook their heads. At the very least, the financial aspect of what they had dreamed of years ago had come true.

The remaining report given that night was short and to the point. Patterson rose from his chair and formally told the Committee that he had found and had begun the training process of another candidate. "His name is Timothy Conolly." he began. "And he's just graduated from a mid-sized college in southern New York."

Patterson projected Tim's picture on the available screen, along with other pertinent information such as his height, weight and his age. "He's been assigned an entry level position with Rich at RDG, but he has just came aboard this week and it's a bit soon to know how he'll work out. Once he gets settled a bit, I'll have to dream up a simple adventure for him, to get his feet wet."

The other nine members, besides the RDG people who had already met Tim, now examined his picture and the other information displayed on the overhead. From Ron's left came a question. "Ron," he began. "I remember my own first assignment, and I can read the kids stats as well as anyone here, but what's your take on him?"

The questioner was John Ferrel, who had come to the Committee roughly three years before May Fong. For a moment, Patterson looked at the younger man as if puzzled by something he saw, or perhaps by the question. Then he continued. "Well, John," came his reply. "You know that I tend to get optimistic at the beginning of the process, and that I tend to paint promising pictures when you people ask me that question."

Ferrel also knew from experience that Ron Patterson could be the most unrelenting of coaches as the development process went on.

"I really think, though, that Tim here might truly be an exception. But I don't know. We'll have some indication, soon enough. With Rich's help, I've put him in a fairly difficult situation at RDG and we'll find out if he's got the guts to stick it out. At the same time, we'll also find out if he's willing to be trained."

"Have you told him about either the vision or about the money he'll have access to?" Arthur asked.

"No," Ron replied. "I've told him that there would very likely be a bonus at the end of the year, from RDG. And that seemed to be enough to interest him in taking the job. The fact that he will have access to a million dollars, at some time in the future, would only serve to make a messy situation worse, should he eventually tell me to Go to Hell."

From the beginning of their recruitment, an account of one million dollars was established by the Committee to be given to a successful candidate. Though the original members of the group had all been wealthy, they had also been at least middle aged. And the older men wanted their new members left free to think and work for the betterment of the planet. A million dollars in the bank was enough to provide a great deal of freedom.

That was as much of a report as Ron had planned to make that night. He said so, and again took his seat. Arthur stood up again, and again thanked everyone for coming. As the others filed out of the room, Ron made his way over to where Arthur was still sitting, collecting up his papers. "Well, you old reprobate," Ron said. "I keep expecting one of us to be absent from one of these, and to have to send flowers somewhere. Then I realize that I hope it's not me that's getting them."

"Well you'll be needing them far sooner than I will, you hooligan." was Arthur's reply, as he stood up to greet Ron. "I'm fit as a fiddle. But, you're starting to look a bit worn."

The two men shook hands warmly and then embraced. Ron was now more concerned about something he saw, but Gorman would not know. Then they each sat down and watched as the others in the room milled about or walked out the door. "It's been a long damn time, Arthur. Did you ever think we could keep it going this long?"

Arthur looked over his shoulder and nodded his reply. "I knew when I chose you to train the new kids that you had a chance of doing a good job. I guess now I was right."

"You chose me?" Ron mimicked. "As I remember it, you fought me every step of the way."

"Only until I got you determined enough to take on the job. Then I let you do what I had wanted you to do all along. Now I think you did a pretty good job. So, take a compliment and shut up."

The two men laughed together and chatted a while before it was again time for each of them to leave. "Ron, if you want me to take the lead in training this new one, or if you need any other help, just let me know. You know, it's always good to have a Plan B."

Arthur offered his hand to Ron as he got up to leave. Ron took it and smiled. Then he said, sarcastically: "Sure, that would be fair. If I have trouble with him, we can finish off his brain by letting your accountants have a crack at him. Thanks, but I'll finish what I started. And who knows, things might work out this time."

They chuckled again and Arthur left the room. Still out in the hallway, May Fong and Rich returned to the room for one last discussion. When they reached where Patterson was sitting, they could see that something was troubling him, but Ron changed the subject to Tim and RDG. "You two should leave Tim alone, for a while." Ron told them both. "I want him to get settled in and to become part of the routine at RDG. I'll stop by for a visit in a couple of days, and we'll see how things go from there."

Chapter Ten

On Friday night, his first since coming to RDG, Tim lay on his bed, looked around his hotel room and quietly wished he could spend the next two days back home. It had been a long week and besides being lonesome, he was tired of having to play up to both Mary and Abrams. Difficult or not, though, during his first week Tim had not let what he considered his temporary subordinate status hamper his learning the basics of his new position. Beginning that first Monday, after the "mini-seminar", Tim sat down with Mary, at her desk. He watched her as she worked and as she tried to explain what she was doing. Immediately, it was evident that Mary wanted to impress him with both the complexity of her labors and the speed at which she was able to handle each problem.

Coming to work those first few days was dreadful. Sandwiched between meetings that Mary "had to attend" and other things that came up during their time together, it took the better part of three days for the two of them to get through Mary's explanation of the "build cycle". Finally, though after watching what she was doing and asking her what felt like hundreds of questions, the bells in his head began to go off and Tim finally started to understand. Once he mentally sliced through the details that, according to Mary, "plagued" each product line, the entire process was actually quite simple.

Tim had met with one of the marketing managers, a man named Julian, and because Julian had seemed more than interested in what was happening, Tim wondered how much of the other manager's negative responses came as a result of Mary's attitude.

"We write the forecast, by month, on the planning forms." Mary nodded and he went on. "And finally, because we know the most efficient size of a batch that the bulk people can make, we convert the number of units of finished goods we want to make, into the number of batches of bulk material we can get, and we order the bulk material made, using the traveling requisition card. Then, we make sure that we have enough bottling and packaging material on hand, and we get it on the packaging schedule."

Tim hadn't quite finished speaking when Dave, who had come into the room and was listening to Tim's account of their job, finished his last sentence for him: "And you make sure you get the products on the schedule with plenty of time to spare. The schedule is balanced as far as manpower is concerned and we don't want to have to rebalance the whole thing because you're running out of product."

Since day one, Tim had liked Dave, in part because he reminded him so much of Casey. Pure Navy. His brother had come back home the same way. They had developed a mindset. There were prescribed ways of doing things and that's the way order was kept in the universe. Variations should be rare, if they occur at all.

"Oh, Dave," Mary replied with almost as much contempt as she usually showed Tim. "With as bad as their forecasts have always been, you know you're going to have to redo the schedule anyway."

What Mary said, though in part true, didn't sit well with Dave but he wasn't about to confront her about it. Instead he reassured them both that he would "of course" continue to keep the schedule as flexible as he could. But he did ask if Tim would try to avoid emergencies. Tim responded that he certainly would, while Mary resumed her work.

"As for checking on the packaging supplies," she looked up from her desk to say. "You had better check on them before you order the bulk. Sometimes there's a shortage and it could take longer than usual to get enough to do your job."

On Thursday of that first week, Abrams decided, over what appeared to be objections from Mary, that Tim would be made responsible for the "RDG Gold" product line. These were the oldest and most basic products that the company offered, consisting of only two bulk materials as compared to some of the newer product lines who's products might begin with as many as eight bulks. The Gold line had also had its production bugs worked out, which made it the perfect learning position for a rookie planner. Despite the clear message to everyone that Mary was still the leader in the planning group, Tim was actually relieved to have been given the simpler line.

But now the product line was his. On Friday, partly to get them used to working with him alone and partly to get away from Mary, Tim made appointments and met again with Julian, and with both the "Bulk Products" manager, a man named Bob Hendley who's sole job it was to make the bulk material for the Gold line, and with Mark Renning the Packaging Manager, who oversaw the packaging process for all product lines. The meetings were short and informal, particularly with Julian, but Tim was able to sound out some of the problems that the men had been running into. Julian complained that his Gold Line products had been given less attention than they required because all the real emphasis was being given to the newer lines. "And that makes sense for the company as a whole," said Julian. "But I'm still responsible to take care of the Gold line. And I, for one, am glad to see you come on board."

Friday night, as Tim lay on his bed and wished that he had something to do besides pretend he was interested in what was on television, he got a small dose of homesickness. He didn't want to call home, though. If he did, he would only paint a picture for his mother that he was having a hard time. She would hear the frustration and the loneliness in his voice and she would feel bad, because there was nothing she could do to help him. Besides, after a long discussion back in Longstown, he had finally convinced his parents that he only needed to call them once a week, on Monday nights. Then again, maybe by Monday night he'd feel better about things. That's when the phone rang. "Hello." he said.

"Tim," came the voice from the other end of the line. "It's Ron Patterson. How are you doing after your first week?"

"Well," Tim replied. "It's an odd world, I've stepped into. But I guess it's going okay."

"Good," added Patterson. "Say, unless you've already made plans, why don't I meet you down in the bar there, and we can talk about your first week."

Tim agreed and the two men met in the hotel bar about two hours later. When they both arrived, and after some small talk about the weather and how it was different from New York, Ron asked for Tim's perceptions of his first week as an employee at RDG. Tim hesitated, thinking about how he wanted to respond. After spouting off during his previous meeting with Patterson, this time he wanted to sound a bit more upbeat than he really was. But the older man saw how he really felt. "Tim," he said, smiling "You're learning valuable lessons, these days, that you'll be able to use, later in your career." He paused but Tim paused longer, urging Ron to go on. "Tell me your feelings about Mary Rose. What's she about, besides being afraid of you?"

"I don't think I understand what you're asking me." replied Tim. The question struck him as odd.

"I mean, when she's not at work, what do you think she's like. What about her husband? What do you think her home life's like?"

The question asked for Tim to form an opinion of his coworker at a much deeper level than he had ever bothered with before. It almost seemed like violating another person's privacy. However, Tim's own answer surprised him. "I think she's very unhappy." he said. "And I think that her job at RDG may be the best thing she has going for herself."

Tim watched Patterson for a response, and he thought a bit

more about what he had heard himself say. But it was the way he felt. Patterson nodded. Not so much with agreement, but with understanding. "As for what the relationship is between Mary and her husband," Tim continued. "I don't know. I can only judge by what I've seen in my parents' house, but my guess is that they're probably not very happy."

As Tim finished speaking, a waitress approached their table and asked them if she could get them a drink, and after Patterson gave her a wink and thought about ordering up a "waitress to go", he settled for a whiskey and seven. Tim asked for a rum and Coke.

"Tell me, then," Ron continued their conversation. "How do you feel now about Jack Abrams, and what's he all about?"

It was one thing to talk to Patterson about one of his coworkers, but Tim felt a little more cautious about talking about his new boss. "Well, sir," he began. "I'm having a harder time getting a fix on him. He seems to be allowing Mary, and everyone else for that matter, to behave in any manner she wishes, toward me or anyone else. He's kind of detached. I don't get the feeling that he's personally very committed to the company or to anything else, really. My biggest fear with him, is that he'll let Mary talk him into almost anything, especially where my career developments concerned."

The waitress returned with their drinks, and after Ron watched her leave for a few seconds, he looked again at Tim. "Again" he said. "Your basic take on both of them is absolutely correct. Mary had to undergo a series of operations, a few years ago to correct some "female problems". Since that time, the rumor is that she and her husband, who's name is Mark I think, have been growing apart. At least, shortly thereafter is when she began to put in a lot of unpaid overtime, into her job. As for Abrams, his wife has been a heavy smoker for most of her life, and now she's developed emphysema. And, I guess she's got it pretty bad. He adores her and, since they never had children, she's his whole world. Though, his reports on you are quite positive."

Surprised, now the feelings that were running around inside Tim had to do with guilt and self-centeredness. But Ron had another purpose for telling him what he had. "But don't get all guilt ridden." he said. "You had no way of knowing. And besides, having problems at home is no excuse for misbehaving at work."

"Yeah," Tim said. "I know. But feeling guilty is something that we Irish Catholic kids are trained to do from birth. We're better at guilting ourselves than Jewish mothers are at guilting their kids."

Patterson laughed and the mood was lightened. "Seriously though, Tim," Ron continued. "As time goes on, I would like to continue having these kinds of discussions with you, to keep an eye on where your mind set is. Think of it as another dimension in your job training, but what I'll be interested in, when I talk with you about the people you'll be interacting with, is how you feel about them, or see them as individuals. Try to get a sense for who they are. I think you'll find that you have a flair for it. And, though you must never ask or make a point to learn about someone else's hard times, from time to time you'll hear things. Remember that each human being out there is a frail, yet unique unit. Some of them work hard to conceal their true situations within themselves, while others will tell anyone about themselves at the drop of a hat. But they can usually be read. I want you to try to develop a feeling for people, both for those immediately around you and for the other people you deal with. Being able to sense what other people are feeling and thinking about will be a big help to you in the future."

What Ron had said sounded like other strange things that Tim had heard come out of his mouth. But though Tim had only a rough idea of what the old man was talking about, he again felt stronger inside somehow just talking to him. Ron smiled and reassured him that "trying was all he was asking for." The two men continued sipping their drinks and chatting about what had gone on during the week. Ron also made a point to reassure Tim that, even if he wanted to, it would be very difficult for Abrams to fire him.

"As long as the other people in the company," he said, "particularly the Sales Managers, see you as working diligently to support their efforts, you'll be fine. Those were the guys who pushed to get your position posted, and they will ultimately be the judges of how well you're doing. And remember, as you master the Gold line, you'll have other lines assigned to you. Take advantage of this and broaden your contacts in the Sales group. Prove to them that you're their best friend in the Materials department, and it will pay off for you."

Tim smiled again. He was not altogether comfortable with RDG's "wheels within wheels" style of decision making, where his success was determined by people outside of his direct line of management. Yet, knowing that his fate would not be determined by Mary Rose and Jack Abrams alone, Tim felt as if a large boulder had been lifted off his chest. Patterson noticed the change and he laughed out loud. "Son," he said, placing his hand on Tim's shoulder. "You've got to lighten up a little, and enjoy the stage of development that you're in. I chose you for RDG because you're a capable young man. You'll be fine. Anyway, on another subject, I wanted to tell you that something that could be serious has come up and I may be out of the country for a few weeks or months."

To Tim, being told to "enjoy where you are as you pass through life" sounded like vintage Ma. He felt a moment of insecurity about Patterson's announcement, but it quickly passed. Having talked with Julian and some of the others, and since he now knew Mary could not do much to get him fired, Tim was confident that he could hold his own, with or without help from Patterson. The feeling of confidence felt good.

Patterson had also seen the return of confidence in the young man, and it made him smile. Perhaps he had been right with this one. Perhaps the boy had what it took to go where he needed to take him. As he took himself out of the picture perhaps for the next few months, Tim would have the opportunity to stand or fall by himself, and perhaps develop some of the skills that he would need in the future. Then Patterson seemed to remember something and he reached into his pocket and produced a key. "Let me see the key they gave you when you first reported on Monday."

The only difference between the two keys, as Patterson held them in his hands, was that his copy had what appeared to be a ruby colored, plastic cover where one would hold it while it was being used.

"I'm going to switch keys with you," he said. "And when you start to get a bit frustrated with what's going on around you, just look at this one and remember that you do play a part in the future of the organization. Then relax a little."

For the next thirty or so minutes, the two men made small talk about the company, but Tim intentionally never asked for and Patterson never volunteered any information about where he was going. For his part, Tim had come to expect that he would be informed of things when he needed to know them. As for Patterson, he had no intention of telling even this promising student that something having to do with the Committee had gone dreadfully wrong, and he was going away to investigate other members, one of whom was a dear friend.

Chapter Eleven

SATURDAY MORNING STILL CAME EARLIER for Tim than it seemed to for the rest of the Bay Area. But, as he adapted to his new time zone, he found it becoming easier to sleep in. Last night's conversation with Patterson still churned in his mind and the old man's reassurance that he still had a better than average chance to succeed at RDG gave him an extra warm feeling. But this morning he'd have another project on his mind. He only had three more weeks to find both transportation and housing before RDG stopped paying his bills. And it was very clear that, as opposed to Longstown where you could use public transit to get almost anywhere, owning a car in California was not a luxury. He had to have one. That day, he decided, would be spent pricing cars at the local used car lots. He was sure he could not afford a new car, but maybe he could find one that was only a year or two old. Anyway, time was running out.

Tim spent the morning pricing used cars at various dealerships. And, as he did, he compiled a list of possibilities. That evening, both as a reward and because it was a beautiful summer night, he treated himself to a leisurely drive and dinner in San Francisco. By the time Tim got back home, it was twenty minutes after ten and he was exhausted.

Entering the front door of the hotel, Tim absentmindedly glanced into the restaurant and noticed that it was still fairly busy. As he went up the elevator to his room, he was proud of himself. He had taken the initiative and gone out for the night and had not stayed cooped up alone in his room, letting the television try to keep him amused. And, more importantly, now he would have something fun to tell Ma when he talked to her.

When he opened the door to his room and went inside, Tim saw the flashing light on the phone which meant there was a message for him at the desk. When he called down to the night attendant, she read the message, just the way the caller had left it. "It says here," she began. "Tell him that his mother called and that she was worried about him after his first week on his new job. Tell him we love him and that we'll talk to him Monday night."

The woman on the other end of the line was stifling a laugh as she read the message. Tim was clearly embarrassed, so she added: "That sounds exactly like the call my mom would make if I ever left town." Then she added. "I took the message myself, she sounds very nice."

Tim thanked the woman for her opinion and re cradled the phone. Inwardly, he was tickled to death that Ma had called, and he was proud of himself for not having called her first, even though he had wanted to. It was dumb, and he knew it. But somewhere deep down, he desperately needed to prove to both of his parents that he could make it on his own. Not that he didn't love them or need them. They knew better than that. It was just that, now he was old enough to be on his own and making his own way. But he smiled and his heart felt warmed, knowing that she was thinking of him. And even though it was his mother who had left the message, Tim knew that Da was standing right beside her as she spoke. Later, as he went to sleep to the sounds of Saturday Night Live on the television, Tim Conolly said a silent prayer, thanking God that He had given him the parents that He had.

Sunday passed uneventfully. Tim went to Mass in the morning and later took himself out to brunch, just to eat somewhere that was not the hotel restaurant or room service. Da was never much on going to church, even though he was, by all other measures, the epitome of a good Catholic father. Ma, however, never missed a Sunday. When they were kids, all the young Conollys had dutifully gone to catechism classes on Saturday, and then marched off to Mass on Sunday morning. Once they reached their teens, however, though Ma continued to be an example, each of them had been allowed to attend or not, as they chose. Neither of them had ever actually said so, but Tim understood that his parents had wanted their kids to have a personal faith that was their own and not forced upon them. And Tim and his siblings were each strong in their different relationships with God. This Sunday morning Tim went to Mass for a variety of reasons, but when he left the church he felt less alone than he had when he entered, and he felt somehow stronger for the experience.

Chapter Twelve

Monday morning the alarm clock rang at six thirty, and for the first time since he had reached California, Tim had still been asleep. As he sat up and turned off the buzzer, he had a bit of a headache, which was rare for him. He looked out through one of the opened curtains and saw that the sun was shining and warming the valley. After turning on the television to get the morning news, he grabbed a towel from the neatly stacked pile that maid service had left and took a shower. The water felt a bit warmer this morning and he enjoyed it running down his back for a few minutes longer than was his normal morning ritual. As he shaved and dressed. Tim decided to call down to the restaurant below and have them prepare a large cup of coffee for him to pick up and drink as he drove to work. The waitress who answered the phone asked him how long it would be before he picked it up, and he replied that it would still be about half an hour. She marked the information down and assured him that it would be poured and ready for him then. As Tim finished drying his hair and putting on his tie, he realized how much he was going to miss this place when he had to move into an apartment.

"Well," he laughed to himself. "At least I'll still have coffee. I'll just have to make it myself. Still, I'll miss the maid service and having a restaurant just downstairs."

A large white Styrofoam cup filled with black coffee was waiting for him when he emerged from the elevator and walked to the counter in the restaurant. Tim paid for it and was adding a little cream when a very attractive waitress softly touched his arm and asked him if he "had been taken care of". It seemed an odd question for someone who had only ordered a cup of coffee. As he looked up to respond, the young woman brushed the tip of her tongue across her upper lip as she looked into his eyes. Tim was speechless. She was beautiful and sexy and everything else that young men dream about in the night. In fact, he was amazed that she had spoken to him at all. But she clearly had. For a moment Tim's baser instincts strongly took over and he almost invited her up to his room for the day and called in sick. Blame it on his headache. However, as the young Irish Catholic attempted to get his hormones under control, and as he stumbled for something appropriately witty to say, he began to get a sense from the woman that something was not quite right. Somehow it was too good to be true. She was clearly coming on to him and she was by far the most beautiful woman to have ever done so, in his whole life. But there was something different and somehow "wrong" about this incident. As Tim put a plastic top on the Styrofoam cup, he smiled nervously at the woman and said: "Yes, thank you. I'm fine."

"I'll say you are." she said, as she watched him make his way to the front door of the hotel.

Before going through to the parking lot outside, Tim turned around one last time to look at her. Down to his loins, he wanted to turn around and continue what she had begun. Something stopped him. But what?

His blood pressure had peaked. Perhaps that is what gave him a splitting headache that seemed to spike just behind his eyes. He could see from his reflection in the glass of the door that his face was flushed. On the other hand, perhaps what he saw next was just the angle of the sun coming in through the windows of the restaurant.

Looking back though, at this sensational woman who must have been part of his dreams, there was a reddish glow about her that he might have "felt" before, but he had not seen. Red, with a warm yellow glow. Still watching him from the entry way, she waved. And not knowing what else to do, Tim smiled at her and hesitatingly waved back. Then, quickly, he went through the doors and hurried to the Granada.

Immediately, as his backside hit the seat and the car door closed behind him, Tim felt like a nail was being driven through his head, beginning just behind his eyes. Pressing his forehead against the steering wheel, instinctively clenching his fist, he closed his eyes and pictured the sharpened point of the pain, imagining it lessening, very slowly. His fists shook. Concentrating and breathing slowly into his nostrils, and out his mouth seemed to be making a difference. The pain subsided to the point where he thought he could continue on. He started the engine and left the hotel parking area. The girl, the auras, and the head splitting pain, what was that?

Leaving the parking lot, Tim felt as if he had escaped, but from what? From the clutches of a beautiful girl?

"You're losing it, old man." he said to himself, shaking his head in disbelief and chuckling.

Trying to shut out the pain in his head, or bracing for its return, images and ideas raced through his mind as Tim absentmindedly drove through the now familiar streets that would take him to RDG. She was incredible, and if the world had ended along the way, he might not have known. The pain ebbing, and safely seated in the Granada, parts of his imagination went into overdrive, mass producing images of the beautiful creature from the restaurant urging him to turn the Granada around. Yet something deeper and stronger had flashed "PANIC" across his mind and he had fled. He had no idea why.

In one of the usual places along his route, traffic slowed and then came to a complete standstill, giving Tim a few minutes to organize his mind and to regain his composure. The headache could be just nerves. True, he had been visibly shaken by what had happened, and that didn't happen very often. He'd been around women before, even very direct women. And he had always kept his wits about him. But this one had gotten to him, and gotten to him badly. Maybe she had just caught him off guard. "But what about that aura thing around her?" He asked himself and gingerly shook his head. "That was something new."

After five or six minutes, the cars ahead of the Granada began to move again and twenty minutes later Tim pulled into the parking lot at RDG. It was not yet eight o'clock, but there was Mary's Volvo, parked alone, and in the same space it had been parked in every day since he had joined the company. And, as usual, on the other side of the lot, but in a more random choice of spaces, was Alice Hartcourt's Camaro. "Oh, how delightful." Tim grimaced to himself. "Just me and the 'warmth sisters'."

With the new key that Patterson had given him, Tim unlocked the front door and let himself into the lobby. He greeted Alice with his usually cheerful, "Good morning, Alice." As usual, Alice barely looked up from the magazine she was reading. Also, as usual, she had no greeting for him at all.

As Tim locked the door behind him and approached where Alice was sitting, she eventually looked up to see if he was wearing his badge. Seeing that he was taking it out of his jacket pocket and attaching it to his shirt pocket, she returned to her reading.

Of course, as was always the case, every hair on Alice's head was lovely, bouncy, and perfectly in place. And, what small amount of make-up she wore would be slightly understated and perfectly applied. Alice had been born truly beautiful, and this morning she was wearing a light brown cardigan outfit that would show off every one of her features to its best advantage. But the cold would still be there. And this morning there was something else, the auras and the headache. As Tim looked up, having clipped his badge to his pocket, he quickly, almost as a reflex, diverted his eyes away from Alice and he began to worry about what he was seeing.

Tim looked around the lobby and noted for his own sanity that he could still see objects as well as he ever could. But, when he returned his line of sight back to Alice, there was another "aura", around her. But this time, as compared to the arch of color Tim had seen earlier in the restaurant, Alice's aura was not red at all, but a very dark blue. There it was. Trying not to stare, Tim continued through the interior door and down the corridor to the familiar door that read "Materials Department". There, he stopped and took a breath before entering. This morning, he had paid attention to only two people, and he had seen an "aura" around each of them. On the other side of the door, or at least in their shared office, he was sure to see Mary Rose. And he could almost bet that she too would demonstrate her own "glow". He was right.

As Tim entered the common area of the Materials department, there was no one in sight. As he entered the conference room, Mary was sitting at her desk, and she too displayed an arch of a very deep shade of red around her. Still trying to understand, Tim stared at her for a minute and then said: "Good Morning, Mary. How are you?"

As usual, Mary had been trying to concentrate on her work, but now that concentration had been disrupted. She turned her gaze upward, looked exasperated, and returned Tim's greeting with a forced "Good Morning" of her own. Tim immediately discounted her attitude and worried about his own eyes. Maybe whatever was happening to him was a temporary condition, brought on by stress. All the books he read had said that stress affected people in different ways. Maybe all the change he was going through these days was taking more of a toll on his body than he recognized. Maybe.

Fortunately, though, even with the "auras", Tim's normal vision seemed to be staying sharp, and the pain in his head had subsided. But how long would it stay that way? On the other hand, he was at RDG now and that meant that he had better conceal his problem from Mary, and everyone else for that matter, and continue his effort to get along with her. And that was still not going to be easy. In that way, nothing had changed.

It was Mary's normal ritual to have at least one cup of black coffee in the morning, and usually she drank two or more. As Tim looked around the office, he was surprised to see that her regular coffee mug was still where she had placed it on Friday, after washing it out and turning it over on a napkin to dry over the weekend. And, even though he had just finished his large Styrofoam cup full of coffee from the restaurant, Tim offered:

"Hey, Mary, I'm going over to the lunch room to get some coffee. Can I get you a cup while I'm there?"

What he had asked her was meant to sound professionally friendly. But the question apparently confused Mary, or at least was beyond what she had expected. Once again, she lifted her eyes from the page she was working on. But this time, very briefly, she looked as if she were going to cry. At that moment, the dark red circle that Tim had seen around her lightened dramatically to what was almost a pink. Immediately, though, she regained her composure and the circle became darkened red, once again. "No." she said. "Thanks, but I'll get some myself, later."

Tim left in the direction of the coffee room and almost ran into Jill as she came through the door. But his mind was far away. "It can't be nerves," he said to himself. "At least I don't think it can."

As he walked, Tim thought about his conversations with Patterson and about what the old man had referred to as "a different view of things", or however the old man had phrased it. He hadn't said anything about changing colors, but maybe this "aura" thing was what he meant. But if whatever was happening to Tim was Patterson's doing, how had he done it? And why did it all start this morning? "This couldn't be Patterson's doing," he told himself. "That's impossible."

Tim hadn't seen the old man since last Friday night, and then it was only for drinks. Once again, he decided that the problem must be stress.

Sitting down at a table in the coffee room Tim thought about what he should do. Taking some aspirin was first on his list. Maybe he should go back to his hotel, after all. Maybe the friendly waitress would still be there. "Maybe that's exactly the kind of tension release I need," he thought to himself.

It was a feeling very similar to the one that had caused him to bolt from the restaurant that now compelled Tim to continue to work as long as he felt that he could. As he sat there, amid his own thoughts, other people began to arrive and the coffee machine that Tim was seated in front of became a very popular spot.

Sipping on another cup of coffee and apparently staring off into space, out of the corner of his eye, he watched his coworkers as they entered the room. By this time, Tim expected that each of them would be encircled by his or her own private arch of colored light. But what was causing the differences? This whole experience was now getting too weird for words.

Again, trying not to look directly at the people involved, Tim began to notice a type of pattern in what he was seeing. Apparently, the background hue that most people exhibited was actually a shade of green that approximated the color of a flower stem. Then, within the green color, there seemed to be "blotches" of other colors that usually took up small sections of the arch. Over half of the auras he had seen showed bits of the dark red color which Tim had experienced around both the woman at the restaurant this morning and around Mary. But with others, the bits of red were few and they were blended into the predominant green of the aura. They had not taken over the entire arch.

Another curious observation that Tim was able to make was that the color of each person's aura seemed to change, again as to color and intensity, when it encountered someone else's arch. Maybe that was what had happened this morning. Maybe, even though he had not been able to see the aura yet, maybe the fact that it was there was why he felt so strange around the woman in the restaurant. "Damn/' he said to himself. "I wish I could get a hold of Patterson."

As he had kept his seat, still silently staring into space, the room was filling up to the point where few of the arches could really be distinguished from others in the crowd. Feeling suddenly claustrophobic, Tim had to get out of there.

With an almost forced calm, making his way back to his desk, Tim reminded himself that, if he told anyone about the things he was seeing, they were going to think he was on the edge of something pretty scary. And they would be right. What was worse, he no longer thought that the problem was just stress. It could be a migraine, it could be brain cancer. His imagination ran wild with possibilities. All he could think about though was that Patterson must know what was going on. He had to. But Tim also had to get control himself and that might be more difficult.

Al and Dave had come in while Tim was at the coffee room and they were busily working things out on their scheduling board. As Tim entered the room Al looked up and said: "Hey Chief. How ya doing?".

Probably ten or fifteen years older than Tim, Al was one of those good natured people that just didn't seem to let things get to him. He was very good at what he did and he got along with everyone. In short, he was the perfect choice to sort out the conflicts one finds in a scheduling function. And "Chief" was a name that Al had taken to calling Tim, that first day, after having seen Mary try to embarrass him. Al and Mary went back a few years themselves, and he had apparently seen her treat other people with that same show of contempt. However, as long as Mary had Abrams' ear, there wasn't much Al could do to stop her. But he could be friendly to the "kid" and try to demonstrate that not everyone at RDG was rude or impossible. Tim, for his part, didn't really care why Al was being his friend. He was just glad he was. And he liked being called "Chief". Maybe one day he would be one. Pausing for a moment inside the conference room door, Tim felt dumb for not having thought of Al and the other "nice" people at RDG when he was feeling so down.

"Hi! Guys." he answered.

But there was something else about Al that Tim noticed as he sat down at his desk. The largest part of Al's arch was green, but it was so light in color that it looked almost clear. The only exception was a very dark patch along his right side. Tim almost missed seeing the spot, but he still wondered what it meant. Dave's arch was almost completely green.

For the remainder of the morning, each of the members of the Materials group busied themselves about their own tasks, and Tim tried his best to do so, also. At the end of this week he would have to tell Al and Dave if he wanted to change anything on the schedule. And, with his distrust of Mary, that meant that he would have to recalculate each item in his new product line and make sure she hadn't left him any "bombs". Fortunately, this also meant that he might be able to bury himself in numbers and avoid worrying about auras for a while.

Shortly before noon, though, a report was delivered from the production floor. Tim had seen one like it last week as he sat with Mary, but she had not explained what it was, and he had not asked. This morning Tim would find out about it. The document, which contained a separate page for each product that had been manufactured during the prior week, was designed to inform the managers and the planners as to the actual number of units manufacturing had produced, compared to the number requested, key information for the planners. As usual, the person delivering the documents dropped them all on Mary's desk and left the room. Mary immediately picked the stack up and began to leaf through it, looking for items that she was concerned about. As she went, she separated the Gold Line products from the others and when she had them all, she handed them to Tim.

"These are the production reports from last week." she said. "You only had a few things produced, but here they are."

It wasn't so much what she said, but the way she said it that irked Tim. He looked up from what he was doing, and he intentionally did so a bit slower than was usual. Regrettably or not, this slowed reaction left Mary's hand, clenching his pages of the report, stuck out in his direction. Tim looked at her hand, then at her face, and then at her hand again. After a moment's pause, he took the reports from her hand and said "Thanks".

Tim hoped she had gotten the message, if only a little. She probably hadn't. As Mary returned to examining her own pages, Tim looked over his. For the products in the Gold Line that had been manufactured, the "number of units made" were very close to the number that Mary had requested. What minor discrepancies there were would make no difference in the plan or schedule.

As Mary read her reports, Tim heard an uncharacteristic "Damn" spoken behind him. Then, she quickly left the room and went directly to Abrams office. The door was open, but Mary never entered her manager's room without knocking and without his acknowledging her and waving her in. It was an odd ritual, but this was nearly the only exhibition of routine courtesy that Tim had seen from his fellow planner. As she entered, she placed one of the pages of the production report on Abrams's desk and this time it was his turn to react.

"Damn," he said. "They're going to be pissed about this."

The "they" Abrams was referring to was the Sales group who had promised a small but important group of customers that RDG would be able to ship a new heart monitoring product named Cardiovan, that week. The product had been sold to customers, planned for and scheduled, but none had been put into inventory.

"When were the bulks due?" Abrams asked her.

"They were due late on Friday and Renning was supposed to have packaged them on Saturday." she replied. "Do you know what happened?" he asked.

"Not yet." she said. "I'm on my way back there now, but I thought you would want to know. Sales is going to have a fit."

"They sure are." Abrams answered, as he frowned and stared at the piece of paper that Mary had given to him. But the number "0" in the "units produced" box said it all.

Mary left Abrams' office and exited the area through the main Materials group door. She turned left and headed to the production area where the bulks for the missing product were made. A man named Rick Wilson, with a pronounced southern drawl and who looked to be about thirty-five, had started as a chemist for RDG and had recently been promoted to manage the Cardiovan bulk production. When he saw Mary enter his lab, there was very little doubt in his mind as to why she was there.

Until that week, Cardiovan had been an experimental product that, from a production standpoint, consisted of two main reactive bulks and four mixtures used as buffers. It had been the pet product of May Fong in the Development group, and in the preliminary tests it had worked reasonably well. But Cardiovan had never been successfully produced outside the development labs. This batch was to have been the first. "Unless you've got bigger boots than the two sales managers that were just in here," he said to her, "this dogs had as much kickin' as he needs."

Mary stood there looking at Wilson, not knowing for sure whether she should continue into the lab or not. Finally, perhaps out of southern chivalry, Wilson smiled at her and waved her in.

"What happened, Rick?" she asked him as they both took seats around one of his lab benches.

"Well," he replied. "The bulks for Cardiovan are not as easy as the ones they make for the Gold Line. And we've never made one this big before. The punch line is, when we added the last ingredient to reagent number two, something went wrong, and all we got out of the batch was layer after layer of particulate matter. Or what we technically refer to as 'CRAPPOLA'."

Mary's mind was racing around for acceptable alternatives and coming up empty. Wilson continued: "May Fong is coming over this morning, and between the two of us, we'll try to identify what the problem was and how we can fix it. Until then, there's not a lot we can do about it." The room went quiet for a moment, then Wilson continued again: "If I were you, though, I would spend the next few hours verifying that we have enough of the makings of Cardiovan to produce another batch of the stuff, or those boys from Sales are going to want your boss' hide up on the shed next to mine."

"Rick," asked Mary. "Is it only the number two batch that went bad? Could you make another number two batch to go with the number one batch and the buffers that we already have?"

"No," was the reply. "We have to make them up in tandem or they won't work. What we have already is just so much wasted material."

As Mary returned down the hallway to her office, she passed May Fong who was walking in the direction of Rick's lab. The two women knew each other and what each did for RDG, but they were not social friends. As they walked past each other, only May said "Good Morning". Mary looked and smiled, but said nothing.

Abrams' door was closed when Mary re-entered the Materials area.

"He's in your room, with the 'boys'," came Alice's voice from behind her. "They're talking about Cardiovan."

When Mary walked into the room, there was Abrams, Al, Dave, and Tim. But they were talking about baseball and the Oakland A's chances of making the World Series, not about Cardiovan.

"There you are Mary," Abrams said. "There's going to be a meeting at three o'clock to talk about what we can do about getting another batch of Cardiovan. Between now and then, I want you and Al to physically verify that we have enough of everything to make at least two more batches. If we need something, get to Roberta immediately. I want to be able to tell them at the meeting exactly what we're short of and when it's due. I've already talked to Roberta and she knows that this is our number one priority."

In addition to supervising Dave and the scheduling board, Al was also responsible for the warehouse. So, it made sense that he should help verify that everything needed was available. It also made sense that they should check the items physically, and not merely trust the computerized inventory numbers. With the move and everything else that was going on, nobody wanted to have to tell the Sales people that they ran out of something, no matter how good a reason there was.

"And Tim," he continued. "It'll be good experience for you to be at the meeting, as well."

Tim said "Okay" but the invitation annoyed Mary and the aura around her shifted darker. Tim offered to help, if she needed some in preparation for the meeting, but Mary replied that she would rather take care of it herself. Inwardly, she would have liked to have sent Tim to look through the warehouse with Al. But Abrams had specifically asked her to do it, and she would. As the clock ticked onward to three o'clock, Tim noticed Mary's arch of color grew darker and redder.

RDG was on the route of a catering truck that "everyone called "the Roach Coach" and most of the employees" bought their lunches from it. During his first week, Tim had decided that it was worth the drive to get away from Mary at lunch time, so he ate his lunches at a restaurant that he had found that first weekend. Today, however, the situation was different. He wanted to observe all that would happen in response to the Cardiovan problem. When "the roach coach" arrived, Tim bought a grilled cheese sandwich from the woman running it and returned to his desk.

The Cardiovan meeting was set to be held in the same conference room that Tim had gone to when he attended the "mini-seminar" in the development building. This time, however, most of the chairs had been removed and a long table put in their place. The materials group, consisting of Mary, Al, Abrams and Tim, arrived just before three. May Fong and Rick Wilson were already there, seated next to each other, across from the door. That's when it struck him. Unlike every other person Tim had seen since leaving the restaurant of his hotel, May Fong had no "aura". She and Wilson smiled at them as they entered the room. Tim tried not to act any differently than the others, as he took a chair next to Al at the table, and again, he tried not to stare. But now he was terribly confused.

As they took their seats, Abrams asked if they were expecting anyone else to join them.

"He said he might be a bit late," replied Rick. "But Dwight Stone, the sales manager for the cardiac products asked me when this meeting was going to be held, and he said he wanted to attend."

As Wilson finished speaking, two men entered the conference

room. The first was a well-dressed, gray haired man who Tim assumed was Dwight Stone. The second man, who still looked relatively unkept, Tim knew now was Rich Barlow, the president of RDG.

As they entered the room, those already seated around the table began to stiffen in their chairs, and their combined auras darkened considerably. Except for May Fong.

"Well," said Barlow. "Where are we with Cardiovan?"

Rick spoke: "We have a pretty good idea that the problem was with the pH of the last reagent. It's not really part of the procedure, but because this was our first batch, we were checking everything we could think of."

It was strange, but as the people around the table listened to Rick as he described how thorough he had been, all the auras in the room lightened considerably, even Dwight's. However, his was the first to darken again and then turn more of the dark blue color as the subject of the meeting turned to how the production people were going to prevent the problem in the next batch.

"We've run a pH check on the material in inventory and the material that May used to qualify the test batches. What we found was that, though they came from the same source, their pH readings are slightly different. That difference may be enough to foul things up. Quality Control checks incoming material for pH, and the material we used passed within tolerances, but what we think we've learned here is that the "specs" have to be tighter."

"Do we have enough material with the right pH to use for a second batch?"

Dwight asked the question and Tim watched his aura turn even darker as he waited for an answer that he was prepared to jump on.

"That'll be a problem," Rick replied. "We have enough of the same material that went bad to make five more batches, but what we have of the lower pH material is nowhere near enough to make even a small batch."

From the color change around him, this was exactly the response that the sales department did not want to hear. Rich Barlow, who'd remained quiet, now looked over to Jack Abrams and asked him to find some acceptable product. "And if we can't get it here by tomorrow, let Dwight know so he can get in touch with his customers."

"Roberta is already working the issue with her vendors," Abrams replied. "But this is the first we've heard about the pH problem. Sitting here, I don't know how big a problem it is, but we'll keep everyone informed."

Dwight and Rich Barlow left the room, and May and Rick Wilson busied themselves trying to re-verify the acceptable pH criterion. When they finished, Abrams picked up the conference room phone and called Roberta, who took the new information and said she would let them know as soon as she could.

Walking back to their office, Al and Mary knew that they had gone into the meeting as prepared as they could have been. Now, Purchasing had to find and get usable material delivered. Then, May and Rick would have to verify the pH reading and make a new batch. Tim thought to himself that a little prayer might be in order, but he kept that suggestion to himself.

Pretending to make some notes to himself on the pad he had brought with him, Tim thought about what he had seen go on in the room. Finally, Rick got up from his chair and left the room, leaving only Tim and coincidentally, May. As they too prepared to leave, Tim once again introduced himself: "I don't know if you remember," he began. "But my name is Tim Conolly. We met here, in this room, at a 'mini-seminar' last Monday."

May smiled at him and reassured Tim that she was not too old to remember people that she had met, even briefly, just a week ago. "But, if you stay away for a month or so," she laughed. "Then maybe you have to reintroduce yourself."

May's eyes almost lit up when she laughed and her smile was almost too large for her face. Tim liked her immediately. But he still didn't know how to ask the question that he wanted to. Finally, he said: "Have you been feeling okay? I noticed you didn't say much in the meeting."

"Tim," she said, as she gently touched his arm."It can be very difficult to do, but you can learn, not only to turn your own aura off, but you can learn to see or not to see those around others, as well"

"You know?" Tim said, and as they stood in the doorway he impulsively gave May a big hug. "I thought I was going over the edge. It's not just me." Then, as he released her from his bear hug and held her shoulders at arm's length. "My head is splitting. What is it? And why am I seeing things? Tell me what's going on, please."

"It's not a bad thing," May began, turning serious and trying to reassure him."Try to calm your mind, concentrate on the point of the pain, and it will flow away." She watched his eyes. "Try this," she said, holding Tim's hand, inhaling, and counting slowly backwards, releasing her breath. "Calming your mind seems to help."

She watched him as he followed her direction. Soon he felt the throbbing behind his eyes lessen, then actually go away. He continued the exercise for a few moments, watchfully waiting for the pain to return. When it did not, Tim turned to May for more information. She held out her hand to stop him from asking. "It is not my place," she said, "to go into great detail about the auras you see. That is for Ron Patterson to continue with you. He's the one who gave you your key." That May knew about Patterson and about his mentor relationship with the old man, brought a thousand questions into Tim's mind. But May held up her hand again to stop his asking. "I will tell you this much," she began. "For now, you can stop what you're seeing by distancing yourself from the key that he gave you. But you should try to stay with it as long as you can. You can learn to control the headache and control what you see, if you work on your concentration."May paused for a moment as if she was carefully choosing the next words she would say. "At this point' she continued. "You should try to feel for personal interpretation of what the colors mean. Then, they can be of use to you."

Tim nodded his head as if he understood. Then May had one more thing to tell him.

"You have nothing to fear. The pain will moderate given time, and there is no danger from what you see," she said. "In fact, after a time, the auras can be very calming. But you and I must not discuss the subject again, unless there is a dire emergency. The use of the auras is, in part, a mental training that only time and experience can master."

May then left the room and walked back to her lab. She was deeply concerned that Tim's new ability to see the auras would bother him to the point of discussing it with someone else. In many ways, that in itself could be dangerous. As Tim returned to the Materials area and to his desk, he pulled the key from his pocket. He was still concerned about what holding the key had done to him, physically. But his chat with May Fong, albeit short, learning that what he was feeling and seeing was directly related to the key itself, and the discovery that there was someone else in the world that knew Ron Patterson, all worked to make him feel more assured.

"Maybe she's right," he said to himself, as he returned the key to his pants pocket. "Maybe, if I could learn to use it a bit." A few times during the day, the headache would rise again, and he had to excuse himself from the room to follow May's exercise, and each time he did the relief lasted a little longer.

As Tim sat down at his desk and pulled out the forms required to rework the production plan for the Gold Line, out of the corner of his eye he attempted to monitor the color of the aura around Dave.

Dave had taken a number of forms from his desk and he seemed content to absorb himself in the business of his job. As Tim watched, Dave's aura remained the same peaceful green that Tim had seen around him before. Then, Dave began to quietly hum to himself. Though Tim could just make out what the song might have been, and even though Dave's ability to carry any semblance of a tune could be left to debate, Tim was glad for the break in the silence. But just as the "music" began, Mary's reddish aura noticeably darkened. Dave apparently knew very well that he was having an effect on her, as little by little, flecks of light blue began to appear against his green. Outwardly, Dave still had his eyes and apparently all of his attention trained on the papers in front of him. But as Tim sat watching the flecks of blue grow and darken as Dave slowly increased his volume, Tim knew somehow that his quiet and strictly non offensive co-worker had developed his own way to give Mary a little taste of "payback". A few minutes later, and roughly half way through the fifth rendition of whatever tune Dave was attempting, Mary picked up a material requisition form from her desk and she quietly stormed out of the room, heading to Roberta's office. Immediately, the blue flecks in Dave's aura darkened briefly and then slowly returned to green. At the same time, the humming stopped.

"That was a nice tune, Dave." Tim said. "Does it always work that well?"

Dave looked up from his work as if completely surprised, ignorant of what Tim was talking about. "What?" he said, wide eyed. "Did you say something?"

Tim just shook his head and chuckled to himself. "*No,*" he answered Dave. "I didn't say a thing."

Even though Tim had believed May Fong when she said that his ability to see the auras was not something that he needed to be afraid of, it was by watching the "encounter" between Dave and Mary that he had somehow understood its power. Beyond their behavior, he literally could see the "truth" about people.

Chapter Thirteen

For the remainder of Monday afternoon, Tim busied himself doing his paperwork and expanding his observations to the other people in his department. By then, it was late in the afternoon and most of those with more private work areas had closed their doors and contented themselves to work alone until five o'clock. As the afternoon wore on, their colors began to show a slightly reddish hue, which Tim later decided was caused by the trauma of a long work day. But what did that say about Mary, whose aura was constantly and consistently red?

A1 and Dave had disappeared from the area shortly after four thirty, and Tim was sure they had left and were half way home by the top of the hour. Mary left shortly after five. For his part, Tim still had a few figures he wanted to check before leaving. It was almost five thirty before he sat up and realized he was getting hungry.

As he walked out the front door of RDG at around five forty, the custodians were arriving and somewhere in the now empty building he could hear a phone ringing. Tim chose to ignore it. Since he still didn't know more than half of the people who worked in the building, it didn't make much sense to try to take a message. The odds were good that he wouldn't know who to give it to. In only a few minutes Tim was in a drive-through line at a McDonalds. He ordered a fish sandwich, fries and a cola. Fifteen minutes later, he was back in his room.

"I am going to miss this place," he said to himself as he entered the room and noticed that the maids had been in, and that they had done their usual splendid job.

There were new towels in the bathroom and his bed had been made. And apparently, if a guest was staying for an extended period of time, they changed the sheets on Monday. As Tim took off his jacket and hung it up in the closet, he looked over to the table next to his bed and noticed that the message light on the phone was blinking. He laughed to himself and he knew that it must be Ma. She couldn't wait until he had called her tonight, and she would probably say she had forgotten about the time difference. That would be like her.

It was almost six o'clock locally, so it would be almost nine o'clock back home. However, his sandwich was getting cold, so Tim decided to take a few minutes to eat. Then he would make his call and give the family "worry warts" a rundown of what was happening. Again, he was glad that he had some interesting things to tell them. Eating alone though, was still a problem. He crossed the room to turn on the television. But before he reached it, his phone rang again.

"Hello." he said.

Tim expected that the voice on the other end of the line would be Ma's, or maybe even Ron Patterson's. But instead, it was Patrick calling. "Tim?" his brother said. "Is that you?"

"Yeah, Ding Dong." he answered. "You're calling my room. Who did you think it would be?"

"Well," said Patrick. "I've been trying to get a hold of you for about the last half hour. Ma's in the hospital and she's in pretty bad shape."

Tim stared into the phone, silently. Then he shook his head. "What do you mean?" he asked. "What happened?"

There was a moment's pause at the other end of the line so Tim repeated himself, trying to sound calm but determined to be told. "Pat, tell me what happened?"

"Well," his brother began. "We all had dinner about four thirty, our time. After that, Ma was going down to one of the stores downtown, to shop for a dress. Mary Margaret had invited us all over for dinner this Sunday and she wanted to have a nice dress to wear."

"Okay," said Tim. "She's been downtown before. What happened?"

Pat paused, and then, almost in tears, he said: "Tim, some son of a bitch grabbed her, dragged her behind the store, and beat the hell out of her. She's in surgery now and the doctor says she might not make it."

A feeling of both helplessness and then rage swept over Tim standing there, three thousand miles away, knowing that he should have been with her. As he looked down at his hands he could see them trembling. "Where's Da?" he asked.

"He's here at the hospital. They say that it will be at least a few hours before they can tell us anything definite, but he's not going anywhere. Tim, he's a wreck. If you can get back here, you should."

Mentally, Tim calculated how much cash he still had and he tried to remember how much his ticket had cost him on either of his trips to California.

"Tim," Pat added, but he obviously didn't want to have to say the words. "There's something else. Da doesn't know it yet, but I talked to one of the doctors in the hallway about an hour ago. He said that there was a pretty good chance that the bastard tried to rape her, too."

What he heard amplified his anger, but Tim's voice remained calm. "Have you talked to Casey and Mary Margaret, yet?" he asked.

"Mary Margaret's here. But Casey's out on a ship. I talked to one of his officers and told him that there had been an emergency here. He said he would get the message to Casey, and if they needed to, they can fly him back to the base. From there, he can get a ride back home."

"Okay, good." Tim said. "Tell Da that I'm going to catch a 'red-eye' back there tonight and that I'm going directly to the hospital. In the meantime, I want either you or Mary Margaret to be with him all the time. I don't want him left alone, even for a minute. Okay?"

"He hasn't been, and he won't be, Tim. But get here as soon as you can."

As Tim hung up the phone he sat down on the bed. "Why?" Almost as an involuntary response, Tim's fists tightened and he began to beat them on the mattress on each side of himself, saying "I should have been with her." As his hands began to hurt and to bleed from the pounding, Tim held them to his stomach and bent over at his waist, his eyes shut, clenching his jaw, too angry and sad to cry, shaking. Nothing made sense. She never hurt anybody, and most of the people she knew loved her. Unbidden, Tim's mind seemed to recall childhood memories and to send their emotions to his heart.

"There is a price," he said to himself as he sat there, "to loving people. Sometimes they need you, and sometimes you aren't there to help them."

"I should have been there." Tim said again, into his fists. "She was all alone while that bastard was hitting her. Nobody was there to stop him."

Slowly and painfully, Tim lifted himself up from the bed and he made his way to the sink in the bathroom. Once there, he ran cold water over his fists, splashed water on his face and began to consider what he would have to do to get back to New York, tonight. His first call was to the airlines.

"Sir," said the female voice. "The next flight to LaGuardia leaves at eight twenty and goes to Chicago. Then, after a fifty three minute layover, there is a connecting flight to New York."

"That would be fine," said Tim. "Please reserve me a seat now, and I'll pay for it when I get to the airport. Will that be okay?"

"Yes sir," she said. "Would you prefer the smoking or the nonsmoking section?"

"Nonsmoking if you have one. If not, smoking is okay." "We have either, so I'll reserve a nonsmoking seat. Would you prefer an aisle or a window seat?"

"An aisle seat would be better."

"Okay, Mr. Conolly," she said. "You have an aisle seat reserved for you on flight Three-Twenty-Seven to Chicago, departing at eight twenty this evening and connecting with flight Four Seventeen to New York. Is there anything else I can do for you this evening?"

"No," Tim replied. "Thank you very much."

As he hung up the receiver, Tim pulled his wallet out of his pants pocket and counted his cash again. He would have just enough for a round-trip ticket to New York and back. The problem was that he wasn't sure that he wanted to come back. It wasn't logical, and he knew it. But if he had been home when she went to the store, it was possible that he would have gone with her. If he had, this wouldn't have happened. Again, he slammed his fist down this time on the table, spilling the phone on the floor.

"Damn"

The time was now nearly quarter to seven, leaving Tim only an hour and a half, or so, to catch his flight. There really wasn't much that he could do about the situation once he arrived, but there was never any doubt in his mind that he was going. The real question, in Tim's mind, was how long he would stay. Or maybe he would never leave again. Who knew?

After picking up the phone and making sure he hadn't broken it, Tim started packing. He decided to take all of his personal belongings with him. He also thought about RDG.

"I can call Abrams from Longstown and tell him what has happened. If he wants to get rid of me, and he can do it politically, this might be his chance. Either way, though, it doesn't matter."

As he continued packing his clothes into the two suit cases that he brought with him, Tim was surprised that somehow everything fit. They would definitely not be as neatly folded as they had been a week ago when he had first unpacked. But they all fit, even the extra things he had gotten after he arrived. But what should he do about the car and the room? Since he had no place to keep it, Tim decided to turn the car back into the rental agency and save RDG some money. If he came back, he could rent another one. But the room was another story. As he understood the terms of the hotel's agreement with RDG, the company had rented his room for a defined month. And they had paid for it, up front. Tonight, he would remove all of his belongings, so that if he decided not to return to California, he could just call the hotel and tell them. But if he did return, and did so before what remained of his four weeks was up, the room should still be paid for and available.

Almost as an after thought, Tim took the red tipped key that Patterson had given him out of his pocket and put it into the toe of one of his shoes. "I'll have enough trouble without having to cope with you on this trip," he said as he stuffed a sock into the shoe behind it. Then he shoved the shoe into the bottom of his suit case.

As Tim finished packing his bags, and as he was carrying them to the elevator, it dawned on him that he had never thought to ask Pat if they had caught the guy. And now he wanted to know.

Somewhere, in the place in his heart that Tim reserved for his relationship with his mother, it made him feel a bit closer to her that his first thoughts had not been about getting even with the guy who had grabbed her. Ma had never taught him to hate. When it had been important, and when he had not taken the time to think about his reactions, his thoughts had been about taking care of Da and the others. Ma would have liked that. She would have liked that, a lot. And she would have been proud of him.

However, being protective of the rest of the family was only Tim's first reaction. As he walked across the parking lot to where the Granada was parked, it was anger that bubbled to the surface. Using the seat of the vehicle as a poor substitute for the hotel's mattress, Tim again pounded his fists against it. But this time he wasn't crying. This time he realized that what he felt was not grief. In his mind he pictured striking again and again at the anonymous face of the man who had assaulted her.

"You bastard," he shouted, hoping that someone thousands of miles away might hear him.

A few minutes later, the Granada started right up, and minutes after that, Tim drove the car into the "Rental Returns" area of the airport. There were signs telling him where to park the car, and when he had done so, he carried his packet of paperwork over to the small return's office, there in the lot. Once again, a young girl was at the counter, smiling widely at him. Her badge said her name was "Carol". Tim gave her his packet of papers. She took what she needed from the packet and returned the remaining items. Then she smiled at him again and said: "Thank you, sir."

"Are we done?" Tim asked.

"Yes," said Carol. "That's all we need to do. Have a nice flight."

Tim glanced at his watch. It was now seven fifty-five on Monday night. The terminal itself was fairly empty, so there were only a few people in line ahead of him when he reached the ticket counter.

"Yes sir," said a woman in her mid-thirties, who's badge read "Ann". "Can I help you?"

"Yes, I think so," said Tim. "You should have a reservation for a Tim Conolly on the eight twenty two flight to New York. I need to pay for it and verify my seat assignment."

"Yes sir, Mr. Conolly," said Ann. "You've been assigned row twenty-one, seat D. It's a non-smoking, aisle seat. Is that okay?"

"Oh yeah," he replied.

Tim gave the woman what amounted to half of his remaining cash and he wondered about what would happen if he left now but decided to come back. And what if he didn't, how would he get paid for the week he had spent at RDG?

"It won't be a very large check," he thought to himself. "But it'll be big enough to get around on if I live at the house. They'll probably just mail it out."

Once on board, and the plane was in the air, he tried to nap, not only to get much needed sleep, but to escape the boredom of the long flight. As soon as he closed his eyes, though, Tim's thoughts turned to the image of his mother. Not as she might be after the beating, but as she looked on the day he left for California. He had kissed her cheek and had given her a long hug that he had hoped she would keep with her until he returned home. And, in a strange way, he hoped that somehow, she still carried it with her. Maybe it would help her get through this.

Trying to sleep was hopeless. Failing that, Tim pretended to read a magazine. At times his mind would race ahead in time and he began to visualize a score of scenarios around what he would find when he arrived at the hospital. And then what? What was he going to do once he got there? If Ma died would he be duty-bound to kill the guy for revenge? Is that what she would want? What would Da want him to do? And how could he identify what his own emotions were? In his heart Tim questioned whether or not the anger he felt was even real, or was he just expending energy to keep himself angry because that was what was expected of him? And how did turning one's cheek figure in when the offense is not against you, but against a loved one? As he thought about these things, sleep was out of the question.

When they landed in New York, the crowd around the carousel where Tim went to retrieve his bags was far more awake and animated than they had been aboard the plane. Perhaps these people were more used to being up all night. Perhaps they felt as bad as he did but only looked better. It didn't matter. Tim waited until his bags came up on the belt from below, and when he had them in hand, he started for the cabby stand, outside. Looking at his watch, and doing some quick calculating, the local time was just six fifteen.

Tim was carrying enough money in his pocket to pay for a one way cab ride to Longstown, but he knew that not every cabby was going to be interested in driving him that far out of the city. As he approached the first cab, he was fully expecting the driver to turn him down. And he was not disappointed.

"Longstown?" the man said incredulously: "That's more than an hour out. I don't go that far."

Then, from a distance off and behind him, Tim heard a familiar shout. As he turned around, there was Patrick running in his direction, waving his arms and continuing to shout his name. He dropped his bags and waved back. Patrick was now running as fast as he could, but he stopped shouting. In a minute or two the two brothers were together. First, they hugged.

"Damn," said Patrick. "I was scared that I was going to miss you. I called the airlines and tried to figure out what flight you might be on, but I wasn't sure. I've got the Impala over in the short-term parking. Are these all your bags?"

Tim had barely gotten out his reply as Patrick picked up the heaviest of his bags and began to march in the direction of the car. When they arrived, his brother opened the trunk and tossed in the suitcase. Tim added the bag he was carrying and Patrick spread them out as evenly as he could, so that the lid of the trunk would close. Then Patrick got into the car on the driver's side, and reached over to unlock the passenger's side door for Tim. Soon the brothers were on the road and away from the airport.

"Who's with Da?" asked Tim. "I told you not to leave him alone, even for a minute."

"Simmer down little brother," replied Patrick, a little rougher than he had meant to. "You've just arrived and there's those of us that have been taking care of the situation all along. Da's fine."

Tim shook his head and apologized. "I appreciate your coming out to get me, Pat. I didn't mean to come across like that."

"Ah Tim, we're all upset." Patrick replied. "But Da's fine. Mary Margaret's with him. He hasn't left the hospital since they called him, but he did manage to get an hour or so of sleep on one of their sofas."

"How about you, Pat? How are you holding up?"

"Don't worry about me. I'm okay." he said. "But I'm glad you're here. Casey called and said that he would be here as soon as he could. That means maybe later today, but probably tomorrow."

"How's Ma doing? Have you talked to the doctor again?"

"Tim," he said. "She hasn't woken up since it happened. And the doctor says that, in all honesty, she might not. He says she's in pretty bad shape. They're doing everything they can, but he just doesn't know."

The words were not easy for Patrick to say, and he avoided Tim's eyes as he said them. They were obviously not what Tim had wanted to hear. But the facts were the facts and Tim needed to hear them.

"What about the rape?" he asked.

Patrick looked at his brother and Tim knew what the answer was.

"Do the cops know who did it, yet?"

"Oh yeah," Patrick said. "They know who did it. A guy named Adams. But because there were no witnesses, they're not going to book him on anything serious."

Tim couldn't believe what he was hearing. Patrick continued: "The detective in charge, a black guy named Sumner, says that he's going to hold 'the suspect', as he calls him, on an attempted robbery charge, while they collect enough evidence to book him on assault and battery, or even attempted murder charges."

"What about rape or attempted rape charges?"

"Well, Sumner didn't say much about those, except that they're even harder to prove in court. He says that he has a witness that heard Adams bragging about having found a new way to come by some spending money, but that might be considered hearsay and not allowed at a trial. Besides that, he says that if Ma doesn't come out of it and clearly identify the guy, it might be tough to prove any of it."

The two brothers didn't have much more to say to each other and that fact made them both uncomfortable. Next to what had happened, nothing else seemed to make any difference. They both made attempts at small talk, just to fill the silence. But they each knew how the other one felt, and they both understood. Finally, Tim asked another question: "Do you know the guy?"

For a long moment Patrick stared ahead, as if watching traffic. Then he answered. "Yeah," he said. "I know him. Or at least I know who he is. He's a laborer from Albany who came to Longstown to work on the new Post Office expansion. Our carpenters local got that job a few months ago and we've been hiring laborers out of the hall. He's a big guy and strong as an ox. His first name's Carl, but everyone just calls him Adams."

"Well, he's not going to walk away from this, I promise you."

Chapter Fourteen

Every hospital that Tim had been inside had somehow managed to look and smell exactly the same. White walls and beige or green linoleum on the floor seemed to be a requirement. And everywhere he looked, there were medical personnel, mostly women, walking briskly from room to room, carrying clipboards. And that smell. Whatever caused it, that odor always made Tim think that it might be healthier to stay outside. Surely it couldn't make the patients feel any better.

He and Patrick had made good time and it was still early enough that there were very few visitors inside the hospital. Patrick knew where Ma's room was so he led the way. They passed two nursing stations, walked down a long hallway, and then went through a set of doors that read "CRITICAL CARE". As they walked through the doors, Tim saw Mary Margaret coming out of a door that was marked A-5. She looked tired. No doubt the entire ordeal had taken its toll on her, as well.

"Mary Margaret," said Patrick, pointing to Tim. "I found this poor little puppy walking around the airport, looking lost. Do you think we should keep him?"

Once their eyes met, Tim and his sister smiled at each other, and they hugged each other for what Patrick felt was entirely too long. "Come on, you two." he said. "You'll have plenty of time for that later."

Mary Margaret frowned a bit, and putting her arm around her younger brother. She gently tried to reconcile him to the fact that, since Ma hadn't "come to" yet, it may mean that she wouldn't wake up at all. Suddenly, though, from inside room A-5, Tim heard Da's voice shout: "Mary Margaret, get the doctor. She just moved her hand and she may be waking up."

Mary Margaret ran down the hallway in search of a doctor. Meanwhile, Tim and Patrick hurried inside the room where Da had shouted from. There on the bed was Ma. Her eyes had indeed opened, but they looked glassy, and it seemed as if she were having trouble getting them to focus. As she lay there, and as they watched her, she tried to smile but she looked very confused. And when she tried to speak, the only sounds she could make were faint and jumbled. But Ma's eyes were open. Da took her hand, kissed it, and held it to his cheek.

"Good morning,' gorgeous," he said to her. "We thought you were going to sleep the whole day away."

Around his mother's head was a large gauze bandage, and another slightly smaller bandage covered her chin. Her left eye was badly swollen, and there was a single dark circle under it that looked like something Tim had once given Casey, accidentally. The right side of Ma's upper lip was also swollen to about twice its normal size and her lower lip looked as if she had required stitches to close up a cut. Tim was shocked at the sight of his mother laying there that way, but she was alive. And she seemed to smile a bit. To Tim, she looked wonderful.

In a few minutes, Mary Margaret and a gray-haired doctor she found in the hallway, entered the room and chased everyone but Da out into the corridor.

"You'll get to see her as soon as we know she's really out of trouble," the doctor told them as they left.

Once the three "children" were out in the hallway, Tim wanted to hear more about the police investigation. He told his sister what Patrick had told him on the way to the hospital, and he asked them both if there was anything else that either of them could add. For Mary Margaret, half of what Patrick had told Tim was news. In fact, staying with Da as she had, she hadn't even thought about what the police might be doing. "What do you think will happen?" she asked her brothers. "Will Ma have to go to court and identify the guy?"

Actually, Maeve Conolly's children knew their mother well enough to know that, when she was well enough to do it, she would be more than willing to face her attacker. If the police caught the man and needed her to identify him to a *court*, she would gladly do it. And she would look him in the eye without any hint of fear or intimidation. What they were unsure of was how seriously the legal system would handle the case.

"I've heard about some of these *guys*," said Patrick, "There were two of them in the papers a couple of years ago. They went around robbing gas stations, and they even killed a guy. The cops found them and arrested them, but their lawyers pleaded them down to some minor charges, and they never did do much time. Maybe two or three years. In the meantime, the victims are scared to be in their own houses."

The three of them sat for a while on a small bench in the hallway and waited for any further word about Ma. After about thirty minutes, Mary Margaret got up to call her husband at home. Since he didn't want to upset his dad or his sister, Patrick took the opportunity of their being alone, just he and Tim, to ask his brother a question: "Even if the cops do charge Adams, what do you really think will happen to him?"

"How do I know?" replied Tim. "I studied business in school, not law."

"You know what I mean," Pat said. "You think Adams will get off light, don't you?"

The short answer was "Yes". From newspaper and television

accounts that Tim had heard, the criminal justice system in the state of New York seemed to be a huge inefficient bureaucracy that would rather release a guilty criminal or let him cop a plea to a lower charge, than try him for the crime he committed. It was easier for the lawyers that way. The truth was that Tim feared Adams would be allowed to walk away, and legally there was probably not much he or his family could do about it. "Legally" that was the way the system would probably work.

As Tim sat there with Patrick, it occurred to him that with all the turmoil that had been going on since his brother's phone call last night, he had not seen or been looking for auras around the people he had seen.

"Maybe May Fong was right." he uttered. "By having the key with me or not, I can choose to see them, or not to."

Patrick had still been sitting next to Tim, thinking about Adams getting away with what he had done, when Tim had mumbled this to himself. Though Patrick had not heard exactly what his brother said, he had heard a woman's name, and he asked Tim to repeat himself.

"Oh, it was nothing." Tim replied. "Just something that one of the women at work said yesterday after a meeting."

"Wow! little brother," Patrick said with his eyebrows raised. "Only in California a week and you're already meeting women at work and after meetings."

Tim laughed at his brother and hit him gently on the arm with his elbow. "You're hopeless," he said. "I only wish it was true."

Mary Margaret returned to the bench where Tim and Patrick were sitting and reported that everything was fine at home and that everyone there was praying for them. She sat down next to Tim and she took his hand in hers.

"I wish your homecoming could have been under better circumstances, Timmy."

Tim switched hands, then wrapped his arm around his sisters shoulders. She had been giving her strength to Da and everyone else, as she had always done. But, for a while as he held her, Mary

Margaret rested a bit on his shoulder and she cried. Now it was his turn to be the strong one. That's how his family worked.

The door to room A-5 remained closed, leaving Tim and his brother and sister outside. What they had seen in room A-5 had to be good news, didn't it? Hadn't she smiled? Out in the hospital corridor, the Conollys all worked hard at maintaining their positive facades. But nobody seemed to be very convinced. The doctor and Da were inside. And the doctor hadn't looked like he was overly concerned. But why was it taking so long? There was clearly nothing they could do. Maybe a prayer? Soon time began to drag. Tim thought about RDG and what was going on there.

Or at least as much of what was going on there as he understood. But, with a three hour time difference between Longstown and the Santa Clara valley, it was still too early to call Abrams to let him know what was happening. And he certainly didn't want to leave a message with either Mary or Alice.

Tim sat on the bench in the hallway again and Patrick sat there next to him while Mary Margaret paced. But none of them really wanted to talk much. Also, the effects of the flight were beginning to combine and to have an effect. Within a few minutes he was dozing.

Though Tim almost never remembered dreaming, as he slept he saw himself seated with a much younger version of himself, in a room with windows that looked out over an ivy covered hollow at the foot of a low hill. A young woman, with an absent air about her, sat there and she talked in loving terms that Tim could not hear but that he understood, about the nobility and beauty of the leaves and vines. Initially, he and the youngster were sitting to one side, but they had moved to the overgrown hollow itself. Tim could see the woman more clearly now. She was lean and supple, wearing a floppy hat and her spring dress looked to be of the lightest of material, like gossamer. As she sat there, near the center of the opening, she was clearly waiting and expecting others. She seemed worried that she was to remain alone. Tim let his eyes leave the woman for only a moment and then return. But the beautiful woman, with doeish eyes and quiet brown hair that floated in the breeze, had moved to the top of the small hill, looking over what appeared to Tim, to be a small stone. Then from the opposite end of the hollow, as if emerging from the very ivy itself, others began to follow her. First there was only a single form. It looked to Tim to be very much like, but slightly different than the woman herself. Then there were two more, then ten, then a score. Finally, other men who had apparently been sitting in a row with Tim and his young companion quietly rose up and crossed the meadow. They too walked slowly up the mound. After a moment spent watching and wondering, Tim saw his younger self also cross the opening and begin slowly up the hill, after her. Tim jumped up from where he sat, and ran after the youth, catching him part way up the hill. Tim wrapped his arms around the youngster, not wanting to control him, but to be with him as they reached the top. And when they reached the top, both the woman and the child had left him.

Suddenly, back inside the hospital, Tim awoke to the sounds of people rushing in and out of room A-5. Outside the door Mary Margaret and Patrick were trying to remain close to the door, but out of the way of doctors and nurses going in and out of the room. Then, as suddenly as it had started, the commotion stopped. Even though his mind was still foggy, from where Tim sat in the hallway outside, he could watch the faces of those who were in the room, as they each realized that there was nothing more to be done. Then, in a very quiet, business-like manner, the doctors and nurses folded up their equipment and filed out through the door. None of them spoke. Soon they had disappeared back into their daily routines.

The only people remaining inside room A-5 were the gray-haired doctor and Da. A few minutes later, the doctor came out into the hallway. Tim hadn't noticed before that his shoulders sagged a bit, and there was sadness in his eyes. The doctor spoke in quiet tones to his sister and then to Pat. And then he too walked through the doors marked "CRITICAL CARE" and the family was left alone. Ma was gone.

Chapter Fifteen

According to what the doctor told Pat, there must have been a blood clot that had formed, but then dislodged and traveled to her heart. When the clot arrived there, it got stuck in one of her main arteries and pinched off the flow of blood.

"That's what happens when someone has a heart attack." Pat told the rest of them. "And that's what they think happened."

Of course, a priest was called, probably by the old doctor, and he gave Ma the last rites of the Church. Da remained next to her bed, still holding her hand. As the priest finished and departed, and as Tim watched from outside in the hall, Mike Conolly slowly placed his wife's hand on her chest, and kissed her cheek one last time. Then he stood himself up as tall as he could, and slowly walked out of the room.

"Come on kids," he said. "We've no more business here."

Mary Margaret rushed to her father's side and tried to wrap her arm around him, but Da would have none of it. Nevertheless, she stayed by his side. Patrick and Tim followed behind them. Outside the hospital, Da and Mary Margaret climbed into her car, a wood paneled station wagon, leaving the Impala for Tim and Patrick.

"We'll go straight to the house," Mary Margaret shouted to them, as the boys walked toward the car. "You're coming, aren't you?"

Tim was sure that they would follow her to the house, but Patrick surprised him and shouted back: "No, you go ahead," he said. "I want to stop by and have a word with that cop."

Between the numbness that protected him from his emotions, and all of what had happened that morning, Tim was too tired and too busy to think about being angry. But now that the worst had happened, Patrick had to vent his feelings. Once they were inside the Impala, Patrick turned to his brother and with a tone that scared Tim a little, he said: "Now the son of a bitch has killed her. And now the cops are either going to nail him, or I'll do him myself."

Tim looked down at his brother's clenched fist as Patrick smashed it down onto the seat of the Impala. The knuckles of his other hand were white, wrapped around the steering wheel. Tim didn't think he had ever seen Pat look this way, but he didn't want the situation to get any more out of hand than it already was.

"Now that the charge has to be murder, I'm sure the police will do everything they can to nail him," Tim answered his brother. "But let's go see this guy Sumner, anyway. I want him to know that this case is not one that people will lose interest in, or let slide."

After a moment, Patrick nodded in agreement and relaxed a bit, then started the car. The police station was only a fifteen minute drive from the hospital, but this time the Conolly boys used the time to talk. The biggest thing going, as Patrick had said before, was the union's new contract to build the Post Office extension. That project alone was keeping most of the union members working. And that was obviously good for everyone in Longstown. As he listened to his brother speak, Tim always noticed the hint of pride that Patrick felt in being a part of the union, and the son of another long time union member. Longstown, above all else, still belonged to them, and the unions would continue to take care of the economy there. But what also dawned on Tim, as he rode past the town's landmarks, was how little he felt a part of it, any more. True, it had only been a week since he left for California. But, as he sat there in the car, Tim realized that something within him had changed. Maybe it had always been different for him. Perhaps he was always destined to live another way, and in another place. Maybe.

When they reached the police station, but before they emerged from the car, Tim stopped his brother and said: "Pat, we don't want to go in there and start pissing people off. Okay? First, let's go in, and get a feel for what this guy Sumner has in mind. Then, if we don't think he's doing as much as he should, we'll go over his head. But remember," Tim slowed what he was saying a bit, and looked for agreement in Patrick's eyes. "He may be willing to take care of it, and do the right thing. And we should give him that chance."

"All right, 'Mr. Psychology'," Patrick replied. "But when we get in there, I'll do the talking."

That was fine with Tim. At least Patrick had met Sumner before and that familiarity might be helpful. Anyway, Tim had learned how to find out what he needed to know, without necessarily confronting people. He could do it if he had to, but it was always his choice. However Patrick's method, the one often spoken of regarding bulls and china factories, could often be just as effective.

As the brothers entered the station, they were greeted by an Irish sergeant at the main counter. Patrick asked the sergeant if he could talk to a detective named Sumner and the sergeant called his office to see if he was there. As it happens, he was.

"Detective Sumner will be down in a few minutes." he told them, putting down the phone. "You can wait for him over by those tables."

The tables the sergeant referred to looked more like benches, but were also usable as a writing surface. They had been grouped in circles of two or three, to give each group some amount of privacy. At any rate, Tim and Pat were not there to take notes, and neither of them felt much like sitting down. As promised, it was only a few minutes before a relatively young man walked over to where they were, and shook hands with Patrick. Then, turning his attention to Tim, the man offered his hand and said: "Hello, I'm, detective

Sumner. I've been assigned to investigate the incident involving your mother."

Tim shook the man's hand and introduced himself, even though the officer already seemed to know who he was. Patrick cleared his throat and then told Sumner that Ma had died in the hospital, about an hour ago.

"That makes the charge murder, doesn't it?" he said.

Sumner thought for a moment, he frowned and then replied: "Well, not necessarily." he said. "In this case, there is no hard evidence that the suspect Adams was the one who actually did it. All we have is the fact that he's new in town, has a big mouth, and that he can't verify where he was at the time."

"What about finger prints on her clothes, or blood stains? There must have been something that you can use."

Sumner looked at Patrick, frowned again, and shook his head. "Well for one thing, the guy must have had his hands covered, because there were no prints of any kind left at the scene. As for blood on his clothing, Adams would have had plenty of time to get rid of whatever he was wearing between the time he committed the crime and the time we found your mother. Frankly," Sumner continued, "without your mother's testimony to identify him, our case against Adams falls apart and I'll probably have to let him go."

"What do you mean 'let him go'?" asked Patrick. "That son of a bitch just killed my mother. And you're going to let him go?"

Tim had to physically stand between his brother and the policeman, pressing Patrick against a wall, to prevent him from landing a punch. If he hadn't, Tim was sure that Patrick would have ended up in jail, and his brother would very likely serve more time for his assault on Sumner than Adams would ever serve for his crime. Of course, at first, Patrick didn't see it that way.

"Pat!" Tim looked his brother in the eye and shouted. "That's enough. You know he can't just hold people without proof. He's only doing his job. He doesn't make the laws."

Tim had surprised himself by being able to pin Patrick against the wall, until his older and stronger brother regained his senses. Once he had, Tim released his grip and the two of them straightened themselves up. Detective Sumner had shown the good sense to back up a bit, away from Patrick. He was still standing there as the brothers approached him.

"How long do you think you can hold Adams with what you've got?" Tim asked the policeman.

"Well, he was picked up last night and held until now. In all honesty, I should walk up there and let him go right now. But I can probably hold him until he gets a lawyer up here, and that could mean tomorrow."

"Well, if you could hold him for as long as possible," Tim said. "We would appreciate it. We're going back to where it happened and see if we can find either someone else who might have been there, or any other evidence."

Sumner began to warn them that the police had already been over the area quite thoroughly, but Tim held up his hand as if he knew what the policeman was about to say. Sumner nodded that he understood. Tim sincerely doubted that he did.

The discussion had been brief and to the point. And now Tim understood exactly how much justice his family was likely to get from the city of Longstown. What would be done would have to be done by them. But how?

Chapter Sixteen

PATRICK HAD USED THE TIME driving between the police station and their neighborhood to curse Detective Sumner and all the other "tin plated bureaucrats" that made up the police department. Meanwhile, Tim had remained fairly quiet. Finally, just as Patrick drove the Impala into the driveway, Tim turned to his brother again and asked him not to tell Da what Sumner had said about releasing Adams, unless he was specifically asked.

"Just don't volunteer anything," he asked. "Da's had enough to deal with."

Then an idea struck Tim, which he shared with Patrick before they went inside. "Maybe Sumner doesn't have the final say in what happens in this case." Tim began. "Maybe what you and I should do, even before we go back to where it happened, is to go see the District Attorney. Maybe we can convince him to keep Adams in jail a little longer, and maybe the DA. can push Mr. Sumner to try a little harder."

Pat was all for going over Sumner's head. But that bit of business could wait until after they checked on their father. Tim had meant all along that they should go later that afternoon, so he agreed. He, too, wanted to see Da and to make sure that everything was going as well as it could. As he waited for Patrick to open the trunk, Tim looked at Mary Margaret's station wagon parked at the curb, and knowing she was still there instinctively made him feel better. His sister would stay as long as they needed her to, but she had her own family to worry about and she couldn't stay away from them indefinitely. He and Patrick would stay with Da for a while and give Mary Margaret a chance to spend some time at home. She wouldn't want to leave, but she should at least have the choice. Then, later in the afternoon after she had taken care of her own family, if she could come back, then Patrick and he could go see the District Attorney. Tim also hadn't called Abrams yet, and that call was now overdue.

As the boys retrieved Tim's bags from the trunk of the Impala and walked up to the front door of the house, Tim was again struck by how familiar the whole scene was, but how little he felt a part of it. Inside the front door, the walls and the furniture were the same as they had always been. That, in itself, wasn't shocking. But today Tim felt more like a visitor than family member. And that hurt a little.

Two women from the parish had come by with plates of food for the family. But nobody had been home, so the women had gone, leaving the food on the porch. In all likelihood, Mary Margaret had brought it inside. Now she was in the kitchen. Da was nowhere in sight and Tim guessed that he was upstairs, resting.

The boys set the suit cases on the entry way floor, out of the way of foot traffic. When she heard them come in, Mary Margaret put aside her kitchen labors and ran to meet them at the door. She hugged Patrick and asked him how he was doing. Pat said he was "fine" and let the subject drop. Then she turned her attention to her youngest brother. With her arm firmly around his shoulders, she asked him the same question, but with a more protective tone.

"And how are you coping, Timmy?"

Tim adored his sister and she, of course, knew it.

"Well," he told her. "I had planned to be gone a bit longer, but it's nice to see everybody again."

It wasn't much of a joke, but Mary Margaret did appreciate his attempt.

"How's Da?" Tim asked her.

The quick answer was that he was doing as well as could be expected under the circumstances. But that answer was not the information that Tim wanted, and Mary Margaret knew it. "Well," she began. "He's upstairs trying to sleep and trying to make sense of it all. And he's trying to imagine any kind of life that's worth living, without her. They've been partners in everything since they were just kids back in Ireland. Now that she's gone, he's a little scared. And, for all of his bluster, he's never been alone before."

"Should I come back, and stay with him?"

The question was blunt and to the point, but then so was Mary Margaret's answer. "What are you going to do for im, if you come back from California? It's nice of you to consider it, and your being here for a while is a big help. But after that, Da has to pick himself up and go on. He has to find his own answers to his own questions."

"How can I help him?"

"Well," Mary Margaret replied, as she took his hands in hers. "Stay around for a few days and help us make the funeral arrangements. There's really not much to it, but do what you can. As for helping Da, if he needs to laugh, laugh with him. And if he needs to cry, do that with him, too. He knows you love him and that you'll miss her, yourself. Just be supportive."

As they sat there together, Tim told Mary Margaret everything that had happened at the police station, and about their plans to get to the District Attorney's office before the end of the day. Once she was sure that he and Patrick were okay, and that they didn't mind her going, she agreed to go home for a while and return later in the afternoon.

"It's not going to be easy telling the kids that their Gramma has gone to heaven," she said. "But going to heaven is a part of coming into this life. And, thinking about it that way, it's really not such a bad deal."

Tim offered to go with her, but Mary Margaret declined, saying that she would rather gather her little family around her, in their own living room, where they would all feel safe, and she would tell them, herself. Then she would need to spend some time with each of the children, but she would get back as early as she could. Once again, Tim was impressed with his sister's strength. But, though she was being strong for all of them, he was still a bit concerned about how she was handling her own loss. Ma had told him once, though, a long time ago, that Mary Margaret and her husband Greg, were the one couple she knew of, who were the most like she and Da. They worked well as a team. As Tim watched his sister drive away, he hoped that Ma was right.

"Everyone needs a place to cry and someone who will let us." he said to himself. But he was sure that his mother had said it first.

It was now just a few minutes after noon, which made it a few minutes after nine in California. Tim could feel that, after being up virtually all night, his body was beginning to demand some sleep. But first he had to tell Abrams what had happened, and what his plans were. Then he would check in with his father, and if Da was still okay, he would go up to his old room and fall asleep.

Tim had written down the number for RDG on a card his first day in the office. Today, not wanting to misdial and add an extra cost to his parent's phone bill, he pulled out the card and reread the number. Then he dialed and waited for a voice on the other end of the line. After three rings, Tim heard the sound that could only mean that Abrams was not answering and that his call was being forwarded to Alice Hartcourt. "Damn," he said to himself, but he was sure that Patrick had heard him.

"Hello," came Alice's voice. "Mr. Abrams's office. May I help you?"

"Alice, it's Tim Conolly. Is Jack just out of his office, or is he not coming in today? Do you know?"

There was an audible quiet, once Alice recognized who she was speaking to, but she did answer that "Mr. Abrams" had gone to a meeting in Rich Barlow's office.

"But where are you, this morning? Mary and Al have been looking for you for almost an hour. Something about making a change in the schedule. Mary left for a minute, but Al's still in the office. I'll transfer you."

The next thing Tim heard was the ringing of still another phone. But this time it was Al who answered. "RDG, Scheduling Department," he said. "Al speaking."

"Al, it's Tim. Alice said you and Mary were looking for me this morning. Is anything wrong?"

"Yeah," he said. "Well no, not really. We just need to move one of your production runs back a week to fit Cardiovan in, and I wanted to tell you about it. Mary checked out your new plan and she said it would probably be okay. But I still wanted to make sure it was okay with you. Where are you, anyway?"

Glad that it was Al he was talking with, Tim told him exactly what had happened last night, after he had left the office.

"Wow, I'm sorry about your mom. That's tough, guy. Are you okay?"

Tim answered that he thought he was, but that he wanted to make sure that Abrams got the message that he would probably not be back before Monday morning. And he gave Al his parents' telephone number to give to Abrams.

"It's the same number he used to offer me the job, but he may have lost it. After all, it's been a whole week since he hired me."

Al heard in Tim's voice the implied apology for taking off so soon after he began his new job. "Don't worry about this place, Chief. Abrams is basically a good guy and he'll understand. And the rest of us can probably keep the place going for at least a week, even without you. At least I think we can."

They laughed a little and Al assured Tim again that he would get Abrams the message. Tim started to tell Al how much he appreciated talking to him. But Al stopped him in mid-sentence and said: "Tim, go get some sleep. You've been up all night and you're starting to babble. I'll talk to Abrams and give him your number. If he wants to talk to you later, he can call. In the meantime, we'll take care of things."

"Thanks guy." Tim said as he hung up the phone. "I'll talk to you later."

Having made the call took a huge weight off Tim's shoulders, making it emotionally possible for him to try to relax. Patrick had settled down on the couch in the living room and had begun to read the morning paper. But he had been up all night also, and soon the open paper was spread across his chest and Tim could hear him snoring. Tim was not far behind. But first he had to go upstairs to see his father.

Moving away from where the phone was, Tim tried to avoid those places on the floor of the old house, where he knew his weight would make the floor creek. He laughed at himself. The way Patrick was snoring, it would take a lot more noise than he was likely to make, even doing so intentionally, to wake him. But still, Tim moved across the living room floor, trying to make as little noise as he could. Outside in the sunshine, he could hear the sounds of neighborhood children playing.

"Going to heaven is part of coming into this life," he said to himself, remembering the way that Mary Margaret has phrased it. "And then the world has to start spinning again."

As Tim reached the bottom of the stairway he couldn't help it, but the strongest memories that came into his mind were of he and the other kids sliding down the old banister, and of how Ma used to shout from the kitchen that they had "better not be doing what I think you're doing." Of course they were, and since Tim was the youngest and usually the last one down, he was usually the one who would get caught in the act. But, though Ma would pretend to be stern with them, secretly Tim always knew that she wasn't really angry, at all. And none of them ever did get punished for doing it. Today he wished he could slide down the old banister again. And that Ma could shout again from the kitchen.

Picking up his bags from where he and Pat had put them, he

started up the stairs. Because he knew that both the third and the fifth stair would creak if he put his weight on them, Tim almost instinctively stepped over them and continued on until he reached the top. When he did, he set the bags on the floor, and looked down the hall toward his old room. Then he stopped. The door to his parents' room, which was immediately to his right at the top of the stairs, was opened just slightly, but not enough for him to see inside. Before he could knock and enter, his father spoke to him from inside. "C'mon in Timmy," he said. "I'm awake."

At that moment, just as Tim opened the door a bit more and entered his parents' bedroom, he looked at Da in the muted light of the room. For the first time in his life, he had been afraid that his father would look like one of the hopeless old men he had seen downtown sitting on the benches. Fortunately, his fear was unjustified. Da was tired, but he showed no signs of giving up.

"I'm sorry Da," he blurted out as he sat down next to his father, who was laying on the bed. "I should have been with her."

Until that moment, Tim had buried his emotions behind his feeling of responsibility to his family. And he had come up the stairs to be an added strength to his father. But now Tim found himself laying on his father's chest, just as he had done as a small boy, and he was sobbing. Da put his arms around his son and he held him for a long minute. Tim sat back up, stood up next to the bed, a bit embarrassed. "I'm sorry. I didn't mean to come in here and do that, Da." he said. "I wanted to come up here and make sure you were all right."

Slowly, Da sat up and put his legs over the side of the bed. Then he gestured toward the windows. "Would you mind opening those curtains behind you, Tim?" he said."

"I think it's time for a little light to enter in here today. This room was always too dark when closed."As he was told, Tim turned around and opened the curtains, and the entire room seemed to light up. When he returned his attention to Da, his father was putting on his shoes and tying the laces. The sun's entering into the room seemed to have revived the older man and returned some of the sparkle to his eye. Da stopped what he was doing for a moment and he said: "Timmy, I've been laying here in the dark for a while. And I've been talking with God and with your mother."

Da paused and Tim wondered what revelation he would be given, next.

"Now, it makes me damned angry that He chose to take her at all, and even madder the way it was done. But she lived her whole life trying to do what she could to be more acceptable to Him, and my feeling is that, for some reason, He needed her with Him even more than we needed her down here. And if that's the way it is, then that's all there is to it. She and I will be together again soon enough."

Da said what he had with conviction, but Tim wondered how deep that conviction went.

"So where are the other kids?" Da asked. "I hope they're not all downstairs crying, or worried that I'm about to do something stupid."

"No." Tim responded. "They're not. Mary Margaret went home to tell her family and to help them get through it. But she's coming back in a few hours to check on you again. Patrick's down on the couch, snoring under the newspaper."

Da laughed at the familiar image, and looked at his son again. With the curtains opened, he could see that Tim was exhausted.

"I think I'll go wake up your brother and he and I will go down to the market. I'm afraid people will be coming by and I don't think there's much in the house to offer them. Besides, it will do me good to get out for a while and 'blow the stink off'. You, Timmy boy, had better get to bed before you fall down. You look terrible."

Tim stood there, smiling at his father, and he didn't know what he should do. He thought he was supposed to be with his dad. To give him support. Now his dad was sending him off to bed. It was almost laughable. However, just before Da left the room and went downstairs to wake Patrick, he turned back to Tim and chided him, saying: "You do remember where your old room was? I know it's been almost half a month since you slept there, but we haven't sealed it off just yet."

They both laughed, and it felt good. Then Da went down the stairs to wake Patrick, while Tim picked up his bags where he had left them, and proceeded down the hallway to his room.

The boards outside of his bedroom door creaked, just as they had since he was a boy. And as he turned the knob, juggling his bags and trying not to let them drop, and opened his bedroom door. Inside the room he was home again. Years ago, when Mary Margaret was still living at home, he and both of his brothers had slept there. Later, when she had married Greg and gone to live with him, Casey got his sister's room because he was the oldest. Tim remembered thinking that it was not totally fair, but once Ma said that it was okay with her, the debate was closed. Tim and Patrick reluctantly shared the room until Casey went off to join the Navy.

As with most brothers, Tim and Patrick had grown very close over their years together. But when Casey left home and Pat moved out of "their room", into "his own room", the two of them seemed to develop apart from one another. Sure, they still loved each other as brothers do.

And perhaps the divergence had been inevitable, given each of their personalities. But Tim always thought that he could trace Patrick's love of doing physical work and creating things with his hands, to the day he got his own room, his own "space". And perhaps it was in reaction to their separation that Tim decided to go to college and take another path for his future. Anyway, regardless of why their choices had been made, now both he and Pat were at peace with the lives that lay before them. Tim chuckled at himself again.

"At least I thought I was, before I ran into Patterson."

Tim carried his bags over to what had been his old dresser, and he proceeded to unpack. Each piece of clothing was returned to the very spot, in the very drawer he had taken it from a week, or so, ago. His socks went into the sock drawer. His suit jacket, which was going to need some pressing before he could wear it again, he hung in the closet and hoped that some of the wrinkles it had collected, would "fall out" being on the hanger. When Tim pulled his shoes out of the bag, though, he stopped for a moment and thought about what he was going to do with Patterson's key. Finally, he decided to keep it with him, and to let himself see the auras again. After all, he would be home for a few days and maybe, safely at home with his family, he could get used to, or learn to handle, the head aches and to seeing the colors. He put the key into the pocket of the pants he was wearing, tossed both the shoes he was wearing and his dress shoes from the bag into the closet, and lay down on his bed.

Chapter Seventeen

Tim had no misconceptions that the District Attorney's office would be any more helpful that Sumner had been, but he was determined to give them a chance. Perhaps someone there would have the guts to step outside the safety of their procedures and actually do what was right. Maybe not. But if they wouldn't make that step, was he prepared to take care of Adams on his own? And what did that mean, exactly? Was he prepared to kill the man? And if he did kill Adams, wouldn't the cops hunt him down and charge him with murder? How ironic, he thought to himself, if he wound up spending the rest of his life rotting in a cell, because he decided to carry out what the cops and the lawyers were paid to do. Or could he do it and escape paying the price? That would be a rough form of justice, wouldn't it? Perhaps, this time, two wrongs would make a right.

As Tim laid on top of the bed and stared up at the ceiling of his room, he let his imagination run free.

After all, there were literally hundreds of methods to kill someone. Some were easy and direct, like shooting them or stabbing them with a knife. But these had the "negative feature" that the perpetrator could probably be identified and prosecuted. That thought returned immediately to Tim's not wanting to spend the rest of his life in prison. Another "negative feature" of the direct physical approach was that, for all of Tim's youth and vitality, being a laborer, Adams was likely to be much bigger and stronger than he was. No, if he did the deed himself, he wanted to find a way that would have the same results, that Adams would be dead, but that didn't require Tim to take the man on, physically. And there wasn't much time. Today was Tuesday, and he had to be back at RDG by Monday morning.

Of course, maybe he didn't have to kill Adams on this trip, at all. And, maybe having Adams die under criminal circumstances would pin too much suspicion on him and his family. Perhaps he should come back six months from now and do it. But in six months, Adams could have disappeared.

These thoughts and hundreds like them swirled through Tim's head as he laid there. Finally, he corralled the images in his mind and he slept. And when he slept, once again he dreamed of the slender young woman at the bottom of the knoll and of the boy, who sat next to him. Again, it seemed that his mother had said "good-bye".

By three o'clock, Da and Patrick had returned from the market and Mary Margaret had been able to rejoin them at the house. Pat came up the stairs to wake Tim.

"Hey, Timmy." he said, as he gently shook his little brother. "Mary Margaret's back and it's time we went to see the DA."

Tim woke with a start, eyes wide, and he scared Patrick a bit by sitting straight up and looking at him as if he were a stranger. Instinctively, Pat stepped back, half expecting his brother to leap off the bed at him. As he sat there, Tim's body was covered with sweat, as if he had been awakened from a nightmare. And perhaps he had.

"Tim, are you okay?" Pat asked, as he watched his brother's eyes dart around the room.

After a minute spent remembering where he was, but not too

many seconds before Pat would have run downstairs to get Mary Margaret to help him, Tim calmed down and he reassured his brother that everything was "fine".

"I just needed to get my bearings," he said. "What time is it, did you say?"

"It's just after three. And if we're going to the DA's office today, we had better get a move on. I waited as long as I thought I could before get you up. But now it's time to go."

Tim nodded, grateful that his brother had given him the time that he had. However, as he sat there, he desperately wanted to drop back down onto the bed. But lost sleep was something that he would have to make up later.

"The prosecutor's office is across the street from the police station, so maybe whoever we get can call over to Sumner and stop him from releasing Adams." Tim told his brother, as he got up and put on a clean shirt.

As Tim was putting on his shoes, Patrick opened the curtains and let the sunshine in. Then, as he looked at his brother, what he saw nearly took Tim's breath away. Patrick was standing there, waiting for him to get dressed, but all around him was an aura that was a more vivid red than any Tim had seen before. And somehow Tim knew that the color signified that his brother was in pain. Outwardly, though, Patrick looked very much as he always had.

"Pat," Tim asked, somewhat hesitatingly. "Are you okay?"

Patrick answered immediately that he was "fine". Then he insisted that they get going. Without seeing the aura, Tim would never have known.

A few minutes later, the boys rumbled down the stairs. Da and Mary Margaret were sitting at the table in the kitchen, having a cup of tea. Just as if it were any other day. And perhaps it was. As he looked at her in the well-lighted room, Tim could see that the majority of his sister's aura was the deep green color of someone who is content, and in her element. The only area of exception was a hint of red around her heart, and that bit of pain was not surprising under the circumstances. He paused for a moment, leaned against the wall, and began breathing deeply. Inhaling, and slowly releasing. He waved his sibling off when they showed concern. "Just a bit of a headache", he told them, as the pain subsided.

Mary Margaret had always been a nurturer, walking in her mother's footsteps. And it had always made her happiest to remain calm and to care about, and care for, others. Tim loved her a lot.

As Da sat there, though, sipping his tea, his emotional state was a totally different story. His father's aura held every color Tim had ever seen, including the dark blue he had only seen before with Alice Hartcourt. In addition, as compared to the others', whose colors remained fairly constant, Da's aura seemed to pulsate and to change colors, moment to moment. It was this sense of instability that worried Tim the most. Outwardly, though, his father seemed as calm as any of them.

"And you two are off to the DA's office?" he asked as the boys entered the kitchen. Patrick answered.

"First, we're going to go back to the police station, and then to the District Attorney's office to see if they have anything new on the case." he said. "Then we might go downtown to see if we can find any witnesses that the cops might have missed."

Da motioned to them to go, but as they left he warned them not to get in the way. "Let the police do what we pay them to," he said. But he doubted if they heard him.

The boys had heard, but having already talked to Sumner, neither of them was willing to let it stop there. And they both felt the anger and the frustration of knowing that one of them might have to tell their father that Adams had been set free. As they climbed into the Impala, and as Patrick turned the key to start the engine, Mary Margaret ran out the front door toward them. Patrick rolled down the driver's side window to find out what she wanted.

"I want you two to keep me up on whatever it is that's happening," she told them. "I wouldn't go into a lot of detail about it with Da just yet, but I want to know. Okay?"

Tim leaned toward the window and reassured her that she would know as much about the "investigation" as he did.

"Don't worry," he said. "You'll know more about it than you ever wanted to, before this is over."

Feeling better, Mary Margaret ran back into the house and the boys drove down the street. Patrick chuckled to himself, as if keeping Mary Margaret updated was a foolish idea.

"Timmy," Pat began. "I love Mary Margaret as much as any man loves his sister, but you're not seriously thinking about filling her head with the details of a police investigation, are you?"

The question shocked Tim, who always thought he knew his brother pretty well. And it shocked him even more because it had a smell of sexism that Patrick must have picked up outside of the family. "What do you mean?" he asked. "Of course I'm going to tell her. Just because she's willing to stay with Da is no reason not to keep her up on what's happening."

Pat didn't offer any more comment, and Tim let the subject drop. He did wonder though, if maybe Patrick's own sense of loss wasn't affecting his judgment.

"Now," Tim asked. "What is it that we want to accomplish by talking to the DA.? Do you want to do the talking again?"

Pat replied that he didn't know the DA any better than Tim did, but he thought he should again be the one to speak "for the family".

"Well do you think you can do it without blowing your stack again?"

Pat took the question as a personal affront and, in a way, Tim had meant it that way. "What you did with Sumner was stupid. And you almost got yourself arrested." As he spoke, Tim put his left hand on his brother's shoulder and laughed at the situation. "I'd have a hard time explaining to Da why I didn't bring you home."

Pat didn't think the situation was nearly as funny as Tim did. As he shrugged Tim's hand off his shoulder, he promised that he would try not to let his temper get out of hand again. "But maybe, this time you had better do the talking. You educated types," meaning Tim and the District Attorney, "might get along better than we working stiffs. Sumner's just a cop. But whoever we get on this trip is likely to be some hot-shot lawyer."

As it happened, the representative of the District attorney's office they were introduced to was an overweight and shabbily-dressed man of about forty five, who had only the vaguest idea of what the case was about. His name was Barkley. "Let's see," he said, obviously paying attention to the contents of the file marked "Conolly" for the first time. "Victim found unconscious. No first-hand witnesses. No prints. Circumstantial evidence pointing to a migrant laborer named Adams." Barkley looked back at Tim and Patrick and shook his head. "In short, fellas, we've got no case against this guy. Law says we have to let him go."

As Barkley closed the file, Tim pulled it from his hands and began to leaf through the documents. Barkley made no effort to stop him. There were two pictures marked "crime scene". One was also marked "North", meaning that the picture had been taken from north of the scene. The other picture was marked "South". There were also two photographs of Adams. One of these showed his profile, the other, taken from the front, showed his face. This was the first time that Tim had ever seen the man, and he would see that face in his dreams for a long time. Leafing through the report, Tim was also able to glean the "residence" address that Adams had given at the time of his arrest, and the address of the bar where he had actually been picked up.

"You can add 'victim now deceased' to your file, Mr. Barkley." Tim told the man, as he shoved the file back into his hands. "She died this morning."

The news had no visible effect on Barkley, and he responded saying: "That means there is no one to even accuse Adams of the crime. And it probably means that the boys and girls across the street have already let him go. I'm sorry, but that's the law."

As he faced them, Barkley shrugged his shoulders and raised his hands over his head, as if he was physically reinforcing the message that he had given them since they arrived. The case was closed, and there was nothing left for him to do but to file it away. Barkley left Tim and Pat standing in the hallway where they had met, and disappeared.

Far from satisfied, however, now the boys were angry and they asked the first person they saw, another man who looked like he might work in the building, where the office of the actual District Attorney was. Once they had been given directions, Tim and Pat went down a long corridor, as they were told, and they arrived at a large office with a sign indicating that it was, indeed, the office of the District Attorney. When Tim asked a woman, who had been sitting at a desk, just outside, he was informed that "Yes, this is the office of the District Attorney, but Mr. Laird is at a conference, out of state. Would you like to leave a message? Or, perhaps someone else in the office might be able to help you."

Tim briefly described to the woman what had happened during their meeting with Mr. Barkley, and that they were far from happy with the way the department was handing their mother's case. "The guy just killed my mother," Tim told her." And all the cops and the attorneys want to do is to get it off their case load. Is there anyone around here that we can talk to, to get some action?"

"Well," replied the woman, who clearly now wished she had not been there for the brothers to ask. "You could fill out a complaint form and mail it to the address on the back. "Then she reassured them, saying: "All complaints are individually reviewed as they come in, and you will be contacted if there are any further questions."

Somehow the woman truly seemed to expect that knowing that this option was open to them, would actually help make Tim and Patrick feel better. Of course it didn't. But the boys now knew that they had exhausted their options. At least their legal options. The woman they had been speaking to then picked up a stack of files from her desk, and she too disappeared down a long hallway. Once again, the boys were left standing alone. Fortunately though, as Tim and Pat turned around to leave, there were large signs in the connecting corridors that pointed the way out. Tim was frustrated but he had to chuckle. "This is textbook bureaucracy, Pat" he laughed and shook his head. "We, as tax payers, have had to run into two very unhelpful idiots, called 'public servants'. And then we have trouble finding the big guy's office." Pat was nodding as Tim continued. "Then, when we finally get to his office, he's securely out of town. Now, I don't really know that whoever does the planning around here actually meant for things to happen this way, or if it's just great good luck on their part."

"However," Tim continued and he pointed to the exit signs. "When we do get ready to do what they really want us to do, namely go away and not bother them, all we have to do is turn around and follow the signs. This way, if you please, sir."

"And, you know Tim, " Patrick added, and he knew something about the subject from his dealings in the union. "The best thing about rules, for people who don't want to work hard, is that they give people official reasons for not doing it."

What Tim did not discuss with his brother were the auras of the two "public servants" that they had run into. Both of them were green, but they were a very pale green. And the absence of color, even a contented color such as green, seemed to underscore how little of themselves they had invested in whatever job they were doing.

"Pat, do you know where Glory Lane is?" The question surprised Pat, but Tim continued. "2935 Glory Lane is what Adams gave as his residence address when they picked him up. Isn't that over by the Post Office?"

"Yeah, it is." Pat replied. "There's a bunch of low rent apartments there that some of the guys from out of town have been renting instead of taking the train home every night.

"And the report said he'd been picked up near a bar called 'Sleepy Teds'. Do you know that place?"

Pat said he did, and asked, "Do you want to go down by there?"

"No. That's okay. I just wondered."

Pat started up the Impala again and the boys drove home, in silence. Finally, Patrick asked the question that they were both thinking to themselves: "If the cops and the DA's office aren't going to do anything about Adams, and they set him free, what are we going to tell Da?"

There was a short pause but then Tim answered the way they both knew that he would: "We're going to tell him the truth."

Chapter Eighteen

Da took the news better than Tim had expected. His aura, though, was now far more red than it had been earlier. But again, it fluctuated, as if he didn't know quite how to react. Finally, he motioned for all of his children to come around him and they hugged each other for a very long time. During the hug, Da said a prayer and they all cried a bit. Then the four of them sat around the kitchen table.

"Kids," Da began. "Your mother was always very proud of the bunch of us. Never forget that. And never forget that she loved us all more than any of us knew."

Once again there were tears flowing around the table, but Da continued: "But she's gone from us now." he said. "And she would want us all to continue the lives that she helped us start."

Tim looked down at the table and he noticed that, though they were each leaning forward and concentrating on what Da was saying, none of their hands were touching. Since he was sitting between Mary Margaret and Patrick, he reached out and joined hands with both of them. Da, who was sitting directly across from Tim, reached out and completed the circle. Even with Ma gone, even through the tears, the family would never really be separated.

"Okay, then," said Da, as withdrew his hands and the circle broke. "We need to notify the parish that we need to have a viewing, a memorial service, and a burial."

"Da," answered Mary Margaret. "I've talked to Father Berry and he's agreed to perform the services. I thought maybe Thursday for the viewing and Friday for the funeral, if that's okay with you."

"That'll be fine," he said. If Tim had not seen his father's aura, he would not have known that the finality of having the services seemed to startle him. Still, Tim didn't know what to say.

Da stood up, poured himself another cup of tea, and he asked if anybody else needed a refill. They had all managed their share and so declined. Tea cup in hand, Da sat back down at the table.

"You kids remember something else," he told them. "The bastard that did this thing will not escape judgment. In the end, everything evens out, regardless of how we try to prevent it. Nature has a way of doing that, even when we're not around to help out."

Oddly, Da's comment on things working out, even if they were not there to help them, seemed to relieve some of the red surrounding Patrick. The color change around him was dramatic. And immediately, Tim wondered if, maybe, Patrick's "pain" was somehow connected to other peoples' expectations of him. Perhaps Patrick, as the oldest son present, thought that he would be the one expected to avenge the family. And now Da had told him, and everybody else, that revenge wouldn't be necessary. Somehow, nature would take care of things. Anyway, Tim was delighted to see the change in his brother. Seeing it happen, he began to understand how much physical impact parents can have on their grown children.

As the family sat there, the phone rang and everyone hoped that it might be Casey calling. He did call later that evening to reassure them that he would be home the next day, but this call was from Mrs. Reineker, from the parish. She and some of the other women had planned another food delivery for them, "if it would be convenient". Da, at first, thought to say no. Clamping his hand over the phone, he looked at his children and rolled his eyes.

"We can bloody well feed ourselves," he said.

Tim disagreed, and this time he prevailed.

"These women were Ma's friends," he told them. "They knew each other for a long time. We should let them help. It's not really for us. It's to honor her and what she meant to them."

Tim had made his point. After what he would later refer to as "Timmy's speech", Da spoke into the receiver. "Gloria," he said.

"Thank you for calling. We would love for you and the other ladies to come over whenever you like. The house is a bit of a wreck just now, but Maeve would have loved the thought. And the kids and I would appreciate it, too."

Da hung up the phone and told the kids that "They'll be coming by in an hour or two to check on us for the priest."

That the parish priests had nothing better to do with their day than to check on the comings and goings of the Conolly clan had been a running joke between he and Maeve since the day they moved into the house and Da had offered drinks to the neighbors. Today, the joke just seemed appropriate.

After a while, as each of them made sure that the others were doing okay, Da went back upstairs to see if he could take a nap. Once he had gone up, Mary Margaret again went home to see to Greg and the kids.

"I'll be back as early tomorrow as I can." she told her brothers. "And if you need anything, you've got my number. By the way, Tim, the kids would love to see you before you have to go back to California. Try to stop by, will you?"

Tim said that he would, but he didn't know exactly when, and his sister didn't press him. When she left, Patrick and he were, once again, by themselves. But it was as good a time as any for what Tim wanted to ask his brother. "Pat, can you loan me some money, for a few weeks?"

Tim said that he would, but he didn't know exactly when, and his sister didn't press him. When she left, Patrick and he were, once again, by themselves. But it was as good a time as any for what Tim wanted to ask his brother. "Pat, can you loan me some money, for a few weeks?"

When they were growing up, it had always been Tim who had saved his money and Pat who asked him to borrow some. And Tim had always loaned it to him, without question nor comment.

"Sure kid," Pat answered. "How much do you need?"

"Well, for a ticket back to San Jose and living expenses until I get paid by RDG, I'd like to borrow about fifteen hundred dollars. Is that okay?"

Pat's eyebrows went up, not because he had any problem with loaning Tim the money, but because it was a lot more than he expected to be asked for. However, this was not the week to give his brother a hard time.

"Sure. I'll have to get it out of the Credit Union for you tomorrow, but that shouldn't be a problem. Is tomorrow okay for you?"

"Yeah, I don't really need it until the weekend. But thanks a bunch. This whole thing just happened at a bad time for me."

Tim immediately realized just how stupid his comment was, under the circumstances, but Pat knew what he meant and let it drop. "Just pay me back when you have it," he said.

Chapter Nineteen

The ladies from the parish came by later that afternoon, and brought with them a pot roast, a plate full of potatoes, and some corn. Da was still upstairs asleep. And though Tim said he was sure that his father would want to thank the women himself, Mrs. Reineker insisted that he let his father be.

"I'm sure we'll talk at a better time," she said. Then, as Tim and Pat thanked them for their kindness, Mrs. Reineker and the other women left. After not eating since much earlier that day, the smell of the food awoke the boys' appetites. Within minutes of the women's departure, half of what they had brought had been eaten.

"Remember," Pat said. "Da hasn't had anything but tea all day. And though he may not want anything yet, when he does, he'll make up for it."

The food had been delivered in separate containers, so it was easy enough for the boys to cover the remaining portions, and to keep them as warm as possible. Pat thought that the dishes should be kept warm in the oven under a low heat. His brother agreed.

With the house now quiet except for the sound of the television set, and with Pat nodding off on the couch, Tim sat down and mentally made plans for that evening. He wanted to spend a few more hours at the house with Pat, and wait until the sun went down. Then, hopefully without having to tell anyone why he wanted it, he planned to borrow the Impala and take a drive to find 2935 Glory Lane. Until now, he and Pat had done things together. From now on, though, he would operate alone. Around seven o'clock, Patrick woke up and they watched a movie together. But by ten o'clock, he was fast asleep again and it was dark enough for Tim to go.

"I'm going stir crazy just sitting around here. " Tim told his brother, in case he was just lying there with his eyes closed. "I think I'll go for a drive. Do you need anything from the store?"

There was no reply and Tim thought for a moment before he woke Pat up to tell him that he was going out. He knew that it might be a tactical mistake. Pat slept like a rock, and he was fairly sure that he could have gone and come back well before his brother woke up again. On the other hand, though, if Pat did wake up and could not find him in the house, there might be more questions asked than Tim wanted to answer. More importantly, Pat had the car keys for the Impala in his pocket. As it was, Tim had to shake his brother pretty hard, just to get him awake enough to hand them over. However, before Tim left through the front door, he could heard Pat snoring again.

"Maybe he won't remember." he said to himself as he left.

After ten o'clock, most towns the size of Longstown folded up and went to bed, particularly on week nights. In fact, Tim wondered as he drove through the darkness, where he would have gone had Patrick answered that he did want something from the store.

Without traffic, the drive to the area of town near the Post Office should have taken about twenty minutes. Tonight, though, the fact that Tim was stopped by every signal that he came to, and once stopped made to think about the gravity of what he planned to do, the drive was taking about ten minutes longer. .But he decided to take as much time as he needed. Nobody would question why he would have trouble sleeping tonight. He would take enough time to drive past where Adams was living, and then he wanted to find the bar where the police had arrested him. Maybe then he could get back home before either Pat or Da knew he had gone.

Tim checked his watch when he first saw the Post Office building, on his right. The main building itself was only a few years old, but it was already said to be too small to be effective. And the Postal Authority had decided that it needed to be larger. In addition, the local job market had been tight and the construction trades had political muscle in Longstown.

Glory Lane was a five block stretch, about a quarter of a mile south of the downtown area. It was one of those neighborhoods that Ma had warned him to steer clear of when he was younger, where trouble could find a person even if they weren't looking for any. And Ma was usually right. The dark of night was broken by a string of streetlights, but they did little more than buzz and cast a dim circle of haze for a few feet. Outside of the circle, darkness took over.

Tim tried to get a complete picture of the neighborhood in his mind. The majority of the buildings on Glory Lane had stood there for decades.

Others, though, were much more recently constructed multi-unit apartment buildings. Already, the grass lawns carefully planted in front of these new units had been allowed to die. And broken down cars took up space on the street.

The building at the address that Tim had read in the District Attorney's file, 2935 Glory Lane, seemed to be one of the newer buildings, but it was as run down and neglected as any of the others on the street. He drove the Impala past it and continued down to the end of the block. There, on the corner was a small neighborhood bar called Sleepy Ted's. From its address, painted over the front door, Tim knew that this bar was where Adams had come after the attack. This is where he had bragged about what he had done.

Tim pulled the Impala over to the curb and parked well away from the nearest light fixture. Looking into his rear-view mirror he could see the front door of Sleepy Ted's. If anyone went to drink there, that was the door he would probably have to come out of. Just ahead of him, as he sat there in the dark, Tim could see the front door of the apartment building that Adams would probably go into, after drinking away a portion of his pay check. This Friday, there would be a memorial service for Ma. And this Friday night, Adams would pay for what he did.

Chapter Twenty

The plan that Tim formulated as he sat in the Impala and looked around the neighborhood had to be kept simple.

"There's going to be a shooting, around here," he said to himself. "And it's going to be at very short range, so I'm sure it kills him."

Tim was surprised at his own ability to consider the details of how he was going to kill Adams, almost without concerning himself with the horror of it.

"Some time before two o'clock in the morning, when the bar closes," Tim began again to himself. "I'll park the Impala on a side street just around the corner there. Then I'll get out and wait down at that end of the block until I see him come out of the bar. If Adams comes out of the bar alone, and if he comes directly home, I'll begin walking toward him, on the same side of the street. If I can walk fast enough, and he's drunk enough, we should pass each other just before he reaches his building. Then, I'll just push a gun into his chest and blow a hole in his heart."

Tim thought about what he had just said to himself, and then he added: "If I'm lucky, and if I do it quickly enough, the sound will be partially muffled and Adams will look like any other drunk, laying down in front of the building. And hopefully, no one will pay much attention to him until I'm out of the area."

Two pieces of the plan still needed to be worked out as Tim left the area around Glory Lane, and made his way home. "First I've got to get a gun." he said. "Then I've got to have a solid alibi."

For obvious reasons, Tim wanted to use a gun that could not be traced back to him or to anyone in the family. He planned to get rid of it immediately, but in case the police actually got around to looking for a weapon, and "God forbid they were actually motivated to do something with it should they come across one", Tim didn't want to leave any kind of trail for them to follow.

He would need to go out of state, probably to New Jersey in order to buy it. Fortunately, that was not a problem. From Longstown, with two or three hours of hard driving, he could get there, buy the gun and be on his way back home. If what he had heard about the gun laws in New Jersey was true, he probably wouldn't even need an ID.

During tonight's return trip to the house, Tim seemed to hit all the green lights that he had missed on his way to Glory Lane. Twenty minutes later, he could see the house. As he rounded the corner, Tim shut off the Impala's engine and the car glided silently into his parents' driveway. When the boys were in their teens, if they had been out, either together or separately, and especially if they had missed their curfew and were expecting to be in trouble when they arrived home, both Tim and Pat had learned to turn off the engine in order to arrive as quietly as they could. Casey had learned to do it first and had later taught the younger boys how.

In theory, if one or both of their parents had been waiting for them to come in, and if they were laying in their bed while they waited, before the guilty party arrived, their parents just might have fallen asleep. In that case, again according to the theory, it was just possible that the "condemned" might get a lighter sentence if it was delivered when cooler heads prevailed in the morning. The ploy had never worked exactly, but each time the situation arose, it was felt to be worth an attempt.

Over the years, Tim had gotten the "silent landing" down pretty well, tonight coming to a complete stop only three feet from the closed garage door. Inwardly, Tim was pleased that, after not having done it for a while, his accuracy was still pretty good.

Inside the house, there had been only the one light left on in the living room, and that still seemed to be the case. Tim closed the front door quietly behind him, and he listened to see if he could still hear Pat snoring in front of the television. He heard nothing. In fact, when he entered the room, he saw that Pat had gone upstairs and that he, or someone else, had turned off the set. Looking down at his watch, it was almost twelve thirty. Maybe there was nothing to worry about. Tim decided to go upstairs, himself.

Turning off the light in the living room and groping his way back to the stairwell, again Tim avoided the noisy steps and carefully made his way to his room. Once there, he closed the door and turned on his bedside lamp. There at the base of the lamp was a note that Patrick had written. "Tim," it began. "Right after you left, a Mr. Abrams from RDG called. Says that Monday will be just fine. Call him if there is anything they can do."

There was also another message that had obviously come in after the first, and had been scribbled on the bottom of the same piece of paper.

"Casey called MM." It read. "He's coming in tomorrow AM. She's picking him up."

The fact that Mary Margaret was picking Casey up at the airport would help to clear the way for Tim to take the Impala to New Jersey. But he had to make the trip tomorrow. With Casey home, there was that much more chance that he or someone else would need to use the car. And with the viewing being held on Thursday and the funeral on Friday, there would almost surely be errands that needed to be run the days before.

Tim tried to be as quiet as he could as he took off his clothes, put on his pajamas, and crawled into bed. Patrick might still be awake, or maybe Da. Either way, Tim didn't want them to hear that he was still awake and think that he might want to talk. This day had been too long already. And there had been enough talk. Reaching up to turn off the light, Tim noticed that someone had placed a rosary on his table. It had most likely been his sister, but he would not have been surprised if it had actually been Da. For all of his father's bluster to the contrary, he had always demonstrated an abiding faith in God. And, though the various priests that had come through the parish might not have blessed his lack of homage to their rituals, nonetheless, Tim had never seen his father waver more than a step or two from what Ma called "the straight and narrow". But, whether he had strayed or not, she had still loved him.

As he lay there in his bed, every part of him, physical or emotional, reported its exhaustion. He conjured up a vision of his mother's face. Not the bruised and battered version of it that he had seen at the hospital, but the youthful and smiling image of her that he had always carried in his heart.

"Why'd you let it happen, God?" he asked silently, watching the ceiling of his room for some kind of answer.

But there was no sign. And the answer that came to his mind, "because God wanted her with Him", made less sense to Tim now than it ever had. Immediately, he thought about Adams and about what the man had done.

"If I take him out, will you overlook my actions the same way you overlooked his? He killed her, God. And he's getting away with it. Will I be forgiven, to go on and live my life?"

No one brought up in a Catholic family got very old without knowing that God "watches over the falling of a sparrow". But as Tim silently shouted his question to the ceiling of his room, he answered the basic question that sat quietly at the pit of his stomach:

"Yes God, I know that killing Adams is a sin. It's vengeance. And I know that killing him is a mortal sin that should send me to Hell forever. But, God, it's going to happen."

For Tim, the situation held a strange twist of irony. His parents had brought him up to know right from wrong. And they had educated him in the litany of Hell and damnation, which, according to the Church, would surely be his punishment for doing this evil act. However, his parents had gone beyond the role of educators for their children. They had been loving and nurturing people, who had taken the time and expended the extra energy required to be actual examples for him.

When Tim was young, they truly enjoyed his childhood and they allowed him to enjoy it also. And by the time he was old enough to be a man, they had instilled in him the bedrock virtues, such as "Fair Play", that had been passed down to them.

"I'm sorry already, Lord." he said. "But right or wrong, I have to kill that bastard for what he did."

Tim lay in his bed as he turned his back on God, the only friend who had been closer to him than his mother. However, he also half expected there to be a feeling that approached the righteousness, even self-righteousness, of doing what was fair and just. Adams had murdered. As he lay there staring at the wall, a quiet tear fell and moistened a spot on his pillow. Perhaps, to do what is "just" in the world, means having to act alone. And perhaps that ultimate aloneness did require turning one's back, even on God.

Sometime later Tim actually fell asleep. Tonight, though, there were none of the peaceful dreams of good bye. But he did sleep deeply. Tomorrow night, unless Casey decided not to reclaim his old room down the hall, as was his right, Tim would again have to share his room with Patrick. This night would be the last he would spend alone until he returned to California.

"And who knows," he thought to himself, as he dozed off. "Even with a troubled aura, if that girl in the coffee shop is still there, maybe sleeping alone won't be a problem, either."

The next morning, Wednesday, Tim awoke just before nine o'clock. By the time he got dressed and made his way downstairs, Da had been up for an hour or so and had begun mixing up a batter for pancakes.

"Well, if it's not our own Sleeping Beauty." he said. "Get yourself a cup of coffee or tea. There'll be breakfast in about ten minutes."

Tim's mind was in a state of "disconnect", so he just nodded to Da and walked over to the cupboard and poured himself some coffee.

"Is Pat up yet?" he asked.

"Oh heavens, yes." his father answered. "Said he had to go down to the job site, down at the new Post Office, to check on a few things. He's taken the day off as a bereavement holiday, but he said there were still a couple of things he wanted to check on. Said he'd be back in time for lunch, though."

Two immediate thoughts occurred to Tim. First, his brother had the Impala, which meant that he would have to wait until later in the day to make his run to New Jersey. That wasn't really a problem, though, since he expected any large store to be open until at least five o'clock. His second thought was that Tim had never known his brother to ever go to a job site when he wasn't expecting to work. In fact, Pat had always said that "if I'm not getting paid to be there, I'll be somewhere else." Maybe, this morning, Pat just wanted to have something to do. But the timing of it was still odd. A few minutes later, Da pulled a large platter from the shelf and began loading it with hot pancakes. As usual, he made more than the two of them could possibly eat. But Da had always prided himself on making sure his family had eaten all they wanted, and then had a bit more. Tim loved his father's pancakes. Within twenty minutes, they eaten the entire plateful and Da had offered to make more. But Tim waved him off. They had both eaten like they had starved for days, and neither of them could eat another bite.

"Well, I guess you haven't lost your appreciation for the finer things." Da chided him as they both sat back in their chairs and wondered on the volume of food they had consumed.

"No sir." Tim replied. "What's good is good. And your pancakes are still the best I've ever eaten."

Da smiled at his youngest son, as he stood up and collected their plates. Then, turning quiet, as he did when there was something on his mind, something that he wanted to be careful about how he brought it up, Da placed the dishes in the sink and turned on the water.

"Tim," he began, with his back to his son. "I don't want either you or Patrick to do anything stupid in the next few days." Tim tried to appear shocked at the thought of it.

Da allowed some water to run into the sink. Then he turned off the tap and faced Tim. "I don't begin to know why any of this needed to happen. That's up to God, I guess. But I don't want you boys to go off and try to make up for it. I want you to leave that up to God, too."

Tim stood up from the table, shook his head, and embraced his father. But, at the same time, he wouldn't let their eyes meet.

"I know," he said to Da. "Don't worry. God will take care of it."

When the two men broke their embrace, Tim sat down at the table again, where his father joined him.

"I'm more concerned about Patrick than I am about you, though." Da continued. "You've always been the one who would think things through. Pat's more likely to act first, give in to his anger."

Da paused and looked away for a moment. The tears in his father's eyes seemed to have a stinging effect in his own. Then Da began again. "Tim, I don't want any more trouble." he said. "Your mom's gone and it's going to be hard enough on everybody. I talked to Patrick this morning, and he said his usual 'Yeah, yeah, I understand.' But I'm afraid of what he might do. Now, I'm going to have this same talk with Casey, when he gets here. But I'd like you to do what you can to keep an eye on things."

Hearing his father speak like that, it was all Tim could do not to sit there sobbing. But that wasn't going to help anyone. Then, as he thought about it for a moment, Tim actually felt relieved that the bulk of his father's concern was with what Patrick might do, not what he had planned. He nodded. The last thing he wanted, for the next few days, was to be the focus of anyone's attention. At the same time, however, he watched his father's aura change. And that was the good news he had hoped for. When his father's concentration became focused on Patrick's well-being, or anybody else's for that matter, the color of it began to revert back to a much healthier shade of green. And, the fluctuations he had seen within the arch itself became less pronounced.

"Don't worry, Da." he repeated. "God has a way of taking care of things."

Perhaps he had spoken blasphemy, but perhaps it was simply the truth. Either way, what he said wasn't a lie. For the remainder of the morning, Tim and his father busied themselves around the house. But they also took the opportunity to talk about a range of subjects, the way they had in the past. As had always been the case, they agreed on most subjects. He and his father had their differences, but it was the fact that they could still discuss things, whether they agreed with each other or not, that seemed to verify that there was still a core of love and respect between them. Nothing had changed that.

By the time Patrick returned, it was nearly two o' clock, which didn't leave Tim much time. However, his brother had been to his credit union and, when Da was in the kitchen and the two boys were alone, Patrick pressed two thousand dollars in cash, into Tim's hand. Then he silenced Tim's thanks, putting his index finger to his lips.

"Just pay it back when you can." Tim nodded.

Because time was short, and because he didn't want to discuss his own plans, there was nothing more said about the loan. Nor were there any questions about what else Patrick had been up to that morning. Instead, Tim asked if it was all right if he borrowed the car, telling his father and his brother that there were some things that he needed to pick up before going back to California. Pat made a face at his younger brother, as if he were very impressed by Tim's "traveling" needs.

"Did you wear out your only swimsuit in the first week?" Pat asked him.

"Yeah," was the reply. "They don't last long when the girls keep ripping them off you. It's really a tough way to live."

Before they had stopped laughing, Tim had gone out the front door. He started the car, and within moments he was driving again.

There were no major freeways between Longstown and the New

Jersey state line. In fact, the most direct route available consisted of a small state road, with only one lane of traffic in each direction. Fortunately though, at three o'clock in the afternoon, there was very little traffic and the Impala made great time. Small farming towns dotted the road, each with its requisite gas station and tiny cluster of stores.

These towns were the communities where many of the current population's grandparents had settled down, after first arriving in the United States of America. Just as his parents had, these people had worked hard to scratch out a living, had raised families, and had done quite well. In addition, because in many of the neighborhoods when the children were old enough to get married and have their own children they simply built a house next to their parents, many of their neighbors were also relatives. They all knew each other and each other's business, but people watched out for each other, and it was a wonderful place to bring up kids.

After two hours, Tim crossed over the New Jersey state line and found himself entering a fairly large town whose name, the sign said, was Maryellen. Over to his right, as he drove down the main street, was a gas station where Tim stopped to look at a telephone book and a map of the area. Just north of Maryellen, he discovered what he had come for, McBrides Gun shop.

Tim had never owned a gun, and he had never even fired one. But he did know a few things that he thought were important. First, the gun that he bought had to be large enough to do the job. It had to have enough firepower to kill Adams with one bullet. On the other hand, he didn't want to have to carry a cannon. Secondly, Tim wanted a gun that was fairly common. What he had in mind was a small version of a Colt 45, since these guns had been around forever, and a large number of people owned them. But maybe there was a better choice.

When he walked through the front door of McBrides, the proprietor was nowhere to be seen. But there were signs that indicated which section of the store housed which sort of gun. To his right, there were more rifles than he had ever seen in one spot before. And on the far side of the rifles, there was an entire wall of shelves which contained literally hundreds of boxes of ammunition. Over to Tim's left were the handguns.

A part of him wanted desperately to run out through the front door again, and to drive back to his life in New York before this nonsense went any further. But he had made up his mind. Tim walked over to the display counter that housed the various types of handguns that McBrides was selling. Some models had barrels that looked to be more the length of rifles than of pistols, but others were more in line with what he was looking for. After he had stood in front of the case for a minute or so, a man came hurrying down one of the store's aisles, walking as fast as he could.

"Can I help you find something?" the man inquired.

As Tim hesitated for a moment, the man opened a gate, let himself behind the counter, and began to open up the display that he had been looking at.

"Were you looking for something particular?"

During the drive to Maryellen, Tim had concocted a story that he now told the man behind the counter. "Well, I don't know a thing about guns, except that you point the business end at something and pull the trigger. But now I think I need to buy one." he almost stuttered. "I live in a pretty rough part of town, and we've had some robberies. But, up until now, that hasn't been much a problem since I really didn't have anything worth taking."

The man behind the counter was nodding as Tim spoke, but he kept quiet. He had heard the story, or one of its variations, before. But he didn't want to squelch a sale.

"The problem is, " Tim continued. "My girlfriend moved in with me last week, and now I'm scared that some thug's going to break in to get at her. And if something does happen, I want to be prepared."

The man behind the counter was still nodding. "Well, do you mind if I make a few suggestions?" he asked.

Though Tim had lied about the reason for the gun, the truth

was that he did need to buy one, and that he needed help in selecting the best model.

"If I were you," the salesman began. "I wouldn't want to go less that a .38 caliber. That's the size of the barrel."

Tim couldn't tell if the man was being condescending or if he just wanted to start his education at a low enough level. He decided to believe the latter.

"If someone is crazy enough to break into your apartment, you want to make sure you stop him. Of course, you could go larger, but you probably don't need to."

There were no other customers in the store, and the salesman seemed to be enjoying educating him, so Tim let him go on.

"Now, the standard gun makers have been in business for over a hundred years. And the guns that they make are either a silver color like this one here, or a dark blue like this one over here."

As he spoke, the man behind the counter picked up and let Tim examine five different guns from the display. He hadn't been looking at the clip loaded, more military looking models in the other cases, so the salesman kept his focus on the revolvers. "They call them revolvers because the cylinder 'revolves' to the next chamber after you fire it,"

The guns all felt pretty much the same to Tim. Some were a little heavier and some felt a bit lighter. But, since Tim was only planning to use the weapon once and then throw it away, he wasn't overly concerned about its weight. Finally, he asked the salesman which one he personally would buy.

"Hopefully, I'm never going to have to fire the thing,"

Tim began. "But if I do need to use it, I want the gun to finish the job. Which one would you pick?"

Without hesitation, the salesman picked up a dark blue gun that the sign said was called a "Bodyguard".

"This is a thirty eight caliber model. They've sold millions of them over a lot of years. And, for what you're talking about, it's as good as they come."

The salesman handed Tim the gun and it fit nicely into his grip.

With one hand behind his back, and the other extended in front of him, Tim held the gun as if he were aiming it down at the far wall of the store.

"Son," the man behind the counter said. "If I were you, I'd spend some time learning to fire that gun before I needed to use it. Some police departments hold classes, and I advise anyone who owns a gun to take at least one of them."

Tim nodded that he agreed. But the man continued: "In the meantime," he said. "Don't hold the gun up that way, with only one arm. In any kind of emergency, it takes longer to get control of it." Then the man came out from behind the counter. "Here, if you shoot right handed, support your right hand by putting your left hand underneath it. Like this. And bend your knees a little."

As he stood there, ready to fire the unloaded weapon, Tim tried to picture how he could incorporate this stance into his plans for Friday night. He thanked the salesman for the lesson.

"I think I'd better see to those lessons," Tim chuckled to the man. "In the meantime, you had better sell me some bullets to go with this thing."

The salesman walked over to the wall where all the ammunition was on display, and he returned with three boxes of .38 caliber shells. The price of the shells and the gun itself came to three hundred fifty-three dollars and twenty-seven cents. Then, after the salesman wrote up a sales ticket, and rang up the sale on the cash register, he brought another book and some yellow forms up from beneath the counter.

"Now, I'm going to need some ID with a picture on it." he said. "And, at the same time, I'm going to need for you to fill out this form."

Suddenly the game became more complex. Tim knew that he had been badly mistaken about just how easy it would be to buy a handgun. And he knew that if he bought the gun and filled out these forms, the police would probably find out about it. Surely, they would check. But, if they did check and they found out he had purchased a gun, they would still need to find his gun in order to prove that he had done the crime. On the other hand, as the situation now stood, even if he didn't buy the gun, if the cops came to McBrides, this salesman would spill his guts about his wanting to buy one. And if he didn't buy it now, when faced with filling out these forms, wouldn't that look just as incriminating?

In the end, Tim filled out the required forms and bought the gun. Though the actual gun he bought was not the one in the display, the salesman had taken it out of its box and allowed him to hold it before any money changed hands. Then the gun went back into its box, and it and the three boxes of ammunition were placed into a bag. Tim picked up the bag and thanked the salesman for his assistance. In his heart, however, Tim was worried about what he had just done.

Starting up the Impala for the return trip home, Tim reached over and turned off the radio. It was just five o'clock, and time for the news.

"Thank you, very much." Tim responded to the voice. "I've had enough news for today."

There was a bit more traffic on the way home than he had seen earlier, but he made use of the delay trying to decide what his next step should be. Should he just fly back to California and forget about it? After all, if Adams was shot to death, he and Patrick would be at the top of a short list of suspects. And there was pretty good chance that the police would find out about his buying the gun. They would want to examine it, and if they did, they would very likely be able to convict him of the crime. The question, in Tim's mind, was "Should I do it anyway? Should I take the chance?" Was the chance to kill the bastard who had raped and murdered his mother worth the price that he might have to pay, that is, if the police and the DA's office bothered to do their jobs? Tim hadn't left Maryellen before he knew his answer.

"Whatever else happens as a result," he said to himself.

"Adams is going to die."

Along the road home, about half an hours drive after he returned to the New York side of the state line, there was another road that veered off from the one he was on and it looked as if it wound around through the surrounding hills. That would be good.

Compared to the well paved surface that he had been driving on, this road was more like a dirt path that had been cut out using a bulldozer. And it was probably used by the local fire district as an access road. But for Tim's purposes, it would do nicely. He slowed the Impala down and then turned onto it. The surface was marked with cracks in the ground and the going was slow, but he followed the curving route it took until he was sure that he was at least a mile away from anyone else and not visible from the road. Then he turned off the Impala's engine and looked around for something to use as a target.

All around, there were rolling hills, interspersed with clumps of tall grass and an occasional tree. And being summer, the grass had given up the green color of growth and had taken on a dried white. The clay that made up the ground itself was almost ashen, and covered with small rocks. These rocks had, most likely, been a problem to the people cutting out the trail, but for today's use they were perfect.

Tim removed the gun from the box and began to load it. Holding the gun in his left hand with the cylinders exposed, and with one bullet at a time in his right, he inserted the ammunition into the chambers until they were all occupied. Then he set the cylinder in place. The gun was ready to use.

What he had in mind was to take up to six practice shots at the rocks, just to get a feel for the gun before he had to use it. On the other hand, he didn't want to waste any time and be away from the house any longer than was necessary. And he certainly didn't want to be seen firing the gun.

Carefully holding the gun in his right hand, he opened the Impala's door and got out. There were five rocks, in a loose sort of pile, about thirty feet away from him. Tim stepped away from the car, and closed the distance to about twenty feet. Then he raised the gun to the level of his eyes, supported his right hand with his left, and bent his knees slightly. Positioned as the man at the gun shop had showed him, he fired three times at the pile of rocks. They shattered as two of the bullets found their mark, the third hitting the dirt behind the pile. The surrounding area echoed with the sounds of the shots, and the loudness of the noise startled him. However, by firing the gun, he had felt the kick of the recoil and now he knew he could handle it. Aiming the gun should not be a factor either, since Tim meant to actually place the barrel on Adams' chest before he pulled the trigger. But the noise could be a problem.

Getting back into the car as quickly as he could do it, Tim placed the gun into the bag again. Then he started the engine, turned the vehicle around and headed back toward the paved highway.

"What if I hit a bump and the damn thing goes off?" he thought.

Stopping the car, Tim reached into the bag and removed the gun. Emptying all six cylinders of their contents, he returned the three unused shells to the box they had come in, leaving the three spent cartridges laying on the seat next to him. For safety, that should do the trick. But what was he going to with the gun and the ammunition between now and Friday night? If he threw the bag and the boxes into a trash can before he got home, he could dump the bullets into his pants pockets. And, once he got home, if he didn't have to stop between the front door of the house and his bedroom, he could stick the barrel of the gun into the waistband of his pants and pull his shirt down over it. Once he got up to his room, he would put the gun inside one of his dress shoes and the bullets into the other. Then, if he put a pair of socks over the opening in the shoes, even if Pat moved into the room with him, the weapon and the ammunition should go undetected. And it would only be for a couple of days.

In a few minutes, with the empty gun hidden for the moment in the glove compartment, Tim returned to the paved road. Then, as he drove along, one by one he threw the spent cartridges out into the countryside. A few miles later, after he had thrown out the last one, he drove behind a store in one of the small towns and threw away the box that had held the gun. In another small town, he threw away the boxes for the shells. Aware that the effort was probably not going to make any difference, Tim still didn't want to take any more chances than he had to.

"Besides," he said to himself, dryly. "Just because I'm going to kill a guy, doesn't mean I have to be a litterbug."

Chapter Twenty One

PATTERSON BROUGHT THE SOUR FRUIT of his investigations to the other three remaining original members of the Committee. The initial information had come from Sherry Minton, but Patterson had made use of other inquiries and other resources, government and private. He met first with Tom Damond. Damond, who stood well over two hundred pounds, was over six feet tall, with grey hair at his temples. With the infectious smile of a salesman, Damond had made his original fortune in California real estate. Yet at seventy-one, his eyes and his mind were as clear and as sharp as ever. He offered his guest a drink, but Patterson declined.

Damonds' study reflected both his taste in dark wood paneling, plush high-backed chairs, and his passion for hunting. The main feature of the room was a bear carpet, teeth attached and glaring, along with the heads of a deer, an elk, and a Bengal tiger. Each had been a moment in his life he treasured. Pictures of other animals filled the walls overhead, Patterson might have thought he was in the wilds of Africa, instead of

New Jersey. But after hearing and viewing the evidence, which included copies of initial shipping documentation for medical equipment sent both to and from Port au Prince Haiti and Miami, Damond sat quietly, his head down, as he rubbed his graying temples.

Patterson said, "That had to be the way they were going to get the drugs in. It's not clear what they were going to do, or how they were going to get the drugs distributed from there. But that wouldn't have been hard."

"Did it have to be heroin?" Damond asked. "Did he have to involve us in that?"

Patterson sat quietly, neither leading nor reacting Damond, after a few minutes absorbing the information, and trying to make some sense of what Arthur might have been thinking, raised his eyes and asked, "Can we contain the damage? I don't think we can let the drugs get to the U.S."

"I think so," was Patterson's reply. "We can stop the drugs from getting to the States. I'm working on that." Then he paused and said the words they had both wanted to avoid. "The problem is still, what do we do with Arthur."

After a pause, continuing, "If we can't trust him not to do something like this, something that puts us all at serious risk, how can we have him around? He knows everything that's going on."

Damond laughed nervously. "Guess we should have thought about a retirement plan." Paterson nodded, and Damond continued. "No one has ever been ousted, or retired from the Committee."

Patterson turned his back on Damond, and continued walking around the room, seemingly to look at the pictures on the walls. With a voice that sounded like sadness itself, he asked the last, but hardest question. "And, even if we can or should remove them from the Committee, can we afford to have someone who knows as much about us as Arthur does, run free even after he's left us?"

"You want to kill Arthur?" Damond asked, looking up at Patterson, searching for an alternative. "And there have to be others involved besides Ferrel. Do we kill them as well?"

"The only other Committee member I'm sure is involved is Ferrel. Arthur's taken him under his wing, and his signature is all over the paperwork." Paterson turned to Damond, and judged what he saw on his old friend's face as despair. "We have to conclude that he is equally guilty, though I'm sure it must have been Arthur's idea. I'm just sorry he hid it from the rest of us."

For one of the Committee members to come up with a personal project was common, even expected. Each of the men had his own ideas of what projects they took on, and they had each been both the instigator and the advocate for any number. But problems had come up. Near investigation by police and other government agencies had needed to be stopped, and the Committee had learned its lesson. As a "safety valve", for their collective protection, they had all decided, they had all agreed, on the absolute need for the sharing of information, the counter-signature process, and mutual oversight on all projects. But the easiest way to oversee projects was to watch the flow of money, and that was Arthur's function.

"If he hadn't known it was wrong, and if he hadn't known we would object, he would not have kept it between himself and Ferrel." Paterson now looked at the other man, not sorrowful, but angry. "And yet, he did exactly that."

Patterson thought about what he was saying, silently for a moment. Then he looked again to Damond. "And he was the one who got the kid involved."

After sitting together, Damond poured them each a brandy. This time Patterson accepted, and they contemplated just what they could do.

"It's about the worst thing they could have done, involving the Committee in not only killings, but narcotics, as well. Damn, I hate that stuff." Then, after a minute, he asked, "Why do you think he did it?"

After a pause, Patterson responded, "I think he thought he was doing what was right. In his heart, Arthur's a good man. And he, like many of us in the past have done, was willing to justify what they were doing as "the ends justifying the means".

The two men said, in unison, "But he went too far."

Patterson and Damond met next with Ken Pope, coming to the same question and conclusion. Pope was small and thin, and spoke in an Americanized German accent. On seeing Paterson's reports and data, mainly consisting of purchase orders, and bills for hotels and airplane tickets, Pope seemed less than convinced that Arthur had actually done anything they could consider an evil deed. "After all," he said. "You have evidence that he has planned to do something. And he spent a lot of money that no one else was asked to approve. But planning something and doing it are two different things. I can't, I won't condone having a man killed." He paused, looking at Patterson. "if that is what you're proposing, Ron. For what? For planning something?"

Pope paused, watching the other men's reactions, and continued, growing angrier, not at Arthur, but at Patterson and Damond. "You two," he said pointing his finger, and looking them in the eyes. "It's you two who have gone too far. Arthur has spent decades, helping all of us. Helping us help others. And you two are willing to throw him away, and even have him killed? For what? For planning something, with no proof he's actually done anything, just planning something you don't understand. Well no. I won't have it. I'd rather rip the Committee apart than be a part of this."

Pope turned threatening to the others, continuing. "And I won't allow you two to do this to him either, no sir, I won't."

Patterson listened and watched his old friend doubt him, defend Arthur, and as he threatened both himself and Tom Damond. Pope's anger was palpable in the room. After a moment's hesitation, Patterson reached into his satchel and showed the other men receipts and police reports from Amsterdam, reports he had until then not even showed Damond.

The reports were written by surveillance and investigative teams, and recorded Ferrel's movements since he left the U.S. in July for England. "When I got the first indication that something odd was going on, I arranged to have Arthur, and especially Ferrel watched.

I thought that if there was travel involved, Arthur would not want to do it. I also don't think he had the stomach for what predictably had to happen."

"Had to happen?" asked Pope.

Damond answered, "If you're going to poison people, you have to know how much to use."

The other men read the documents, searching for reasons to doubt Patterson's conclusion. The truth was there. "On July 25th," he said. "John Ferrel, using the assumed name Carl Jenkins, and using funds from the Committee, countersigned by Arthur, landed with medical equipment in Amsterdam. He had rented a house on the outskirts of the city."

Patterson paused, then continued.

"They spent a lot of money getting him there, involving false documents. According to eye witnesses, one of whom was the man they rented the house from, Ferrel brought together seven drug addicts, gave them heroin for a week or so, then intentionally overdosed most of them." After a moment he added, "Something must not have gone to plan. Five of the addicts died of complete systematic failure, thought to be caused by poisoning, but two of them, including an American girl of about twenty, died of bullet wounds to the head."

After a quiet moment, Pope held his head in his hands. "They murdered seven kids?"

Looking up at the other two men, Ken Pope rose to his feet, placing his hand on Patterson's shoulder. "Ok," he said. "I'll call Chris Walker, and see if he's around. He'll need to be part of whatever we do from here.

The three met with Christopher Walker in his understated, yet large country home in Maynard Massachusetts. Patterson drove, and the ride from Pope's home to Walker's was quiet. Aside from a few stories and questions about life, their wives, and now their grandchildren, each of the men sat contemplating what would have to be done. What could be done?

Walkers' house itself was smaller than any of them remembered from previous social calls. As the car entered the driveway, three small children were playing on the grass near the house. When the car halted at the front door, the children watched, clearly puzzling about who might be visiting Grandpa, but they remained apart.

An athletic young man approached the car before the doors were opened. Patterson lowered the driver side window and identified himself and the others. The young man refrained from saluting, opened the driver side doors, and said, "Mr. Walker is expecting you."

Christopher Walker stood just less than six feet tall, with a slight build, a shaved head, and a now gray handlebar mustache. On seeing him come out of the house, the children came running over, and Grandpa took the time to introduce them to his visitors. Pointing to the oldest, a boy about nine, he said "this is Jack, my first and favorite grandchild." Jack looked away sheepishly, genuinely embarrassed. Then Walker drew before them the older of two girls, each wearing jeans, T-shirts, and tennis shoes. "This is Eva, my oldest granddaughter, and my favorite child in all the world."

Eva was six. She stepped forward, offered her hand to each of the visitors and shook their hands. "Pleased to meet you," she said in a firm voice and with a hearty handshake. "But Grandpa says that about all of us."

Grandpa smiled, ruffled Eva's hair, and said, "But it's always the truth."

The other men smiled, enjoying their friend's happiness. "And this little lady is Caroline. She's both the youngest, and my favorite." Now all three children moaned, and then laughed. Caroline was just three, and feeling very shy. When he picked her up, she buried her face on Grandpa's shoulder.

Setting Caroline down, and sending her and the others back to their play, Walker motioned to the house, inviting them inside. "Can I get you something to drink?"

The young man outside retook his position, near to but not interfering with the children's play.

The dominating features of Christopher Walker's house were shelves upon shelves of books. Walker had been a lawyer by training, and had made his fortune arguing both corporate and international law. Having left his visitors in his study for a moment, he reappeared carrying a tray containing an ice bucket, glasses, and several soft drinks. Once he set down the tray, he opened a nearby cabinet, revealing his liquor.

"Whatever suits you," he said, smiling. "But I have a feeling there's a problem."

For the next two hours, Patterson reviewed the reports and the documents with Walker, Damond and Pope looking on. Each piece of evidence was methodically gone over, and questions asked. Pope and Damond remained quiet, except for the occasional question or clarification. Patterson, at the end, revealed, as he had before, the final report concerning the seven dead addicts. Walker understood, even more than the others, that for Patterson, what was happening had to be crushing him inside. Arthur had been Patterson's closest friend on the original Committee. To all outward signs, however, Patterson was calm and business like. If Damond was feeling anything, he was following Patterson's lead and concealing it. Ken Pope, however, the one of his visitors Walker was personally closest to, was showing an inner struggle, being objective, and yet, not wanting to believe.

"Do you think you know why he did it, Ken?" Walker asked. The question hung in the air.

After a moment, Pope gave the answer. "When we get old, we want to make a last statement, something big. We want to do something that will make a difference. Arthur didn't have a family that I know of, no grandchildren." He paused, looked around at the others. "I can see Arthur thinking it through, logically, precisely. The drug problem is huge. Maybe we could fix that."

It was Damond who spoke loudly. "Ken, we don't sell dope, and we don't kill people. It was never about that."

Chapter Twenty Two

When he arrived home, Tim looked down at his watch and saw that it was seven twenty. Mary Margaret's station wagon was parked on the street, which probably meant that she and Casey, along with Da and Patrick, were waiting in the kitchen for him to arrive. But, with any luck at all, it also meant he could hurry up to his room without running into any of them.

Retrieving the gun from the glove box, Tim got out and closed the car door as quietly as possible. Then he stuck the gun barrel into his waistband and pulled his shirt over it. The metal of the weapon felt icy cold against his skin, but it was less uncomfortable than trying to explain to Da why he had just purchased a gun. Standing on the front porch, Tim breathed in and collected himself. When he was ready he opened the door and moved as fast as he thought he could, without tripping over something. Standing at the stairs, however, and a bit startled by his sudden appearance was Mary Margaret. "Well, there you are." she said.

Tim was more surprised than she was, but he kept his wits about him. "Oh hi," he responded, not stopping. "I'll be right down. I've had to go for the last few miles."

Instead of going directly to his room, Tim took a detour into the upstairs bathroom. His sister laughed and continued on her way to the kitchen. "I guess you heard," she said to the three men sitting around the table. "Our young wanderer has returned, and is currently making use of the facilities."

Casey and Patrick laughed, and Da just shook his head. "You would think that after sitting in all of those classes, he would have learned to hold it a bit longer." joked Patrick.

In the upstairs bathroom, Tim waited for a few minutes and made sure that the gun had remained secured in his waistband. Then he slowly opened the bathroom door, looked down the hallway, and walked swiftly into his room. Safely inside, he closed the door behind himself and listened. Downstairs, in the kitchen, he could hear the rest of his family laughing, and he smiled knowing that it was probably at his expense. As he turned around and pulled the gun free, he saw that Casey's duffel bag had been thrown on the other twin bed in the room, but he hadn't bothered to unpack it.

Not wanting to waste a moment, Tim took his dress shoes out of the closet and sat down on his bed with them. In the right shoe, he placed the .38 caliber "Bodyguard". Then he pulled a pair of black socks out of his drawer and pushed them into the shoe, behind the gun. In his left shoe, he did the same thing with the bullets. When he was finished, he returned the shoes to the bottom of the closet.

On his way back downstairs, Tim made another stop in the bathroom. This time he ran some water and washed his face and hands. As he saw his reflection the mirror, suddenly, he felt guilty. "Save it, pal." he said to himself, in the mirror. "Come Friday night, you'll be guilty enough."

Tim ran a comb through his hair, then walked downstairs and rejoined his family. Casey was there, still in his uniform, and he looked bigger and more muscular that Tim had remembered. "Hey!

Casey," Tim smiled as he entered the kitchen. Casey stood up from the table and gave his little brother a hug.

"I hope you don't mind me bunking in with you for a day or two. It didn't make much sense to make Pat move just because you and I come home."

When they separated, Tim said that he was "just glad you could make it". Then he took the opportunity to make a crack about Casey looking well fed. "At least they're not starving you."

"In the Navy," Casey answered, mockingly raising his right hand into the air. "Everyone loves their supply officer. And because we have all the food, we eat very well."

From the look of the dishes of food on the kitchen counter, the women from the parish had returned yet again. However, Tim's stomach felt a bit queasy, so he didn't eat much. The rest of the family, especially Casey, experienced no such problem. Even Mary Margaret stayed to eat with them. "The kids wanted pizza tonight," she told her brothers. "And since we don't know when all of us will be back together again, I thought I'd come have a meal with you guys, tonight."

As they ate, she also filled them in on the details of the ceremonies. "The viewing is scheduled for between three and six on Thursday. We'll all be there, to meet people and so everyone can pay their respects. There's a short service. Friday, there will be a high Mass at one o' clock." she looked around at the others. "Father Berry, himself, will be doing both. After that, around three o' clock, we'll all go down to the cemetery for the burial. Then there'll be an open house type of a reception, here in the house for an hour or two."

The four men nodded their understanding, and they very much appreciated that Mary Margaret had taken care of things. "Is there anything that we can help with?" asked Casey.

"Yes, there is." she replied. "You three guys, along with Greg, Carol Hubbley's husband John, and Kenny Belerive from the parish, will need to be pall bearers. The casket will need to be carried from the church to the hearse, and then from the hearse to the grave site."

Once again, Mary Margaret, and everyone else, felt better having some duty to perform, and each of their auras reflected it. Casey's, which Tim was now watching for the first time, had been reddish and fluctuating, just as Patrick's had. But now, they both seemed to be settling down. But there was something else strange about Casey's. There was a dark red spot that remained in the area of his midsection. "How's that stomach of yours doing, Case?" Tim asked his older brother. "If I remember right, it used to bother you when things started to get crazy."

Patrick, not being able to see his brothers' aura, thought that Tim's question was a bit silly, and said so. "Well, 'doctor'," he said to his younger brother, "I think we can reasonably forgive him a little nausea, don't you?"

Tim understood why Pat thought the question was an odd one, and because he knew his brother was just teasing him, he let the subject drop. Later on, though after Mary Margaret went home, he would talk to Casey privately and learn that the Navy, since the war in Vietnam was over, not only didn't need any new officers, they were planning to "force retire" some of those who had been serving. And, though his ratings had been very good, Casey did let on that there was a slight chance that he might become part of that process. But Tim could see how worried he really was.

For the rest of the evening, the activities in the house were the same as they had always been. The only exception was that Tim and Patrick volunteered to clean up the kitchen. That had almost never happened. But tonight, the two younger boys wanted to give Da and Casey as much time together as they could. Even though Tim would also be leaving home after the ceremony, Casey had been gone much longer, already. And Da wanted to keep up with all of them.

"It's a shame that Casey couldn't have gotten back before she died," said Patrick, almost matter-of-factly.

Tim watched his brother's aura redden as he was obviously getting upset again, thinking about what had happened to their mother. Tim put his hand on his brother's shoulder to comfort him, and as the fluctuation receded, he told Patrick about what Da had told him. "Da's concerned that one of us is going to do something stupid and get ourselves in trouble with the law."

"Well," Patrick replied. "It did occur to me that the guy should die for what he did. But I don't think Ma would have wanted us to do it."

The way Patrick's aura began to redden as he spoke, told Tim that his brother was far from comfortable with his decision.

"Well, Da asked me to keep an eye on you and Casey, until I have to go back. So don't get any ideas until I'm safely out of the picture."

"Well, for your information, little brother," Patrick replied. "He asked me to keep an eye on you two as well. And I've no doubt that Casey was asked to do the same for us."

Chapter Twenty Three

Thursday, the day of the viewing, was the most difficult day because Mary Margaret had taken care of all of the arrangements, leaving nothing for Tim or any of the others to do. It was her way of coping, of course, but the time dragged.

Tim thought it was strange, but Casey had never asked for more than a brief rundown of what had happened to Ma. Tim knew from his aura that his brother was as hurt by the whole situation as any of them, yet he never asked for details. Pat suggested that "Maybe the fact that she's gone is as much as he can handle for now. Maybe it will take a while before the rest is important." Maybe Pat was right.

Shortly after noon, Tim called the airline and made reservations for his return flight to San Jose on Saturday. Nobody questioned why he wanted to leave so soon. After the funeral, it would be time for all of them to rejoin their lives.

The viewing itself was a simple arrangement, held at the funeral parlor, with soft music almost imperceptible in the background. Tim and his family entered the side chapel together just before three. Mary Margaret held Da's hand, the boys following behind them. The funeral director, Mr. Lindsay, a tall man, impeccably dressed in a dark suit and tie, with gray hair combed precisely, greeted them, smiling, yet showing just the right mix of comfort and service. He showed them the book set up for friends and well-wishers to sign and to leave a brief note if they wished to. There were a few signatures, some with notes, but the family didn't stop to read them. That could wait.

The three women from the parish were sitting in silence inside the chapel when Tim and the others come into the room. The women looked up, but said nothing. Da stood just inside the door, frozen, perhaps fearful, that what he had feared, what he had tried to deny, had actually happened. His beautiful Maeve was laying in the coffin at the front of the room. The coffin was open, and he could just see her hair, her face. Slowly shuffling forward, driven by his sense of obligation to her, to his family, a no longer young Mike Conolly was looking down at his beautiful girl, his partner in life, and his best friend. Her hands folded across her chest, she was, as his eyes had always seen her, beautiful. And he missed her, wanted her, and still felt his need for her smile. Trembling slightly, with tears streaming down his cheeks, Mary Margaret gently squeezed his hand, his daughter knowing only a small piece of his love for her. Watching as his father's powerful hands shook gently, Tim wondered if he had ever seen him cry before. One by one, each of them stepped closer to the coffin, took a moment to be with her, to say what each of them believed would be a temporary goodbye.

Pat stepped forward to wrap his arm around his father, silently squeezing his shoulder. They sat down, each searching for words to comfort the others, each running short. Mary Margaret stepped close to the coffin, reached out and brushed her fingertips across her mother's cheek, looking down, sharing her own thoughts, just between them. Then she smiled, almost laughed out loud, but stifled herself. Tim wondered, but didn't ask.

Casey, dressed in his uniform could not bring himself to step any closer to the coffin, and the dark spot of his aura grew, and grew darker. Knowing his brother was in pain, Tim reached, squeezing his shoulder. His arch turned softer, and he stood there for a few moments. Then he wiped a tear from his eye and joined the others sitting down.

Tim stood alone, looking down at his mother's body in the coffin, and he knew he should feel sadness, and he did. Her eyes closed, he wanted her to open them, wanted to see her breast move as she breathed. He waited, not wanting to accept, and yet, even in death she had an aura, colorless, almost purely invisible, like heat as it rises from a highway. The vessel was empty. She wasn't there. She had gone.

The front row of pews in the chapel, were reserved for the family and they sat quietly, sometimes mumbling prayers, sometimes just thinking of her. Tim rejoined them, and felt his father's hand on his arm. He smiled and said, "I'm ok." Da smiled back, and nodded. Soon, Father Berry entered the room and led the mourners in prayer. He spoke from his knowledge of her, and retelling them that, though they missed her, she was now with her Father in heaven, in the place which had been prepared for her since the beginning of time. And that she was happy there.

Tim watched the priest, and he listened. And he watched Father Berry's aura become a genuine glow when he spoke about his mother, and when he spoke about the love of God. Tim nodded his agreement along with the others in his family, and he listened as those in the room whispered their acceptance. Ma was gone, and she'd gone to a wonderful place. The God of the universe did keep his eyes on each blade of grass, and each sparrow in the sky. Tim believed this, and the thought did comfort him, and he could see that it did add comfort to his family.

"But tomorrow night Adams is going to die."

Friday morning the sun was shining, and the world was spinning as if it were any other day. Da was making pancakes again when Tim came downstairs. Casey and Pat had gone to the market to buy some orange juice and a paper.

"Good morning Da. How'd you sleep?"

His father had only been able to sleep a few hours each night since Monday. But no one, not even Tim, could tell. "Good morning son," he smiled. "Here, eat these while they're still hot. You'll have to drink either coffee or milk with them, but your brothers should be back soon with some juice."

"Thanks," he said. "Can I pour you some coffee?"

"No," his father replied. "I've got a cup going already. I hope Casey didn't wake you up when he finally went up to bed last night."

The night before, after cleaning up a bit, the boys and Da had decided to get out the cards and to play a little poker. Immediately, Tim discovered that by reading the other players auras, he could tell how good a hand they held. This worked particularly well with Patrick and his father, whose colors would fluctuate wildly if they had anything better than jacks in their hands. Casey's aura was a bit less dramatic, but still readable. In short order, Tim had won most of the chips on the table. But winning that way was too easy. And it really wasn't fair. Four hands later, after a "terrible run of bad luck" Tim had lost all of his chips and went up to his room. But he never did hear his brother.

"No, actually I didn't hear him at all. In fact, if his duffel bag hadn't been moved and the bed messed up, I wouldn't have known he'd even been up there."

"Well, he said you were sound asleep, and snoring like a buzz saw."

Tim was sure that his snoring was not quite as bad as Da was making it sounds, but he did know that he had gone right to sleep. Just then Patrick walked into the kitchen carrying a container of orange juice and a box of doughnuts. Casey followed him in.

"It smells great in here Dad," Casey said. "And I could eat a horse."

Pat poured each of them a small glass of juice and they all sat down to eat. As they finished, the phone rang and Tim answered. On the other end was Mary Margaret.

"Tim, remind the others that we have to be at the church by twelve thirty. The first row on the right will be roped off and reserved for us, so tell everybody not to sit anywhere else. Greg and I and the kids are planning to get there a little early, but you never know with kids. We might even be a bit late."

"Okay, don't worry about us," Tim told her. "We'll all be there early, and we'll take care of things until you arrive." "Thanks Timmy," then after a slight pause she said. "I'm really glad you're here."

For the services, Da put on a black suit that he had seldom worn, and Patrick planned to wear slacks and a sweater. However, it only took a few minutes in the heat of July before they all knew that the sweater idea was impractical. Fortunately, though, using other clothes that Pat had in his closet, and what Tim and Casey had brought with them, the boys were able to put together an ensemble that went with Tim's extra jacket. Casey wore his blue dress uniform.

By twelve fifteen Mike Conolly and his sons were dressed and loading into the Impala for the drive to the church. Once in the car, though, none of them felt like talking. Tim sat in the back with Pat and stared out of the window. Once again, there were children playing in their front yards, as if today were any other day.

When they arrived at the church, Mary Margaret's station wagon was parked in the lot next-door. Da turned and parked next to it. Just after twelve thirty, Tim wondered what they were going to do for the next half hour before the service began. He also wondered who would come. As cars began to arrive, though, and as the parking lot began to fill up, Tim felt relief, and then a deep-seated pride, that nearly one hundred and fifty people, Ma's friends, or their relatives, as well as union members who were there to support Da and Pat, had come to see her off.

During the high Mass that Mary Margaret had arranged, and that Father Berry was now performing, Tim's thoughts returned again to the .38 caliber pistol in his shoe back at the house, and his plans for that night.

"What if Adams doesn't go drinking tonight?" he thought to himself. "Or what if he goes someplace else?"

The answers to the questions were simple enough. If Adams

broke his pattern, he would probably be alive tomorrow. Tim was not about to push his way into Adams apartment and confront the larger man there. And, since he would be returning to California tomorrow, whatever was going to happen, had to happen tonight.

"But if he walks down Glory Lane tonight, he's going to die."

For the remainder of the service, Tim went over, step by step, what he had to do to be ready. Loading the gun, parking the car and walking to a position at the end of the block. Then he would wait.

After an hour that seemed far longer, the Mass was over and the family stood outside being comforted by their neighbors. Mrs. Reineker and some of the other women offered to continue bringing food over. Da thanked them but he said that it wouldn't be necessary after the reception. "Casey has to go back to his ship," he told them. "And Timmy's heading back to California tomorrow. Patrick and I appreciate what you've done already, but we have to start doing our own cooking sometime. Though I doubt it will be near as good as what you ladies have delivered."

As the family and their neighbors made small talk outside the church, two black limousines drove up in front. A young man, wearing a black chauffeur's cap, got out of the first one while an older and much taller man, the funeral director Mr. Lindsay, drove the second car. Pulling in ahead of the limos was the hearse.

The funeral director found Mary Margaret and handed her a small stack of dashboard signs that read "Funeral". She quickly began to distribute them to the mourners who would be coming out to the cemetery. When everyone was ready, Tim and his brothers, along with the other pall bearers, were asked to bring the casket out from the church.

As he walked toward the alter, where the casket was, Tim worried to himself how heavy it might be. And what if they dropped it? The funeral director had come with them, and he placed them on each side. Casey was the biggest man, and he was positioned at the front on the right. Patrick was positioned across from him on the left. Tim and Kenny Belerive took up the middle positions, with Greg and John Hubbley behind them. Each of the men was given a boutonniere for his lapel and instructed that during the ceremony at the grave site, they would be instructed to take the flowers off and to lay them on the coffin.

When they reached down to take the handles of the casket, the director said: "Now, all at once, lift."

As they each took up their portion of the weight, Tim was relieved but surprised at how light his burden was. The director walked to a position down the aisle toward the door and they each turned in his direction. Casey led the way, stepping with his left foot and then with his right, the way a procession might be held in Arlington. Under his breath, he spoke the words "right" and then "left". The other men heard him and followed the cadence.

Step by step, the casket was brought down the main aisle of the church, down the front steps, and into the opened rear door of the hearse. The driver closed the door and left Tim and his brothers, if only for a moment, looking through the window at the box that held what remained of their mother. Tim managed to look away before he cried, but a single tear crossed Casey's cheek.

"Come on, son" director Lindsay told Casey, as he put his arm around him. "It's time to go."

Da and the boys got into the first limo while Mary Margaret, Greg, and the kids climbed into the second for the ride to the cemetery. As the door closed behind him, Patrick broke the tension with a comment about the length of the service. "I was afraid I was going to fall asleep before he got done." he said. "Either that or retire."

"Do you know what kept going through my mind as 'old Berry' droned on and on during the ceremony?" Da spoke thoughtfully.

"What Da?" asked Tim.

"It occurred to me, if only briefly," he began. "That your mother was probably up in heaven, laughing her head off that I finally had to sit through one of these things without excusing myself to go outside. Between her and 'old Berry', they were always trying to get me to sit through as many of his damned ceremonies as possible. Said it would do me good."

The mental picture of their mother in heaven and laughing helped everyone, even Casey. It was a short drive, and soon they arrived at the cemetery. As they came to a halt, each driver got out quickly and opened their limo's door.

"Okay gentlemen," the director said to the six men, "if you could take up your same positions at the rear of the hearse, you'll carry the casket up to the burial site."

Once again, Casey spoke the cadence softly enough not to be heard by those in attendance, but the pall bearers kept in step. Slowly away from the cars, then up a small hill and over to their right, the six men carried the casket. Careful not to misstep, they placed it above what would be her grave, on a device that would lower her at the appropriate time. The family took their positions at the foot of the grave.

Once again, it was Father Berry who performed the graveside service. When he finished, roses that had been given to Mary Margaret and to Da, along with the boutonnieres from Tim and the other men, were laid atop the coffin and it was lowered into the ground. One by one, beginning with Da, the family members and some of her friends, sprinkled a bit of dirt on the casket and said goodbye. After another round of condolences and "thank yous" the service was over and the limos drove the family back to the church.

"Mrs. Reineker and some of the other women have told me that they're going to miss getting together in the afternoons to cook for you guys," began Casey. "It seems that it was quite a lot of fun for them."

Da smiled and said that they were good people to help out during a hard time, but enough was enough. He and Patrick would just have to get used to each other's cooking. During the services, particularly during the one at the grave site, Tim had watched them all. Each of their auras had nearly glowed the red of emotional pain at some time, and it grew worse for them all at the grave site. However, once the casket was lowered into the ground, there seemed to be a collective understanding that Ma was somehow "Okay". And eventually their auras all returned to a more natural green to reflect that feeling.

"I was very proud of all of you kids today, the way you all pitched in and helped." Da told them. "And your mother would have been proud of you, too."

Chapter Twenty Four

During the reception, while they were all still nicely dressed, Tim made small talk and accepted condolences from most of the people as they came, stayed a politely brief while, and left again for their own homes. As they arrived, Mary Margaret would greet them and thank them for coming. They would smile and say something nice about Ma and about how much they would miss her. Then Mary Margaret would point out the food and the punch bowl that had been placed on the kitchen table, and the newly arrived guests would move on and try to find another member of the family. Over in one of the corners of the kitchen, Casey was exchanging "war stories" about his time off the coast of Vietnam with some of the older men who told him their stories about World War II and Korea. This group of men could get a bit loud, laughing or when someone made a vain attempt to sound like an explosion. But each man in the group told some tale about his experience and it seemed to add to a sense of bonding between people who had been through similar situations. And that was the point. Ma would have loved to have been there.

Meanwhile, before a group of neighborhood women had surrounded Da, pointing to Mary Margaret, he excused himself and began to make a fresh pot of coffee. As he finished adding the water and moving the switch to the "on" position, Da saw Tim slip out through the front door. After setting up another row of coffee cups, and checking the punch bowl again, Da wound his way through the crowded front room and followed him outside. Tim was sitting on the front fender of the Impala, staring up into the bright blue sky, and tapping his fingertips on the hood of the car.

"What is it, son?" Mike asked. "Are you okay?"

With a sense of cold anger in his voice, he said. "That son of a bitch killed her Da, and those bastards downtown aren't going to do anything about it."

Tim leaned over, picked up two stones from the ground, and he hurled the first against the side of the house. The stone missed a glass window pane by an inch, and made a noise that may have been heard down the block. Da took a step toward him, but he stopped. Then Da also leaned over for a stone himself, took a few steps toward the target wall and, putting his full weight behind the throw, hurled stone against the wall as well. The second crash of a stone against the wall sent the people at the reception to cringe, and then look out the window. Da waved to them, smiled, then returned his attention to his son.

"Tim." he said, loud enough to be heard, "You have to believe that things will even themselves out."

Tim dropped the second stone he still held in his hand, and he walked over to where his father was standing. When he reached him, he wrapped his arms around the older man and he said: "I know, Da. I know."

The two men walked back through the front door and into the crowd. Inside, no one inside gave any indication they had left, and it seemed as if no one in the house had heard the noise the stones had made. Within thirty minutes, however, the last of the guests had said their good-byes and had gone.

Mary Margaret filled a sink with water while Da and the boys collected dishes and cups from around the house. She offered to wash if Tim would rinse and dry, but Da said that she had done enough. "We can manage around here." he said, as he took her in his arms. "I, for one, wouldn't have made it these last few days if it weren't for you. But we're okay now, really. The boys and I can clean up around here, later. What would you like to do?"

"Well," she answered. "The kids are handling all this pretty well, but I should get them home. If you guys are really okay, that's what I'll do."

Da nodded and he hugged her again. Then, after Mary Margaret had rounded up Greg and her children, Da held her hand as he walked her to her car. When they reached it Da took her other hand and smiled at her. "I want to be clear about something," he began. "Just because your mother's gone on, that doesn't mean you're obliged to take her place."

Mary Margaret pretended not to understand, but Da stopped her before she could respond. "You have your own husband and your own children to look out for. And though we love you, and you'll always be more than welcome back here at this house, you've got to let us make our own way. And you've got to live your own life, too."

Da hugged her again, or rather she hugged him. And Mary Margaret began to cry. During the past week, he had seen the boys all cry and he had hoped that she would find a time to release her emotions, also. But he didn't remember seeing her do it. Now, as they held each other for a few minutes, Da was sure.

"Now you go home, and you and Greg plan to come over next week for dinner."

Mary Margaret was smiling back at him, but she was still wiping the last tear from her eye.

"And don't be surprised," he continued, "if Patrick and I can't turn out a meal to rival your own."

"Okay," she answered. "But don't get too cocky, Ma spent a lot of years teaching me to cook."

"Well, see here, little miss," he smiled at her and they hugged each other again. "Don't forget that I knew your mother a lot longer than you did, and I may have learned a thing or two, myself."

Mary Margaret climbed into her station wagon next to Greg and they drove away. Da waved as they did, and inside himself he could feel a peacefulness that hadn't been there before.

"Death is a part of living," he told himself, quoting something he was sure his wife had said many times. "And, like it or not, those that are left have to go on."

Casey was running the vacuum cleaner in the front room as Da came back into the house. Tim and Patrick were finishing up the dishes in the kitchen. When they had each finished their assignments they joined Da around the kitchen table.

"Casey, when do you have to be back to your base, son?"

"I don't have to be back until Tuesday, before I miss my shift, so I thought I'd make reservations for Monday morning."

"And Timmy, how about you?"

"Well Da, tomorrow. My flight leaves at one-twenty."

"If that's in the morning," Patrick laughed, "I hope you also made plans to get to the airport by cab, again."

Tim laughed and reassured them all that "another red-eye flight was out of the question."

"As it is," he told them, "My body isn't going to know if it's time to get up or lay down, anyway."

Tomorrow would, indeed, be an interesting day. And as he thought about it, Tim had to wonder about how it would all play out. He would want to be at the airport by at least a quarter to one, in order to make his flight. That meant leaving the house no later than twelve noon. And he did want to spend an hour or two with the kids, so he would have to be at Mary Margaret's house by about ten. And, if he hadn't been arrested by then, it all sounded so reasonable. It was almost four o'clock, though, and they were all exhausted. Da and the others turned on the television set, while Tim decided that a nap was in order. "If I'm not up by six thirty or so, why don't one of you guys come and get me and we can go out for pizza or something."

Tim was sure that everyone down there would, very likely, be asleep themselves in a few minutes. But he also wanted to make sure that they would all be home again by at least ten or eleven o'clock, so that the Impala would be available.

"I don't know about pizza," Patrick said, frowning a bit. "But one of us will come get you, and we'll go someplace for dinner."

Tim turned and walked up the stairs, but this time he put his full weight directly on the noisy third and fifth steps. The first one sang out its song and it was followed by the squeak made as he stood on the other one. He couldn't remember the last time he had deliberately stepped on one of these steps, and he really didn't know why he had done so today. When he got to his room, Tim closed the door and immediately went to the closet to check on the gun. Not surprised that the weapon was still where he had put it, he then picked up and shook his other shoe to make sure that the bullets were also there. Then he slipped the key into the left shoe, and placed the pair into the back of the closet. The key was an extra variable tonight, one he didn't need. When the moment came, he'd be ready.

It had always been Tim's habit to spend a few minutes in prayer, before he nodded off to sleep. Sometimes he just said "thanks for the day". But that afternoon, he really had nothing to say. A silent gulf had developed between them. Once again, as he lay there, he went through a checklist of what he had to do later that night. Drive there, park the car, wait for Adams and then do it. When he was dead, walk back to the car and drive home. He noticed he had been squeezing his fist as he lay there. He opened his palm flat, trying to not notice the slight trembling in his hand.

"Keep it simple," he said to himself. "Then get out of town."

Roughly ninety minutes later, Patrick was standing at the bedroom door.

"Hey, Tim" he said. "It's after six and we're all hungry again. And now we all want pizza. Get up and we'll go."

Tim moved a bit under his covers and uttered something that he hoped sounded like "Okay." But Patrick had left before he opened his eyes. For a few more minutes, he laid there in his bed, listening to the voices from downstairs. The television was still on, but the others were moving around, obviously getting ready to go. As if overcome with a sudden burst of energy, Tim threw off his covers and stood up next to his bed. His head hurt a little, but he controlled the pain. His clothes were still piled on the dresser where he had tossed them earlier. As he got dressed again, Casey came up into the room and began to change out of his uniform and into civilian clothes. Once again, Tim looked for his brother's aura and was pleased to see that, with the exception of the red spot that was still evident around his midsection, his emotions had become fairly stable. However, it was then that Tim realized that he could see how his brother was feeling, while the key that Patterson had given him was still on his closet and not in his possession.

"Have I got something stuck between my teeth?" Casey asked, and Tim realized that he had been staring at him.

"No," Tim laughed. "Don't mind me. I just stare at the air a bit when I first wake up. But why are you changing out of your uniform?"

Casey continued to kick his shoes into the closet and to hang up his dress white shirt. "Because, now they're still wearable when I get back to the base. But, with my luck, I'll drop a big gob of pizza sauce on myself and I'll have to spend tomorrow getting them dry-cleaned, again."

As Casey and Tim came down the stairs, Da and Patrick met them at the bottom.

"Patrick," Da asked. "Do you still have your keys? I can't remember where I put mine."

"Sure. Do you want to use them?"

"No." replied his father. "You drive. And maybe on the way home you can teach me how to come into the driveway quietly, like you boys do sometimes."

After a moment of guilt and discovery, after imagining that they had been getting away with something for a long time, the boys all laughed nervously as they got into the car, then they were quiet.

"Your mother and I used to get the biggest kick out of waiting for one of you to be out after your curfew, and then watching whoever it was try to glide in without hitting the garage door. I think Casey was actually the best at it. But maybe that was because he was out late more than the rest of you, and he got more practice."

The boys, perhaps with the exception of Casey himself, laughed a bit nervously, but Da continued. "And then, the next morning, whoever the guilty party was, would come slowly downstairs and it was all we could do not to laugh out loud. But we had our parental duty to do and we did manage to inflict some kind of punishment on the culprit. But it was hard."

As Pat drove across Longstown to the pizza parlor, the boys and Da began to confess other things to each other. They were little things, really. Patrick confessed that once, while in grade school he had sneaked away from the school yard and gone over to the drugstore in town to buy "Poppers".

"You know, those little plastic bottles that, when you pull their string, they go 'BANG' and confetti shoots out."

Da shook his head and commented that it was a good thing for Patrick that he hadn't got caught. "Your bottom would have still been sore." he told him.

The boys also began to share with Da other significant memories that they had of him and Ma, while they grew up. Tim told the story of once, when he was really small, Da had asked him something and he had lied about "whatever it was". However, Da had caught the lie. "You looked at me with a look of disappointment that I'll never forget. Then, looking at me very sadly, you said: 'A man is only worth as much as his word.' Then you walked out of the room."

Sitting in the pizza parlor, Da shook his head, not remembering the incident, at all.

"Well I knew then," Tim continued the story, "that I never wanted to see that look on your face again. And to my knowledge, that was the last deliberate lie I ever told."

The other boys laughed and added their "lessons in life" stories. And each had been a major influence on their growing up. But Da had raised four children and frankly, most of those "key" moments had not really seemed that significant to him or their mother, at the time.

"But you've all grown up to be people that we're proud of, so I guess we didn't traumatize any of you, at least any more than was necessary."

The pizza was ordered and delivered. And, sure enough, Casey did manage to drop a glob of cheese on what would have been his white dress shirt. But the topics of their chatter then became centered around what they were going to do in the future.

"Your mother and I have wanted to go back to Ireland for a week or so, just to see that it was still there. And I think I'd still like to go. If any of you boys think you might want to come along, I'd be proud to show you off."

"Count me in," Patrick replied, almost as quickly as Da finished.

Casey and Tim added that they would love to go, but that, because of their jobs they really couldn't expect to get away again any time soon. Tim told Da and Patrick: "But you two go and check it out. Then later on, you can guide us around."

The pizza, itself, was as good as any Tim had eaten. And the four of them spent the next two hours laughing and sharing stories. Sometimes, as the others talked, Tim sat back in his chair and he listened. When Da enjoyed himself, there was no one who could laugh with more enthusiasm, even if the laughter was at his own expense. And all of his brothers had been given the same gift. No matter what happened in the next few days, Tim was going to miss them.

Chapter Twenty Five

As the four men walked back to where Patrick had parked the Impala, Tim glanced at his watch. It was nearly a quarter till nine. Patrick and Da walked on ahead, giving Tim one of the few moments that he had spent alone with Casey.

"Hey, little guy," Casey said as the two walked. "I know you don't want to get all mushy at the airport tomorrow, but take care of yourself out in California. I expect to read headlines about you out there. But I don't want it to be as a statistic in a story about earthquakes or something like that."

"Don't worry," Tim replied and shrugged his shoulders. "I've already been out there a week, and nothing has happened yet."

"Oh!" chuckled Casey, as if he believed. "Well, that's different."

"Besides," Tim added. "You're out on a ship that's full of rockets and shells, and all kinds of explosives. You take care that you don't get your butt blown up."

"Don't worry about me, the Navy's got more regulations than

you can shake a stick at, for just that reason. Even during the war, it was virtually impossible for anything to happen."

"Well, 'virtually impossible' doesn't mean completely safe. Besides," Tim said. "You and Pat are the only brothers I've got. And now, with Ma gone, we can't make any new ones."

When Tim and Casey reached the Impala, Da and Pat were already inside, and Pat had started the engine.

"You got a late date, Pat?" Casey asked. "Does she have a good looking friend that might go for a uniform?"

"No" replied Pat. "But if I did, I'd know better than to introduce her to a sailor on his last few nights ashore. Remember, I've got to live around here after you two shoves off."

Pat had actually been seeing one of the women down at the union hall, and Da knew. But Pat had asked him not to say anything to Tim, Casey, or even Mary Margaret, until there was something to say. It was hard for Da to keep the secret, but he did.

Pat turned the corner that lead to the house, but as he drove past a fire hydrant on his left, he reached down to the key in the ignition and turned off the Impala's engine. Until then, Tim and the others had been chatting, and not paying much attention. But when they realized what was going on, they all grew very quiet. They were still the better part of a block away from the house, but the Impala had retained much of its speed and they were closing fast. When he had reached another landmark, this time a light pole two doors down from his target, Patrick reached down again and turned off the car's headlights. Da was visibly nervous, but Casey and Tim sat quietly, observing the procedure as if they were calculating style points for Patrick's performance. As the Impala approached the driveway, it was still moving quickly. Patrick carefully applied pressure to the brake pedal and the car slowed down measurably. They all expected to feel the bump, as the tires rolled off the street itself and onto the slightly inclined driveway. However, between the change in direction as Patrick turned into the drive way, going over the bump, and with the careful application of Patrick's foot on the brake, the car slowed down dramatically, and then came to a very quiet stop. Satisfied with his own actions, Patrick turned to his brothers and said: "Learn from the Master."

Da remained quiet, but Tim and Casey began to applaud. Casey, mimicking an announcer at the Olympics, cupped his hands over his mouth and began a monotone of numbers. "Five point eight, Five point eight, and a five point one from the East German judge."

As Patrick emerged from the car, he raised both of his arms in a sign of victory. Then he bowed and accepted praise from the imagined crowd that had watched. When Da got out of the car, though, he walked over to see how close they had come to the garage door. "You know you only missed it by about two feet." he told Pat. "But I'll tell ya, it's a lot easier to watch you do it from upstairs."

The four men walked up to the front door, and when they entered, Patrick went immediately to the television set and turned it on. Da asked if any of the boys wanted a drink or something else to eat, but when they all declined, he walked over to the kitchen sink and poured himself a glass of water. As he stood there, alone in the kitchen, he gazed back into the room where the boys were. In his thoughts, he felt proud of all their children, proud they had now grown into fine young adults. Under his breath he whispered to Maeve: "Darlin' girl, we did do a fine job with them, didn't we?"

Over the sink, Mike washed the tears from his eyes, then he dried himself with the dish cloth that hung there. A few minutes later, he had collected himself enough to go back into the room where the boys were, but Da soon excused himself and went off to bed. They had arrived home shortly before ten o'clock. However, by shortly after eleven Da had gone upstairs, and both Pat and Casey were fast asleep in front of the television.

There was a commercial break on whatever program they had all been watching. And Tim took the opportunity to go upstairs and retrieve the gun and the bullets. Once again, he avoided the noisy steps. Once again, inside his room, he closed the door and made his way to the closet. It was possible that Casey would wake up and come up to bed, so Tim quickly stuck the gun into his waistband and once again covered it with his shirt. Then, just as quickly, he poured the bullets out of his other shoe, into his hand, and then into his pants pockets.

There were more bullets in his pockets now than Tim ever intended to use. And the bulge they made would have been more than a little noticeable to anyone who may have seen him. On the other hand, when everything was done tonight, Tim wanted to be sure that no evidence had been left in the house. He would dispose of the extras somewhere, but for now he would take them along.

Even though that Friday night was a warm one, Tim grabbed a jacket, one of his old ones, and put it on. Then, from one of the back pocket of his pants, he took out Da's car keys that he had "found" in the kitchen, earlier in the day.

Before stepping into the hallway and going downstairs, Tim looked out through the crack in his door to see if anyone had come upstairs. The hallway was empty, as far as he could see, so he hurried down the stairs and out through the front door. He hadn't stopped to look, but he was confident from what he could hear from the living room, that Casey and Pat were still asleep. They would probably never know he was gone. Even if they did happen to wake up, they might just assume that he had gone to bed. So far, so good.

It was nearly twelve o'clock when he got into the Impala again and started the engine. As rapidly as he could without making additional noise, he backed the vehicle out into the street, turned on the headlights, and drove away. For the moment he was clear. Tim hadn't seen anyone and, in all likelihood, no one had seen him. And he was concerned that Adams might make an early night of it. In any case, he would be there. And maybe he would be home again before anyone woke up.

It was already too late for Tim's wish to come true, though. After he had excused himself and gone upstairs, Da had not gone to sleep, but he sat down in a chair at his bedroom window, looking out into the night, and missing his wife. During these last few days, since

Maeve had passed on, that was where he had done the majority of his crying. And each night he had sat there in the dark, crying until he had no more tears and until he had consumed at least two strong drinks. Certainly not enough to get a good Irishman drunk, but the alcohol did seem to help.

Neither the boys nor Mary Margaret had known. But Da had moved a bottle of whiskey and a glass from the kitchen up to his room. Without Maeve with him, sleeping in "their" bed, the place where most of their children had been conceived and where for more nights than he could remember he and Maeve had made each other laugh, made no sense to him at all. This night though, the night of her funeral, Da had begun a strange ritual of both drinking and praying. And somehow he felt that it was all right with God that he did it that way.

Mike had finished his first drink and had closed his eyes, to see her face again, when heard the front door of the house open. And one of the boys came out in the direction of the parked Impala. Originally he had supposed that, whichever one it was, he was running to the store for something. But it was almost midnight and none of the stores would be open. Mike knew that it was Tim who was leaving the house, and he also knew that something was wrong.

The traffic lights along the way all seemed to switch to red as Tim approached them. And once he was there, they seemed to take considerably longer to change back to green. At one stop, while he impatiently tapped his fingers against the steering wheel, a black and white patrol car settled next to him, also waiting for the light to change. The single patrolman inside, glanced over at Tim, and he nodded "hello" just as the signal changed and he drove on ahead. Tim was relieved and happy that he had decided to put the gun into the pocket of his jacket instead of leaving it on the seat next to him, but he wondered if the patrolman's smile could be some kind of sign that what he was doing was somehow "sanctioned". But the ploy wouldn't work. He knew very well that what he was about to do was very wrong.

"At least I can be honest with myself."

The patrol car seemed to be the only other vehicle that Tim shared the roadway with, and he knew that was bad news. However, at that point there was very little he could do about it. He kept driving in the direction of the Post Office, and then on to Glory Lane.

A slight cloud cover blocked the full intensity of the moonlight, making the night just a bit darker than it ordinarily might have been. Once in the area again, Tim drove the Impala up the street, past the room that Adams had taken, and he continued down to the corner, where he turned the Impala around and came back down Glory Lane. This time, however, when he drove to the corner just past Adam's room, he turned left and found a place, as far as he could find from the street lights, to park.

Sitting in the dark, and hoping that no one had seen him arrive, Tim reached into his pants pockets and took out six cartridges. Then he pulled the pistol out from his jacket pocket, and began to fill the chambers one by one. Finishing with chamber number six, he snapped the cylinders back into place, and returned the gun to his jacket pocket. He was ready.

Making as little noise as possible, Tim opened the car door and closed it softly behind him. Looking around for signs of being observed, but seeing none, he walked quickly around the corner to the spot he'd chosen earlier, where he would wait. Near the end of the block, on the same side of the street as both the bar and Adam's room, Tim could see anyone who approached from that direction. Also, once he was in position at the end of the block, whoever came out from the bar would have the lights behind them.

"Sort of his last halo," Tim jested to himself.

The interior of Sleepy Ted's was like that of millions of small town bars across America, around the world. Two light fixtures, over two coin operated pool tables left the seven tables that rested against the walls in partial darkness. Behind the dark wooden bar was a girl named Flow. Do you get it? She had asked, giggling, with a big smile and wide eyes, when Adams first met her months ago. "Flow, and I work in a bar.?"

"I get it," he said, flatly, and he shook his head, not amused.

Adams stood six feet five, and weighed just over 260 pounds. His hair was dark blonde, and he rarely shaved on weekends, leaving him too scruffy to attract women. He traveled alone, and he said he preferred it that way. Every night since coming to Longstown to work on the new Post Office addition, Adams had come to Sleepy Ted's, ordered beer after beer, and sat alone. The regulars were there, sitting at the bar and talking about the weather, the government, and how difficult things had gotten. Most of them had opinions, regardless of the subject. Two women and three men were at their usual seats, and they had Flow to serve them. One of the seats at the bar was empty, because the best looking of the women, Lori, was at the table of a man she had just met. One of the men, one they called Cowboy, dressed in boots and denim, had ridden bulls on the rodeo circuit as a younger man. He'd been a champion in 1967, and had made a lot of money. But in 1969, a bull named Iccarus had fallen on his right leg and crushed it. Cowboy laughed with the others now, told them stories, and ordered his round of drinks. And, aside from Cowboy, Adams wondered how any of them could afford to be there every night.

Adams could hear Lori and her new friend laughing behind him, and Flow continued bringing them drinks, both of them drinking beer. Tall and slightly heavy, now in her forties, Adams thought Lori had probably been quite pretty once. Her long blonde hair hanging down to her shoulders, and her ample breasts, let men over look her slightly bowed legs, and that laugh. Adams shuddered when he heard it, more a cackle now than the pleasant laugh of a girl. And she was loud. The man with her was a newcomer to the bar, probably traveling through, probably with a wife and family at home, but they were not here tonight.

And, like most other women, Adams both loathed Lori, and he wanted her.

As the regulars amused themselves, and the couple at the table whispered softly, and then laughed aloud, in the back ground, a music track played on, love songs mostly, but now and then someone fed the quarter-for-three-songs juke box, and for a moment or two life washed back on those in the bar, reminding them of times in their lives. Better times when everything was possible.

Adams nursed his beer, wishing he was somewhere else, and struggled with his own memories. Other people had come into the bar. Some played pool, flirting with their dates if they had one, or showing their skill at the game to their friends. Food, mostly hamburgers, chips, and a drink was available, for a price. Some ordered food, played their games, and laughed, having a good time in a small town. Then, in time, they drifted out into the warm night.

Carved into the tables were the names of earlier customers, other people who filled the emptiness of their lives with the quiet of a drink. In the middle of his table, someone had scratched the words, MOLLY WAS HERE, and he wondered who she had been. And his mind wandered back to his childhood.

Carl Adams had been born in Redmond Nebraska, roughly thirty miles from the University of Nebraska. His father owned a general store for a while, then eventually lost it, as he lost everything in his life to his need for alcohol. He drank only Jack Daniels, a man's drink. And he was a mean son of a bitch when he was drinking. Carl and his mother, Audrey, would never go looking for him when he was out late. Instead they waited fearfully for him to arrive.

Adams had grown up listening to his mother's cries, the crashing of her body against the wall, and the thud of his fathers' fists as he beat her. Carl trembled in the hallway outside their room, or huddled silently in the corner of the living room as he beat her there.

Yet Carl could never understand why she didn't leave him, or even fight back against him. She just stood there, taking his constant physical abuse, and lay bleeding on the floor when he was finished. When he was young, Carl would run to his mother's side and try to help her, pressing ice against her eye, against her split lips.

When it was over, the following day, his father would quietly look in on his son, assuring himself that he was still there. Sitting down next to Carl on the bed, his father would gently run his fingers through his son's hair. "I wish she didn't make me do that," he told Carl. "But I can't stand the way she looks at me, like I was nothing." Sometimes tears would well up in his father's eyes, and Carl began to understand what he meant. "Women need a firm hand, don't they dad?"

When he was old enough and large enough, his father encouraged Carl to go hunting with him and to play football. He was not a great shot with a rifle, and he found it boring to walk slowly or quietly sit in the forest, waiting to shoot his prey. But football was very different. Nebraska was a state custom made for a large young man who was able to run fast, and who loved the feel of pad to pad, or helmet to helmet hitting. In the eight-to-twelve league, he played linebacker, but as he grew taller and stronger, and with good sure hands, in high school, he was shifted to wide receiver.

Carl Adams was in his element. His father was proud of him, and he came to every game, cheering for his son. Adams was handsome, with a winning smile, and strong as a bull. And though his school grades were low, with a little applied pressure from his coach, Adams was allowed to play for his high school varsity team as a freshman, class of 1970. And everyone, especially his coaches and his father, expected him toget scholarships for college, maybe even to the University of Nebraska.

His high school team, the Redmond Avalanche, won the county championship when Carl was a junior and again in his senior year, and though technically not eligible to play, the coaches took advantage their influence in the school to make the large young man an exception. Teachers were pressured to raise Carl's grades, and most of them complied. Administrators were encouraged to be flexible with eligibility rules. Football was not only a major source of revenue for the school, but both faculty and alumni wanted a winner.

In the spring of 1969, just after the football season had ended, the principal of Redmond High School was fired and quickly replaced by the county's new Superintendent of Schools, Miss Jodie Newman. For years, the voices of parents whose sons had not been allowed to play on school teams, had been ignored. But in the new Superintendent, they found their voice. Threatening to take the district to Federal Court, the parents argued that their sons were not getting fair access to federal or state funds allotted to schools for sports, and that ineligible students were being allowed to play instead.

As he hoped, Carl Adams had already been offered a full ride football scholarship to Nebraska, and he read the reports of cheating in the paper with mixed feelings. He had his scholarship. But he felt bad about future players who would not get to play because of bad grades. However, for her own reasons, and what she called public pressure, Superintendent Newman investigated a sufficient number of cases to convince herself that a series of wrongs had been done. On her own initiative, Superintendent Newman fired and replaced the principals of the high schools involved, suspended Carl Adams and other major players from school, and declared that they would not be allowed to participate in graduation ceremonies. The football coaches, however, were shielded by vocal alumni, and given a verbal warning, with no other consequences.

But as word of the conflict reached the local papers, headlines ran with bold reports of "cheating scandals in high school sports", and University administrators chose to keep it away from their campuses by rescinding the scholarships of any student involved. Adams received his notice in the mail, and pounded his fist on the kitchen wall. "That bitch," he said.

His father went to plead his son's case with the new Principal of Redmond High School, the admittance office of the University, and with Superintendent Newman herself. But the door to Carl's admission to the University was shut tight. Again and again he was told, "Your son can't cheat his way through life, Mr. Adams." Covering their own involvement, the others involved, the coaches and the alumni avoided him like a leper.

Carl could still recite the words of the largest news article about the cheating scandal, and the way the finger of blame seemed to focus on him. In his small Nebraska town, the image of being a cheater loomed over Carl, and though few people spoke of the incident after the dust settled, Carl always knew what they were talking about behind his back. His father couldn't find a job, and he and his wife moved to Dallas. She died two years later in what was officially called an accident. Carl Adams moved east, finding work when he could. Maeve Conolly was not the first women he had beaten, or raped, just the first he had killed.

Adams nursed his beer, and his inner demons, feeling the beer run down his throat, letting it sooth his feelings, medicating the violent images in his head. He had never acquired his father's taste for Jack Daniels, never feeling as weak as he now understood his father to be, or the need for that strong drink. In time he heard Lori and her friend struggle to their feet and make their way to the door. "The bitch got him," Adams said to himself, as the couple opened the door, into the night.

Standing in the dark, concealed as much as he could be, but knowing only too well that his simply being there had changed what was normal for this place, Tim watched the door of the bar, Sleepy Ted's, and he waited. For the longest time, no one came or left. Then, a couple came out into the parking lot. They were drunk, and they were loud. The woman was trying to kiss her partner, while the man tried desperately to find his car keys. He only tried so hard, then he took her in his arms and they kissed, the woman leaning with her back against the car, holding him. A few minutes later, the man pushed her away, and after he emptied the contents of his pockets out on the hood of the car, he found the keys, they got in, and the couple drove away. Then again, a long time passed before anyone stirred in the direction of Sleepy Ted's. Finally, though, a single large man came out through the door of the bar and began to walk in Tim's direction.

"Adams." he said to himself, hoping that he was right.

Instinctively, Tim checked his jacket pocket to make sure that the gun was still there, and finding that it was, he too began to walk, tentatively. Moving slowly, he tried to gauge where their paths would cross, as the other man kept coming. Adams feet scuffed along the sidewalk, as he tried to raise himself up to his full height, as he tried his best to appear sober. Tim listened to his own shallow breathing, and he could almost hear his heart pounding. And the spike of pain behind his eyes was growing. Outwardly, though, he remained calm. The sky was dark and the two men were virtually alone. The gun was in his pocket, and very soon the waiting would be over.

As he walked closer, Tim sized up the man, how much bigger he was, and that his walk was uncertain. Once, Adams nearly stumbled but caught himself before he fell. "You drunken pig," Tim thought. "You're never going to know what happened tonight, never know how you died until you land in Hell."

The muscles in his hand gripping the gun were getting tired and Tim deliberately relaxed them. As they stepped closer, Tim could see Adam's eyes, his unshaved face, he could hear his breathing. Four feet apart, Tim focused his total hatred of the man who had raped and killed his mother, walking his mind through what he imagined happened that afternoon behind the store, feeling anger, and projecting his feeling of horror and worthlessness on the man standing before him. He let his rage for the man rise up into his mind and he stared, gritting his teeth, and looking into Adams blurry eyes.

And, fortunately or not, he allowed himself to think. New emotions swept over Tim. His head felt like it was splitting, and Adams' aura fluctuated violently from reds to darkened purple to a dirty dark yellow. Tim raised his hand to cover his eyes as he braced against the pain in his head. The situation was wrong. Ma would never have wanted this for him, not for him and not for the family. But someone had to make Adams pay. It was something he would do for her. And yet, she would have hated it. He was sure. He felt differently. It was not what she would have wanted. Tears welled up in Tim's eyes, and dripped across his cheeks.

In the darkness of Glory Street, within feet of Adams, Tim realized in his heart that for all his intentions and the hatred he carried for the man, he would not be able to use the gun and kill him. He felt himself a coward, unable to do the one thing that would avenge his mothers' rape and killing. "Damn" The pain in his head felt like a nail against his brain, and his body shook visibly. He was afraid to do it, and afraid of failure. He accused himself of being afraid to confront the larger man. A coward, the realization shook Tim emotionally and shook him physically. The pain in his head spiking, Tim felt waves of sadness and, at the same time, waves of self-revulsion. What would he say to Da, or to Patrick? He knew what his father would do. Tim had this one chance, one shot at Adams. It was dark and he had the gun in his hand. And yet, for all his brave words and planning, tears of frustration running down his cheek, he was unable to do one simple thing.

Feelings of self-loathing and self-hatred flowed over Tim, buckling him to the ground, feeling himself worthless. Tim dropped to one knee as Adams walked closer to him. He looked up from where he knelt, feeling helpless, empty, wanting to die. For a moment, Adams' aura seemed to jump from multiple shades of blue to yellow, but Tim hardly noticed that the pain in his head subsided.

The larger man paused as he approached Tim. Tim pressed his fist against the sidewalk, skinning his knuckles to dull the pain, and he looked up, staring into Adams eyes. Adams smelled of drink and he stumbled closer to Tim, kneeling there. Adams stopped and looked down at Tim, as if he were disgusted "Friggin loser", he grunted, and he continued on.

As Tim returned to the Impala, he immediately recognized the form sitting in the passenger's seat. Again he wasn't surprised. As he got in and placed the gun into the other man's outstretched hand, he heard Patterson say simply: "It's cold, son. That's good."

The tears streaming down Tim's cheeks, spoke more of frustration, humiliation, and his own version of cowardice than of anything good. Putting the pistol into his own jacket pocket, Patterson placed his left hand on the back of his young friends' neck. "If it makes any difference, your brothers sent the word out through the union of what

Adams did to your mom. If nothing else, he'll never work again, at least not in organized labor."

Tim nodded that he understood, and he was glad that Pat had done it, but he still felt shame that he had gotten so close and had failed.

"Tell me two things about what just happened, Tim," the older man began. "First, would it really have helped you or your family if you had shot him?"

"It may have helped me," was the reply.

Patterson nodded his head and agreed that it may have made him feel better, but it would also have caused major problems. Then he asked his second question: "I need you to think clearly for a minute," he said. "At any time, when you and Adams were face to face, did the color of his aura change?"

After all that had happened, the question almost seemed reasonable. Tim rubbed his bleeding knuckles and replied: "Well, it was dark but I saw his aura. The color did change from dark blue to almost a yellow, but not because I scared him. I didn't. I was afraid of him, and mine was probably yellow, too."

"Somehow I doubt that." was Patterson's comment. Then the older man drew back his arm away from Tim and said: "Don't beat yourself up, son. In the end, stopping yourself was the right thing to do, and you may have done more than you know."

Patterson held up his hand to prevent Tim from asking for a clarification of what he had just said. "We'll go over everything in a week or so," Patterson told him. "For now, you just be on that plane tomorrow."

Chapter Twenty Six

Saturday afternoon, the room at the Driftwood was still being held and the rental car company had reopened his reservation, having been instructed to do so by someone at RDG. As he dumped his clothes out on the bed and proceeded to hang them up, things were all very much the same, and yet everything in his life had changed. The chasm between his life now and Longstown New York seemed complete and total.

Saturday night, Tim went down to the restaurant to eat, but also to find out about the girl. When he approached the greeter position, she was there, and she smiled. This time her aura was a gentle green, and before he returned to his room, Tim knew her name, Shelly, when her shift ended, nine o'clock, and her telephone number. Shelly already knew his room number, and she met him that night.

"You look great," he said as he opened his door and saw her standing there. She had changed from her uniform into a short denim skirt and white blouse. Downstairs at the restaurant, she had tied her long dark hair back behind her head, now it hung loose across her shoulders. Tim loved her smile. "C'mon in," he said. After she had stepped inside, Tim backed away and offered her a seat. She just stood there looking incredible.

Tim thought that though he had eaten, Shelly might be hungry, "Did you eat?"

"Yeah," she replied, and seemed to enjoy his awkwardness. She thought it was cute.

Finally, after a moment spent not knowing what to do, Tim stepped closer to her, watched her incredible eyes, and gently let his fingertips trace along her cheek. Then he leaned slightly and brushed her lips with his, once, and once again. He felt her arms around him, responding. Soft kisses, as his fingertips brushed gently through her hair. Gentle caresses as he made love to her. Shelly didn't work on Sundays, and Tim doubted if he would make it to Mass the next morning.

Monday morning at the office was very strange. Al and a few others asked him how he was doing. But what could he tell them? He appreciated their concern but he didn't have much to say.

"Thanks for asking," he replied. "I'll be fine."

Though he had found a new lover, and he knew he would be with her again, Tim was, far from "fine" emotionally. He was drained from his trip. Da had been right about the bottom line, though. Survivors did have to continue on. Maybe that was the hardest job of all.

Thinking about Ma, and he did that a lot on his first few days back, Tim decided to use the fact that he was keenly aware of his own emotions, to achieve something good in a long term way. She would have liked that. Also, since the people around him at RDG might expect him to be a bit quiet for a few days or weeks, maybe he should use this time and his own aura to verify what each of the colors really meant. Then, if he was able to figure them out, maybe he could make them change. But he would take his time and be certain.

For the first two days, Tim decided not to carry the key with him at all, wanting to settle back into a routine with his coworkers and with his responsibilities at RDG. Not having the key created a problem when he arrived Monday morning around seven thirty and couldn't open the locked front door, but Tuesday morning, after adjusting his alarm clock and his departure time so that he arrived just after eight o'clock, he was relieved to find that not only was the main door to RDG unlocked, but the first face he saw in the morning was not Alice Hartcourt's. After resting Monday and Tuesday, Wednesday evening, Tim felt prepared to begin again, and kept the key with him.

"If I can cause the colors to appear in my own aura, then I'll know what emotions they represent."

After work, while driving home, Tim began to think about his mother, deliberately concentrating on just how much he missed her, and on how much missing her hurt. Immediately, his mind's automatic defenses tried to adjust and to help him cope with his feelings, but he subdued them and allowed the pain to flow. As he parked the car and ran up to his room, tears were once again in his eyes and streaming down his cheeks. Safely inside, Tim walked directly to the bed, sat down, and began to tell himself over and over again that Ma was dead and he should have been there to help her, to stop what was happening. After letting the pain build up inside himself, he allowed himself to cry.

After another minute or so, Tim looked up to see his reflection in the bathroom mirror. As he had hoped, all around him was a deep purple and bright red aura, the same general colors that he had seen around Mary. His arch, however, was somewhat brighter than hers had been and more intense. Perhaps the difference was due to his having been more focused on a specific set of feelings instead of what, under normal conditions, would be a combination.

As his mind began analyzing the aura around him, the colors began to lose their sharpness and fade, blending together and then returning to a normal green. Still, Tim had his first verification. The red and purple mix did signify a disturbing degree of sorrow or regret. After spending that evening experimenting, he knew he could safely recreate and catalogue any of the colors he had seen.

Tim met Shelly that evening, they went out for drinks after her shift, and she wondered why he spent most of his time looking at her. But Tim was the first really decent guy she had met in a while. He was a bit awkward and shy, but she enjoyed being with him.

During the following weeks, Tim took the key with him wherever he went. As he expected, most of his coworkers took things around the office in stride. And though they each carried what he referred to as "background pain", their auras seemed to stay basically green, or to fluctuate within what he came to call their "normal zone".

Finally, Tim wanted to know if he could cause other people's colors to change, and if he could change their auras, could he affect the people themselves. He would wait for his chance, but Alice Hartcourt would be his first subject.

Opportunity came knocking the following Tuesday morning, when Freida, the purchasing assistant whose desk shared the common area with Alice's, called in sick for the day. Alice was delighted, thinking that she would have the common area to herself, but when Tim suddenly picked up some of his paperwork and planted himself in Freida's chair, the dark blue shade returned.

As Tim sat at Freida's desk, knowing that he had invaded Alice's "inner sanctum" he busied himself, appearing to work on his plan.

"Are you going to be there long?" she asked.

"No," Tim replied as if answering pleasantly. "I'll just be a few minutes or so."

Using his peripheral vision to watch what was happening, and being a bit unsure that it might not be better to let sleeping dogs lie, Tim remained at Freida's desk much longer than Alice wanted or thought necessary, pretending to work, yet closing his eyes and focusing on her emotions. Could he turn her ugly disposition to something less, something friendlier? Tim pictured Alice as a beautiful, smiling child of six or seven, with golden hair, laughing and playing in a field of wild flowers. He held his mental image there.

But suddenly Tim felt a deep wave of sadness well up from within himself, realizing that, maybe as a child, some part of what he had visualized for Alice must have been true. Maybe she truly had been a happy child. Children were not born miserable and angry. Sadly, something, or some series of things, must have ripped that joy away from her, and that loss of joy, that hurt, must have affected the rest of her life.

When Tim looked up, almost in tears himself, Alice's aura had lost all trace of her permanent blue color and had taken on a blotchy mix of deep red and other blended, confused shades. Tears were streaming down her perfectly made up cheeks. She was trembling uncontrollably.

"Oh, damn," he whispered to himself.

As Alice pushed away from her desk, and hurried from the room, Tim didn't know what to do, so he quietly returned to his own desk again. Yes, the experiment had worked. No, it wasn't as simple as wishing another person's feelings to change, but if he created an emotion within himself, he had been able to transfer what he was feeling into someone else's mind or soul, or whatever. He could change the color of their aura. The process took some time, and was emotionally draining, but he could do it. And then it dawned on Tim that in doing so, the pain in his head had not only subsided, but he actually felt better.

Alice Hartcourt remained in the women's room for almost an hour, and a few of the other women ventured in to check on her. When they came out, no one knew what was wrong with her. "She's just in there crying." they said. But Alice went directly home that day, and she called in sick for the remainder of the week. On Tim's urging, Abrams called her at home Friday afternoon, and was told by her husband that Alice had been hospitalized after coming home Tuesday. He didn't want to talk about it over the phone, but he promised to keep them informed as to what was happening, and when her doctor would allow Alice to return to work. "For now, though," he said. "She's a sick little girl."

Chapter Twenty Seven

When he arrived at his room, Tim lay down on the bed and looked up at the ceiling. Could he speak to God? Would he be heard if he prayed? Tim lay there on the bed, his mind trying to bring order to the events of the last week, but the clock in his head had continued to tick, and it was time for him to cope with something else. It was time he moved out of the hotel. Tim had come to think of the Driftwood as, if nor a home, at least as a convenient base to operate from. It was close to RDG. And, of course he loved the maid service and room service. And Shelly was there. But his free ride on RDG's dime had come to an end. Beginning tomorrow the bills for staying there would come to him.

His move was already scheduled. Tim had packed, and that Friday night was to be his last night staying there. His new place was a small furnished apartment he had found in a town on the outskirts of San Jose called Campbell. It was cheaper, and not too much farther from RDG.

But that night, after the call to Alice's husband, Tim thought about the seriousness of what he'd done to her, even if he did it for a good reason. Sitting up in his bed, tears once again streamed down his face. And there was everything else. His mom had died a senseless death, only days ago. And he resurrected the feeling of powerlessness and self-loathing he felt over the business with Adams. He had tried to kill the man who hurt her, who killed her, but couldn't bring himself to pull the gun from his jacket and kill him. And now Alice Hartcourt was in a hospital because of something he had done. When the phone rang, Tim was not at all surprised that it was Patterson.

"Are you okay, Tim?" the older man asked. "I'm going to be down your way in about thirty minutes and, if you don't have anything else planned, maybe you wouldn't mind if I dropped by?"

Tim had stopped wondering how Patterson kept himself so well versed on what happened at RDG, and yet remained distant. He said, "OK" and rose up to wash his face. When his friend knocked on his door, and stood in the hallway with both Rich Barlow and May Fong beside him, many of Tim's questions were answered.

"I believe you've met my friends here, Tim. If not, this overweight ne'erdo-well is Rich Barlow. And I know you've met May."

Tim responded with a quick yet warm hello to May, but on top of everything else, the fact that the president of RDG had just walked through his door and was now standing in his bedroom, was a bit too much. They all shook hands. He only had a can of soda and some left over Champagne he and Shelly had shared, but he offered them what he had. They declined. Patterson quietly smiled and put his arm around the younger man's shoulders. "Tim," he began. "You've been a big surprise to us, a good surprise, but a surprise, none the less. And there's a bit more about seeing the auras than what little I've told you."

Tim barley stifled a laugh. He could list a few things Paterson had not mentioned at all, but left to him as a surprise, like the colored auras, or the splitting headache pain. But he didn't say anything. Tim kept his eyes on Patterson and the older man continued: "My guess is that you've already figured out some of what I'm going to tell you. But, before I get started, I need to know exactly what was going on between you and Alice Hartcourt last Tuesday."

Supposing that if they came with Patterson, it was okay to talk about everything in front of May and Rich Barlow, Tim began to describe his experiment and how he was trying to effect Alice's disposition. Patterson looked over to Barlow and nodded, but he didn't say a word until Tim had finished. Then he rephrased his question and asked it again. "Were you deliberately trying to change the color in Alice's arch?"

"Yeah," he said. "I tried to change her normally ugly attitude into something more pleasant. I thought that would be better for everyone." Tim looked up at Patterson for his reaction. Then he continued. "Half way through, though, I thought of her as a happy child, and then pictured her the way she is now. It was like I touched a nerve inside her, and I felt very sad for her and sad for what had happened to her, whatever it was. And apparently that's the emotion, that utter sadness, that got transferred to her. I didn't mean to hurt her."

Patterson and the others seemed to have heard what they had come to hear, and there was a strange mix of concern and excitement around them. Barlow stepped in to explain: "Tim," he began. "There's a dozen or so of us now, and no more than twenty people I've ever heard of, that can see the auras and we have each tried, as you have, to understand for ourselves exactly what the colors mean. And once you get the hang of it, it's pretty easy. And the headaches go away in time if you learn to concentrate." Barlow winked at Tim and then said, "If you've ever played poker, you know that being able to see what another person's "emotional cards" are is a big advantage when you're dealing with them."

The others nodded their agreement as Tim looked around at them, then Rich continued: "As I said, there is a group of us who have trained ourselves to see and understand the colors, but as far as I know, until today, Ron here was the only person who's ever been able to change what he saw."

Tim asked, "Why is that?" But the others continued. "What

that means," Patterson added, "is that with practice, you can make anyone you wish to feel anyway you want them to feel, from euphoric happiness to despair, even fear. And they'll feel that way down to the marrow of their bones."

Tim wrinkled his brow and tried to take in what he was hearing, and to make some sense of what it meant to him. Patterson saw the skepticism and confusion he felt, paused for a moment, then went on. "But, as we saw with your experiment with Alice Hartcourt, changing peoples feeling without their consent can be unsettling to those around you, until you learn to control it. But you can do it."

Paterson looked to see the effect his words were having before continuing: "And there's something more I should tell you." Tim sat down on the edge of his bed as Patterson talked. Now Ron sat beside him and continued. "When you and I sat in the dark that Saturday night in Longstown," Tim looked at the floor, not really wanting to think about what had happened that night. After a moment, he looked up again into his friends eyes, and Patterson smiled. "I knew I'd been right about you. You're a good kid, Tim." Tim whispered a "Thank you," but with little conviction.

The older man continued. "Let me tell you what happened that night." Tim nodded. "Adams was a violent pig of a man who enjoyed hurting women, I don't know why. But I do know that he had had several brushes with the law, and several accusations were made by women he knew, and yet no one ever testified in court against him, and he was never convicted of anything. People are afraid of men like that." Tim listened.

"But physically strong or not, a person's emotions, what we see as auras, reflect how people's actions truly do affect them. Our minds try to adjust, but over time people's actions do have consequences, for good of not." Tim sat silently, still listening.

"What you saw first were the wildly fluctuating colors of trauma in Adams aura, probably made more extreme by sitting in a bar, drinking all night. He hated his life and he hated himself. But he had carried that hate for years, and had been doing ok with it. It was only when your emotions of self-hatred and worthlessness were transferred to Adams, did the severely darkened and changing aura around his head change more radically, and then to become yellow. At the same time, you hated him, and held him responsible for you mother. You felt yourself worthless, and you felt that Adams was much worse than that. You wished not only him dead, but you wished yourself dead as well. Am I right?"

Tim nodded. He didn't know how Patterson knew, but he described his feelings, his emotions that night precisely. Patterson put his arm around Tim's shoulder and continued. "And that night while you felt so badly about yourself, thinking you had failed your family, you thought you had merely scared him. But just after he left you there, Mr. Adams returned to his room and he hanged himself. The police found him Monday morning."

Patterson felt badly, having to tell Tim in such a blunt way, and he allowed his young friend to see the sadness he felt. And Tim was torn between how he was supposed to feel. On the other hand, Patterson knew that Tim had to know the truth. "Don't blame yourself for what happened with Alice, son. You tried to do something good, but it got away from you. It's more my fault for not warning you. From now on, though, you'll need to be careful. You and I will talk more, and I can help you."

May broke into the conversation to add, "Alice's doctor finally reported that she would be okay and back to work in a couple of weeks. According to him, a breakdown of that sort is fairly common among people who carry as much anger as she does. And she has carried it for a long time."

"As for Adam's," Patterson said. "You can decide for yourself how much remorse to spend on him."

After an awkward pause, Patterson continued: "But you've got the ability, all right. And since you and I are the only ones that do, and since I'm not going to be around forever, if you're willing we can kick-start things a bit. Your life is about to start getting even more interesting."

At that point, as if on cue, May and Rich Barlow excused themselves from the room, leaving Tim and Patterson alone. Tim stood up as they left, but when the door closed, Patterson motioned for the younger man to sit down again. "If it's okay with you," he said, "I've asked Rich to temporarily reassign you to one of RDG's outside sales offices for a couple of weeks, so that no one will notice that you're out of the office for a while. I've got a problem on my hands and I've got a favor to ask of you. And I think it'll start off your training with a bang."

Patterson's phrasing reminded Tim of their first conversation, when he first stepped off the brink of the familiar, into the unknown, strictly on his faith in the older man. Once again, Tim watched Ron's eyes and began to feel a strengthening and a confidence. It warmed him inside, but then he realized what was happening. Tim reached, squeezed Ron's arm firmly and said, "Stop it, Ron. You don't need to. Tell me what I need to know, and I'll listen. But don't try to control me."

During the next forty-five minutes Patterson gave Tim a detailed briefing about the Committee's origins and goals, the structure of their business holdings, and their absolute need for secrecy. Finally, he told Tim what he had learned about Gorman and John Ferrel's "project" in Haiti. Tim was shocked. "These are friends of yours?" he quizzed Patterson, members of your Committee? Then he asked, "Why not just call in Washington or the local Haitian police? I'm sure the DEA, or CIA has contacts there. They could pick up the doctor and get rid of the drugs."

"The problem," replied Patterson, "is that if there's an investigation, and we all know there would be one, the path of that investigation could lead directly to the Committee. That would be a serious problem." The facts raised his suspicions about the Committee, and frankly about Patterson as well, but after a moment Tim nodded that he understood, and asked Patterson what he had in mind.

"I would like for you to deliver a package for me."

The next evening, Saturday, after Tim finished moving into his new apartment, Patterson joined him there and produced a passport under the name of Bill Morris, but with Tim's picture on it. Tim could only guess how the older man had come by it as quickly as he had. "You'll need to show this to customs, both when you arrive and when you leave. But don't worry," Patterson assured his young friend, watching Tim eye the document suspiciously, "it's perfectly legal, just don't carry your real driver's license with you."

Then Patterson reached into his coat pocket and produced what looked to Tim like an average pencil box that any school child might carry. When he carefully opened the box, Tim saw two dull metallic cylinders inside. With Tim watching, Patterson lifted the two pieces of the bomb up and showed him where the pieces could be attached. Then he showed Tim a red button on the side. "All we need you to do Tim, is to fly to Haiti, and find the lab of a doctor named Coleman. We have the address the equipment was sent to, so finding the place should not be hard." Tim was still listening quietly, thinking but not commenting. "Then you need to get access to the crates, put this bomb inside, and push the red button, and make sure you leave the island the same day."

At 9:57 Sunday morning, "Bill Morris" boarded a plane for Miami, which was followed by another flight bound for Port-au-Prince, Haiti. The flight was smooth and Tim's mission was simple. The first shipment of altered drugs was to be picked up at Coleman's lab Tuesday morning, hidden inside machinery destined for Miami. Tim's assignment was to go to the lab, place the contents of Patterson's pencil box inside the machine to be shipped, and then be well out of Haiti within twenty-four hours. Twenty-four hours after he visited Doctor Coleman's lab, the ship carrying the altered heroin would explode and sink in international waters.

"No problem," he chuckled to himself.

Patterson had furnished Tim with dossiers on John Ferrel and Arthur, but the bulk of the information he was given concerned the scientist, Doctor Richard Coleman. The doctor had earned two Ph.D.'s in addition to his MD, and in the course of doing so, had published dozens of articles. As for any form of a personal life, there was very little. He had a sister living in Athens Georgia, but there was no indication that she and Coleman had remained very close. Tim surmised that the doctor had probably let his work dominate both his time and his life, and that was too bad.

It was Sunday afternoon, at twenty past three local time, when the airline's captain welcomed Bill Morris and his fellow passengers to Port-au-Prince, and quaintly provincial Haiti. As they walked down the ramp, the heat seemed to encase them like a humid cocoon. The air was thick, and in minutes his clothes were as damp as if he had just left a sauna. Flashing his passport to a local official, who seemed far more interested in the legs of a woman standing at the ticket counter than in anything Tim might be carrying, he found a taxi and asked to be taken to one of the city's larger hotels.

"I don't really care which one," he told the driver. "Just as long as it's air conditioned and has good beds."

The cabby smiled overly broadly at his new fare, and assured him that "I know just the one you want." As it turned out, he was right. The room was perfect, and Tim hoped the tip he had given the man had been large enough.

From Coleman's dossier, which did include delivery instructions for some very scientific sounding equipment, Tim knew where he would find the lab, just outside a dot on the northern coast named Monte-Cristi.

Chapter Twenty Eight

Monday morning in Port-au-Prince was not unlike Monday mornings anywhere. They always come too early. And for Tim, who had just adjusted again to west coast time, it felt like he had just gone to sleep when the sun, and noise from the street below, woke him. Rising slowly and trying to make his brain function, he showered and shaved, then went down the elevator to the hotel's restaurant. His stomach queasy, and in no shape for bacon and eggs, this morning orange juice and toast would do nicely.

At nine o'clock, Tim went out through the hotel's main door. The doorman, dressed in a brightly bleached white uniform with gold buttons, asked him if he needed a cab. When he answered that he did, the man lifted one gloved hand into the air and a cab appeared from behind the building. It was hard to understand what he was saying, but the driver of the cab was either a relation or a friend of the man who had driven him from the airport the day before, and judging by how happy the man was to have him in his cab, the tip he had worried about must have been more than adequate.

"Good morning, sir" the driver said, smiling. "Where would you like to go?"

"Monte-Cristi, if you don't mind going that far," Tim replied. "I'd like to take a quick tour of the city."

The cab driver smiled and replied that the road there was bad in spots and that a quick tour of Monte-Cristi was all there was. "But I'll get you there, and I'll get you back," he assured Tim. And again, he smiled.

Port-au-Prince is the capital and the largest city in Haiti, but even there the conditions the people lived under were harsh. The nicer areas, perched high on the hillsides, were set aside for the rich and those with political power. The poor were allowed to infest what was left. Tourism, however, was a main source of hard currency for the government, and outside the inner circle of palaces and state-built monuments, they had made attempts to hide the signs of poverty from visitors. Still, thin and without purpose, the look of hunger and want on the faces of the people, particularly the children, was unmistakable.

The "highway" between Port-au-Prince and Monte-Cristi was far longer than Tim would have liked, particularly since the cab was not air-conditioned. Small settlements dotted the roadside, but he couldn't remember seeing any people there. Meanwhile, the driver began conversation after conversation about life in America, and how he had relatives who lived in Miami, but Tim had become Bill Morris to end a trail, should he need to, and chats with the cabby about life back home were out of the question. The day was getting hotter, and they drove on with all the windows down, but after what felt like a very long and bumpy drive, the cab eventually passed a sign welcoming them to Monte-Cristi.

"I'm looking for a new building on the outskirts of town," Tim said to his driver. "It has to be wired for extra electricity, and probably for a telephone, also."

The cabby was correct in that a complete tour of Monte-Cristi did not take as long as the drive they took to get there. As Tim and the cab driver followed the equipment delivery instructions Patterson had provided, they found themselves approaching what must have been the newest building in town. Dome shaped and made completely out of shiny heat reflective aluminum, the building was set a long ways off any well-traveled road, but it was unmistakably the lab that Tim was looking for. The driver slowed the cab as they approached and he had nearly stopped before Tim could tell him to keep going. "No, don't stop," he shouted, a bit panicky. "I just wanted to see where he was." Tim thought for a moment before he went on. "In the states," he said. "It's considered very rude to just drop by on people, without calling them first."

That anyone would drive all the way to Monte-Cristi to see a friend and then not stop when they arrived made no sense at all to the cabby. He rolled his eyes and shrugged his shoulders, but he continued driving past the new building. Then Tim said he wanted to go back to his hotel. When they returned, Tim gave the man a slightly larger tip than he had given yesterday's driver, and again the man smiled broadly. "Thank you, sir" the driver said. "Maybe you want to go someplace else tomorrow?"

"After I call my friend, I may want to go back tonight," was Tim's reply. "Can you be available around eight o'clock?"

As he walked through the main door of the hotel and into the lobby, a blast of cool air-conditioned air sent a wonderful chill down Tim's spine. As he continued on, the desk where he had registered stood directly ahead of him, and at one end there was a phone that he was sure he would be allowed to use. The hotel's bar was to his left, and Tim was sure there would also be a phone in there. Two additional phones sat on small tables at opposite corners of the lobby. However, not knowing how the phone system worked in Haiti, whether it was different from what he knew at home or not, Tim asked one of the men behind the desk to help him. "Excuse me," he said to an older man who seemed to be in charge. "I'm Bill Morris and I'm staying up in room three twenty-one."

The man behind the desk literally snapped to attention on being spoken to. He smiled and listened intently as Tim continued. "I have an old army buddy who lives up in Monte-Cristi. And I want to call him, but I don't have his phone number. Can you give me a hand trying to get it? His name is Coleman, Doctor Richard Coleman. And, to make things worse, it's probably a relatively new number."

The man behind the desk clicked his heels and said he could have the information in ten minutes, if that would be satisfactory. Tim smiled his biggest "hick town American" smile and patted the man on his shoulder. "Ten minutes would be fine, son" he said. "In fact, I'll just wait for you over in the bar. Ten minutes, you said."

In exactly eight minutes, one of the younger men from behind the registration desk entered the bar and handed Tim a slip of paper with the hotel's logo on it, along with a hand-written telephone number. "Your number, sir," the young man said. "with our complements."

Once again Tim made sure to over tip for the service rendered, and to send thanks back to the older man. Then, using one of the phones in the bar, he called Dr. Coleman and surprisingly, the doctor answered.

"Dr. Coleman," Tim began. "Who I am doesn't matter, but that I know about the heroin and the shit you're mixing with it, should tell you who I know." Coleman didn't answer. Tim went on. "About ten o'clock tonight, you'll get a visit from a mutual friend of mine and of your American boss. He'll be there to check the machinery that's going to Miami tomorrow. For your part, make sure the shipment is loaded and ready to inspect. Once the load is examined, he'll seal it. From that point on, leave it alone until we come for it."

The doctor, not knowing what to say or do, remained silent. Then, as suddenly as the phone had rang, it went dead.

"Sam Junior" had briefed him on what would happen, but there was no mention of anyone else examining the cargo before they put it on the ship. He could have just forgotten. Coleman, however, was realistic enough to know that his part of the plan had been accomplished, and he could be seen as a loose end that needed clearing up. But why would anybody call him if they were sending over someone to kill him?

Opening up the top drawer of his desk, Coleman reached inside and took out the .45 pistol that he had purchased on a trip to Port-au-Prince. At the time he considered buying the gun a heroic gesture. Somehow though, he never thought about having to use the weapon to defend himself. But again, if they meant to kill him why would they have called to tell him about it? Coleman returned the pistol to the drawer, sat down in his chair, and laughed at his own foolishness.

"The man they're sending to examine the load is probably well experienced and doesn't want to be shot dead by a hysterical novice."

A moment later, though, Coleman removed the pistol from the drawer again, made sure it was loaded, and pushed the weapon into his waistband. With his lab coat on it would be hard to notice.

Chapter Twenty Nine

By nine fifteen, Tim had taken another shower, dressed in his "interview" outfit, and made his way to where his cab driver was waiting for him. "Good evening, sir," the man said. "We are returning to see your friend?" Tim just nodded and climbed into the cab. The suffocating heat of the day had gone, leaving behind it a sea breeze, not really cooling, but better. Tim was now more concerned about getting his clothes dirty from the road, than he was about the heat, so he rolled his windows up for the ride. He practiced what he planned to say to Dr. Coleman, and how that conversation might go. "If he says this, then I'll say that." He said to himself, and laughed aloud at himself. The driver heard him, but said nothing.

From the place at the side of the road where Tim got out and left his driver and the cab, there remained roughly a half mile's walk to Coleman's lab. After thinking about an evening spent alone in the dark, the driver offered to come along, but Tim refused, commenting that his old friend's "surprise" would be most effective if he appeared, smiling and alone, "as if by magic." In addition, holding the pencil box in his left hand as he closed the car door with his right, Tim looked the part of a suitor. Disappointed, the driver agreed to wait as directed. Tim added: "If I get lucky, I'll be back in about an hour, but I might be longer. Just be ready to leave when you see me."

The driver hesitated briefly, then smiled broadly again as if he suddenly realized what was going on. Tim's "old friend" might actually be a woman. And she might be someone else's woman. He winked at the young American and responded: "Take your time my friend, and don't worry. I'll be here, ready to go when you've finished." As the cabby's aura lightened dramatically from his normal green, Tim nodded, dropped the subject, and walked away.

The contrast between the heat of the day and the relative cool of the night actually felt refreshing on his skin as he walked the half mile, and reminded Tim of hot summer days followed by cooler nights he'd spent at home. Tonight, however, as he walked along the dirt road, home seemed a very long distance from Haiti, and the "favor" he was about to perform for Ron Patterson was something he had never learned there. A chill ran up Tim's spine that he wanted to believe was caused by the change in temperature.

Again, and again, Tim reviewed what he was about to do. The cab had been too loud and too visible, so he left it in the dark. Coleman would be expecting him, but he'd watch the place for a while in case someone else was waiting, also. Then, if things "felt" right, he would make contact with the doctor, plant the bomb, and get out. Hopefully the picture in the doctor's dossier was recent enough for a good identification, and hopefully too, the doctor would behave himself. But, what if Coleman decided to be a "tough guy", and do something stupid? Tim's answer was that Coleman needed to feel completely intimidated, and he thought he could make that happen.

After a bit more walking and some additional games of "if he says this, then I'll say that", Tim looked ahead and saw lights coming from the lab. Immediately crouching behind a tall dried bush, he listened and watched for any sign of danger. Actually, nothing looked out of place, but a quiet alarm sounded again in his head. Staying low, but moving away from the road, Tim made his way around to the back of the building until he saw the other man.

"There you are," he thought to himself. "And just who might you be?"

The form, crouched behind a bush in the dark, appeared to be a local, probably paid by whoever was transporting the drugs tomorrow to watch the doctor prior to the shipment. Tim thought the practice made sense, and that he would probably do the same thing in their business. But for now, the man's being there presented a problem.

Dark skinned, slender and nervous, twitching as he tried to keep himself hidden, maybe the man was an addict and this was how he earned his "wages". Maybe not. Maybe he just liked sitting in the dark by himself. Either way, he was a problem that had to be solved.

Image by image, Tim began to think about everything he had ever heard or read about, concerning Voodoo. He pictured strange looking dolls and chanting witch doctors. At the same time, he mentally conjured up images of deep-seated fear. Tim watched the man sit there trembling, and he began to manufacture a feeling of dread within himself. Moments later, the Haitian's aura changed fearfully dark, then he screamed, his arms flailing, as he ran into the night. For the next few minutes, Tim rested and waited, wanting to make sure that there were no other watchmen.

Tim listened as the man's voice faded, and he looked at his watch. An hour passed uneventfully. Sure, that he was alone again, Tim concentrated on clearing his mind. When they met, he didn't want Doctor Richard Coleman to feel fear. That would not help. He wanted the man intimidated. Coleman still had to get the shipment on board the ship, and if he appeared too frightened the smugglers might get nervous themselves, and drop the whole deal. No, the doctor needed to be handled delicately.

Moving again as quietly as he could, Tim reached the front door of the lab. However, before knocking, he began to think of movie figures such as Humphrey Bogart and James Cagney, who nobody ever dared "mess with." After all, wasn't that the situation he wanted to create with Coleman? Didn't he want the doctor to think of him as too dangerous to "cross"? But how dangerous? The image of an assassin, both dangerous and silent, popped into his mind, and Tim liked it. At the last minute, though, he realized that his plan was backwards. If he transferred a dangerous image to Coleman, the doctor could become aggressive himself. Couldn't he? And that could be a serious problem. He wanted the man docile. Then again, maybe docile wasn't what he wanted either. Perhaps what he really wanted was for the doctor to be awestruck by him, the same way he always felt about Casey. Tim chuckled to himself because, in truth, he did idolize his brother and he would do almost anything for him. "And Casey could do it with no help from Patterson," he smiled.

Carefully, Tim placed the pencil box in the back pocket of his pants, again focusing his thoughts and concentrating on exactly what it felt like to be awestruck, trying to achieve a pure picture of what it was like before laying eyes on his target. Once he had the images in mind, he tried to send them through the closed door. The attempt was successful.

"Doctor Coleman," Tim began as the door opened. "I believe you're expecting me."

At the rear of the lab there was a collection of large crates, equipment that had been crated, and carefully packed for shipment. Tim could see it from the door, yet before entering, he wanted to see more. He did notice something else, too. There was a bulge under Coleman's lab coat that might have been a gun. The doctor's mannerisms, however, were far from threatening. Opening the door and almost dragging Tim inside, Coleman closed it again quickly, peering out through the nearest window in case his young visitor had been followed. "You can't be too sure," he said, smiling nervously, tentatively offering his hand. "I'm Richard Coleman, and yes, I've been waiting for you."

As they shook hands, Tim looked slowly around the room again and noticed the security tape control box, and he wondered if there had been an outside camera. "How many cameras?" he asked, releasing the other man's hand.

The doctor thought for a moment and answered: "Just two, one filmed you as you approached the door. It's on a motion sensor, and this one here in the corner." Coleman pointed to a small black box suspended from the ceiling that Tim had missed seeing.

"Turn them off at the control box, and bring me tonight's tapes."

As Coleman walked over to the security box, Tim projected to the doctor's mind the strongest mixture of awe and fear that he could muster. Then, when the doctor brought him the tape, he said: "Why don't you give me the gun too, doctor? Or do you think you'll need it tonight?"

Surprised that his visitor had noticed the weapon, Coleman laughed as if embarrassed and he smiled. "No," he replied. "It's just that I didn't know what to expect. And I didn't want any trouble."

Tim had maintained eye contact with Coleman since asking for the gun. Now, as the doctor stood there, his aura flashed, and his mouth formed an embarrassed grin. He offered Tim the gun, Tim took it and placed it, out of reach, on one of the lab benches.

"Can I get you a drink?" the doctor offered.

After considering for a moment, Tim declined. Coleman seemed disappointed, then he too abstained. Since the doctor was no immediate threat, Tim turned his attention back to the shipping crates. There were at least twelve of them and he wondered how many contained the altered heroin. "I'll tell you what I would like for you to do, doctor" Tim began and Coleman waited anxiously. "First, I want you to point out for me which of these boxes have our "product" inside. Then, I'd like for you to begin telling me all about your family, and what it was like growing up around your house."

Coleman didn't understand, but remained quiet. Tim continued: "As you do that," he said. "I'd like for you to go just outside the door there, keeping your eyes away from this room, and continue talking loud enough for me to hear what you're saying. Can you do that?"

The doctor had wanted to be a "partner" in what was happening, but before objecting to Tim's request, he thought the better of it. Tim could be dangerous. This pleasant looking young man was probably a cold blooded killer, and he had certainly been involved in this kind of situation hundreds of times before. Yeah, he liked the kid, but he didn't want to wind up dead. And charm, without violence, probably didn't go far in the drug trade. "Sure," he replied. "I could do that. Or I could do anything else you want me to."

"That's okay," Tim responded calmly. "Tonight's just a preliminary check. Tomorrow the real work begins when the crew comes and hauls it all away. I'm just here tonight to keep everybody honest."

Impressed with the young man's outward calmness, and knowing that it only mattered that he was heard saying something, the doctor began his assignment with a brief description of who his parents had been and the kind of relationship they shared. As Tim nodded and motioned for Coleman to continue. The doctor kept talking and walked outside, closing the lab door behind him. "Can you hear me?" he asked.

"Yeah, fine" was Tim's reply. "Just keep talking" And he did.

The impression Tim wanted to leave was that he was taking a random sample that could be checked now and verified again on the other side. That part of the fiction accomplished, what he wanted was to plant the bomb and get off the island.

Listening only enough to be sure of the doctor's position, Tim moved directly to the crates Coleman had pointed out. Then, looking around the lab, he saw a small crowbar he could use. Opening the first one, which measured about five feet wide and four feet high, he found that the crate actually did hold a piece of lab equipment, the back of which had been opened and the drugs loaded inside. It wouldn't look right if Coleman thought he hadn't known what to expect, so Tim didn't ask any more questions nor make any comments. He did notice, however, that the doctor had stopped talking.

"Are you all right, in there?" he heard.

"Yeah, I'm fine. Keep talking."

Coleman continued as he was told, and Tim decided to open a

second crate, which would carry the bomb. This one was a slightly smaller box than the first one, and it contained a machine with lights that probably flashed and buttons to push, but he had no idea of what it might be used for. On the other hand, since his goal was to spread the boxes and their contents over the bottom of the Caribbean, it didn't really matter, did it?

Next to where Tim had found the crowbar, there was also a Philips head screwdriver that he could use to reopen the back of the crated machine. As he pulled away the panel, a plastic bag of heroin and some cardboard used for packing dropped to the floor next to his foot. In a strange way, it startled Tim how ordinary the bag looked. This was heroin, after all. People died using the normal type, and this stuff had been specially designed to kill. Still it looked like powdered milk. Tim replaced the bag inside the machine and looked within it for a place to attach the bomb.

Even though Patterson had described how to activate the bomb's timer, Tim had never actually taken the cylinders out of the pencil box. As he did now, he noticed first that both pieces were actually made of plastic. And on each end, there were thin metal straps that could be used to attach it and prevent the bomb from falling, maybe exploding too soon. Tim thought about his mentor and somehow wasn't surprised. Gently slipping the two cylinders together, he felt a click. Then he tied the metal strips around a metal base structure inside the machine, and gave it a little tug to be sure it would stay put. He thought it would. Then Tim pressed his finger against the red button. Finished, Tim reattached the back panel of the machine, and used the crowbar to reseal both of the shipping containers. "Doctor Coleman," he shouted. "You can come back inside now. This part of my job is done. The next step for me is in Miami."

Coleman looked at the packaging material that had fallen out of the crates, and it surprised him that more care hadn't been taken. In the end, though, he decided that once the crates were gone from his custody, it was not his problem.

"You can do me a big favor, though, doctor" Tim said as he left the building. "When the men come tomorrow to move the shipment, you can remember that I was not here tonight. Tell them what you like about the Haitian and what happened to the tape, but leave my visit out of it." Tim concentrated on the doctor again and added: "You don't want to see me again, doctor. You really don't."

Once again, the doctor's aura which had reverted to a normal green, now flashed again, and the smile on his face faded away.

"Don't worry," he said, with a nervous laugh. "I was alone tonight, wasn't I?"

As Tim walked swiftly into view, the cabdriver looked at his watch to see how long it had been. Not much more than an hour and a half had passed, and the young man had returned, probably not a good sign. Perhaps the young man's "friend" was not as willing as he had hoped. The driver also noticed that Tim no longer carried the pencil box and he hoped, for his sake, that the gift had not been an expensive one.

Tim looked serious, but not sad as he climbed into the back seat of the cab, saying only: "Let's get back to the hotel."

The driver, thinking that the pain of rejected love is something that each person must learn to carry by themselves, elected not to console the young man. In the end, neither of them spokes until Tim got out, paid the driver another large tip, and went inside to his room.

"It's a shame, sometimes" the driver mused to himself as he pushed the money into his shirt pocket and drove away.

At seven forty-five Tuesday morning, a tired looking Bill Morris checked out of the hotel and boarded the nine fourteen Panamanian Airlines flight to Miami. Patterson would be watching flights into San Jose for the next few days and he would call Tim the following morning at his apartment.

At shortly after ten o'clock, Doctor Richard Coleman began looking out through the front window of his lab, expecting an unknown someone to come for the shipment. Junior had only said to expect them "late in the morning" and he never said anything about who they might be. Still, Coleman had to admit feeling a certain excitement at being so closely involved in a criminal behavior and with actual drug smugglers. Just before eleven, a large, slightly battered moving van rolled to a halt on the road in front of the lab. At first, as Coleman remained inside watching through his window, no one stirred from the vehicle. Then, one lone figure emerged from the cab.

The Doctor stayed where he was, continuing to watch. His visitor, who looked to be neither Haitian nor Spanish and who Coleman thought might be Portuguese, walked around the van, listening and watching, as if he expected trouble.

"A cautious fellow," Coleman whispered to himself. "That's probably good."

After a few more minutes though, the man approached. Coleman came to the door before he knocked, and said: "Good morning, I've been expecting you."

As if expecting a trap, Coleman's Portuguese visitor drew a pistol from his belt and pointed it at the doctor, motioning for him to step outside into the sunlight. The doctor thought he understood the other man's concern and did what he was asked. Holding up his hands to show that he had no intention of resisting, Coleman pointed inside to the boxes in the lab and said: "There's no one else around, and your crates are ready to go."

The Portuguese, still holding the pistol ready to use, pointed the weapon inside, then stepped into the lab, himself. He immediately noticed the empty control box for the security cameras. Coleman followed him inside, saw what the man was looking at and reassured him: "That's empty, and hasn't been used in a couple of days."

The lie was believable enough, with the control box laying open. The man nodded his understanding, yet he held his gun ready and walked over to the crates, inspecting a few at random as to size and approximate weight. Coleman approached the crates himself, hoping his visitor had made arrangements for some additional help and perhaps some equipment to load the crates onto the truck. When he got within five feet of the crates, the Portuguese looked up from the crate he was checking and pointed the pistol at him. "There is obviously no one else here to cause trouble," the big man began. "And the crates are ready to set sail. You have made this step of our business very easy. I thank you."

Coleman smiled, feeling like an accepted co-conspirator, and he shrugged his shoulders as if to say "any time, my friend." It shocked him when he saw the Portuguese pull the trigger of the gun and as he felt the bullet enter his chest. He fell to the floor like a rag doll and died.

The man with the gun fired again, this time into the Doctor's forehead. The second shot was also a signal that brought another car into sight, loaded with very large, strong looking men. At the same time, the rear door of the van opened and three other men began to bring out equipment for moving the crates. Within twenty minutes of their arrival, the men had loaded the crates into the van and were on their way to the loading dock. By twelve o' clock, the crates had been loaded onto a chartered Greek freighter whose eventual destination was Florida. At eleven o'clock that night, however, a large explosion rocked the vessel, blowing a large hole in the hull, and sinking it out at sea. Three crewmen were lost, but the Portuguese captain was never questioned about the death of the American doctor. But then, neither were there ever reports of large numbers of heroin addicts mysteriously dying.

Tim's first assignment had been a success.

Wednesday, when Tim arrived at his apartment, around five thirty west coast time, he unpacked, went straight to bed, and got a good night's sleep. He would call Shelly tomorrow. At nine thirty Thursday morning, though, before he woke up, his phone rang. "Tim," came Patterson's voice through the receiver. "How are you feeling?"

"I'm fine, Ron." he replied. "Did everything work out?" Patterson paused for a moment, and then said: "Well, Tuesday night the Coast Guard reported rescuing the captain and crew of a burning freighter, bound for Miami. There were casualties, and the ship's cargo was a total loss." "Gee, that's too bad." Tim said sarcastically. "But what do we do when Coleman's ready with his next batch. My little act won't work twice."

"Well, that's the other piece of news, Tim. Somebody killed Doctor Coleman yesterday. Shot him in the head."

Stunned as the danger of his trip to Haiti dawned on him. "It wasn't me," he said, immediately. "Monday night, when I left him he was fine."

"Oh, I know, Tim." Patterson quickly replied. "Coleman was shot Tuesday, late in the morning or early in the afternoon. You were on your way home by then. No, the people handling the drugs probably got wind of something fishy, and decided that the doctor was too much of a risk. I was relieved though, to see your name on the passenger list, arriving in San Jose."

"Funny," Tim said, primarily to himself. "I was afraid I might get arrested, either when I was carrying the bomb or when I was at the lab. And I was concerned about the bomb going off early. But I never thought about getting shot."

"Tim," said Patterson. "Even with our advantage, when we deal with dangerous people, there's always a chance of getting hurt or even killed. You should think about that before you say you want to continue."

"Ron," he replied. "I could have gotten just as dead if my plane had crashed when I was coming home, and I do want to continue."

"Good, son, because we still have to deal with the two who began this whole mess. And that's on tap for this evening around seven o'clock, if you're game. I'll come by your place at about six and we'll meet them, just south of San Francisco, at about seven thirty."

"But what are we going to do when we get there?"

"Well, you'll give them a play by play description of what you've been up to over the past few days, and when I tell you to, I want you to clear your mind of everything, just let it go blank."

"Go blank?" He said to Patterson. "What's that going to do?" Patterson paused over the phone, and Tim could almost see him, smiling his Cheshire Cat smile. "Just that, Tim. Just that."

"And then what?" Tim asked.

"Then," Patterson replied. "If everything goes right, you'll learn something. Anyway, you should probably wear you interviewing clothes if you can. I want to keep our meeting with them fairly formal. Okay?"

"Okay." Tim hung up the phone and hoped his blue jacket was still in wearable condition. It was.

At five thirty, Tim was dressed to go, and Patterson knocked on his door precisely at six. Tonight, though, Patterson seemed a bit more preoccupied than usual, even sad. Tim could not see his aura so it was difficult to tell what was on his mind.

Ron had a duffel bag with him when he came to Tim's door, and as they left he threw it in the rear seat of Tim's car. They spoke very little on the drive toward San Francisco. Ron seemed distant, as if trying to stay focused. Tim drove north on Highway 101, and through an industrial area south of the city. Finally, he was instructed to park the car in the "Employees Only" lot, outside a small office building. Another car, a white Lincoln Continental, was already there.

Ron lead the way, as they got out of their car and approached the building. Just before he opened the door, though, he turned to Tim and said: "I am going to ask you to tell your Haiti story, and when you're telling it, try to draw it out as long as you can, leaving nothing, not even the tiniest detail out. And, also try to keep your voice in a monotone. That will help."

Not knowing what else to say or do, Tim nodded that he understood, though he really didn't.

As they entered the building, down a long hallway and to their left was the meeting room where the other two men were waiting. When Tim and Ron entered the room, the others stood up and greeted them at the door. One of them was an elderly man, about the same age as Patterson but who did not look quite as healthy. The other man was not more than a few years or so older than Tim.

"So, this must be young Tim Conolly," Arthur shook his hand, not waiting to be introduced. "I've heard a lot of good things about you, and I'm glad to finally get the chance to meet you." Then he turned to Ferrel. "This is John Ferrel," he said. "He's another friend of ours."

Standing just inside the doorway, Arthur turned to Patterson and asked, "So Ron, what's so all important that you had to get us up here in the middle of the night?"

After a moment's pause, Ron answered: "Arthur, we know what you two, along with Doctor Richard Coleman, have been up to, distributing poisoned heroin."

Neither of the two men answered, nor denied what Patterson had said, so he continued: "Yesterday, the drug smugglers who you made arrangements with apparently killed Doctor Coleman. Shot him through the head. Whether you told them to do it or not, I don't know. I only know that he's dead. Tim here, though, went down to Haiti and stopped the whole process, by placing a bomb inside the crates and blowing a hole in the bottom of the ship before it got to Miami. Now I would like for you two to sit here quietly, and I would like Tim to tell you, in detail, how he went about doing it. Tim... "

Before Tim began speaking, Arthur took a pistol from a holster on his waistband and held it to Tim's temple. "Not so fast young man," he said. "What we did, we did for the general good. And that's what the Committee is for."

Patterson calmly stepped forward, closer to Tim, placing the flat palm of his hand on the young man's arm, and Tim felt himself calming down. Mentally fighting his fear, controlling his own emotions, Patterson watched Arthur's trembling hand holding the gun, and the older man's aura as it began to appear. With his free hand, Patterson motioned for Ferrel to sit down on a nearby chair and the younger man did so.

Returning his full attention to Arthur, Ron spoke softly. "The Committee has never been about killing, Arthur. You know that."

Vividly aware of the gun barrel pressed against his head, Tim felt Arthurs' aura changing. Patterson could see it turn from blue to dark green, and then a paler green. Applying a gentle pressure on

Tim's arm he said, "Go on, son" and Tim began to unfold each step of his adventure to Haiti. Deliberately slow and methodical, and not leaving anything out, Tim tried to ignore the cold metal pointed at his forehead. He added some commentary along the way, and he droned on with the story. At first, Arthur appeared to willingly listen, and his aura grew calmer, lighter. From a pale green, to an almost clear shimmering of light. Ron said, "now go blank, son." And Tim cleared his mind.

Arthur's hand lost its tremble, and the gun fell to the floor as his body slumped. Surprised, yet instinctively, Tim reached out and caught the older man, holding him up and looking behind himself to Patterson, who sadly said. "Lay him down gently, it's ok."

When Arthur was safely face down on the floor, Ron directed Tim's attention to John Ferrel. From his chair, Ferrel darted for the door, but Tim moved quicker, caught Ferrel around his waist, and tackled him to the ground out in the hallway. After a momentary tussle between the two younger men, Tim secured Ferrel's arms behind him and held him steady. Patterson walked up behind them, touched the back of Ferrel's head, and said softly, "Go on Tim, you were going to Monte Christi."

But Ferrel was stronger than Arthur had been, and as Tim began to describe his first cab ride to Monte Christi, he struggled a bit. After a moment, though, he rested his head on the floor and ceased his resistance. "I'm sorry," he whispered. Patterson leaned over the young man and continued his concentration. And finally, he closed his eyes. That was when Patterson told Tim to once again "Go Blank" and he did. The hallway was dark, and Tim could not see Ferrel's aura, but he felt the man go completely limp. Tim stopped his mental exercise and looked to Ron for an explanation. Ron was visibly shaken. "Tim," he said. "Would you go out to the car, get that duffel bag, and bring it back in here?"

By the time he returned, Ron seemed to have recovered a bit and he explained what had happened. "Neither of those two have any family around, so it's unlikely they ever told anybody about their involvement with the Committee. Even Arthur, who started the whole thing to begin with, would never have said anything about it. What I've done, or what we have done here tonight is to completely erase their memories. They're not physically hurt, but when they wake up, neither of them will remember his name, or where they came from, let alone anything about the Committee." Tim remained quiet.

"We'll change them out of their clothes, and dress them in the clothes from the bag. I've removed all the labels. We'll take their drivers licenses, and any other ID they have, and we'll deposit one of them at the San Francisco Police department and the other one down in San Jose. I've made some other arrangements so that, when the police do finally identify who they are, all they'll find is a good deal of money, in various accounts, and nothing about what they've been doing with their lives."

Tim asked Ron, "Arthur knew what was happening, didn't he?"

Patterson stopped for a moment, and nodded: "Yes, he did. He knew." Then after a pause he said. "It's a shame about Ferrel, though. I think he could have done well. But now the Committee is short two members."

Looking to Tim, the older man said, "I'm assuming you're with us." And it was Tim's turn to smile and nod.

Chapter Thirty One

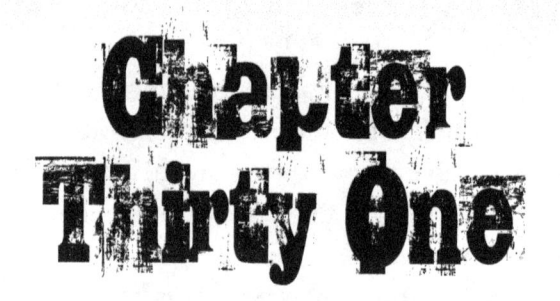

EPILOGUE

By 1986, Mary Margaret and Greg had delivered their last child, a red-haired cherub, their "oops baby", named Becky. Casey remained in the Navy, reached the rank of Master Chief, and looked forward to retirement. Tim had a collection of Post Cards from places he traveled to. Patrick married his girlfriend from Longstown, but it didn't last. Two years later, they divorced, no kids. He moved back in with Da, and the situation seemed to suit everyone. Tim married Shelly a year to the day after he returned from Haiti. They had two children, Thomas and Katie, and they moved to the affluent northern California town of Menlo Park.

In 1988, "The Boy Wonder of RDG" still used the clear glass desk that Patterson had ordered made and delivered to his office two years earlier, on the day when NOSCO was spun off from RDG and Tim became its CEO. The old man said that the desk reminded him of Tim's management style. "Nothing's hidden or forgotten," he said. "And it always functions best when it's uncluttered."

That day, though, May Fong had called to tell Tim that Ron Patterson had been hospitalized.

"Which hospital is he in?"

Patterson had seemed old to Tim the first time he had laid eyes on him. That was almost fifteen years ago. More recently, there had been bouts of this or that slight illness, but the old guy always seemed to bounce back and to be just as lively as ever. And they had shared a lot of time together in recent years, traveling for the Committee. The tone of May's voice, though, was now very different. "They moved him up to Stanford last night," he said. "This time it's his heart. The dirty old man probably saw the backside of some cute young thing, and it was more than he could handle."

They both chuckled at the thought of what May had said, and because they both knew that it was at least possibly true.

After thanking her for calling, and then hanging up the phone, Tim picked up the receiver again and called Stanford Hospital. After initially making contact with the main operator, he was connected directly to the nurse's station in the intensive care ward. "We are not allowed to give out information on patients over the phone," he was told by the nurse manning the station. "However, if you would like to leave a message for his doctor, she could call you back."

"Could we do that, please?" Tim asked her.

"Mr. Patterson's primary care physician is Doctor Nora Schultz. I'll leave her your message."

Tim gave the nurse his telephone number and he thanked her for being so helpful. Within an hour, his secretary had a call for him from Stanford.

"Mr. Conolly," the voice on the other end began. "I'm Nora Schultz, Mr. Patterson's doctor. Are you a member of Mr. Patterson's family?"

"No, doctor," he said. "We're very close, but to my knowledge, he doesn't have any family."

The line was quiet for a moment, but then Doctor Schultz seemed to get a little upset with him. "Well, I don't know how close you are to the patient, but I've got calls here from at least six people who claim to be his nieces and nephews. One of them gave her name as May Fong. Is she not a relative?"

Tim smiled and then tried to cover his mistake. "Oh," he said trying to be as convincing as he could. "I'm sorry. Yeah, they're all related. But can you tell me anything about his condition?"

Doctor Schultz chose her words very carefully, then she replied that she "was telling all family members that Mr. Patterson is very ill. And if they were going to visit him, it should probably be sooner than later."

"Often times," she continued. "Patients with these symptoms do not survive very long."

Tim put down the phone again and tried to think clearly. Then he walked to his office door and asked his secretary to clear his calendar for the remainder of the afternoon. "A close friend of mine is in Stanford. I'll let you know more as soon as I can."

Finding his way to the Stanford campus was easy enough, he just drove up Highway 101 and went west on Embarcadero. But once he entered the Stanford University campus, Tim turned left instead of right and found himself severely lost. Eventually he stopped and asked directions from a student who was riding a bicycle along the road. Even with directions, though, finding the Medical Center, as the student with the directions referred to it, was obviously not designed to be simple. But Tim persisted and eventually he found his way. Outside of the hospitals main building there were a group of older men, each wearing a blue smock. One of these men approached Tim's car and asked him what department he was looking for.

"Intensive care, I think." he replied. "A friend of mine was brought in for heart trouble."

"Well," the man told him. "Intensive care is on the second floor. You can park right over here." The man motioned to an open space, right up front. "If you have any trouble finding it when you get inside, just ask the woman at the information desk."

Stanford was touted as one of the premier hospitals in the United States, if not the world, but as he emerged through its doors, he tried to shake the memories that lingered from his mother's passing. Beneath a sign that read "Information" sat an older woman, who Tim assumed was a volunteer. He asked her to verify where his friend was being kept and, after calling up the information on the screen of a computer terminal, the woman told him.

"Mr. Patterson is still in Intensive Care. That's on the second floor. Just go down this hallway to your right and you'll see the elevator. Once you get to the second floor, you'll go through a set of double doors and the nurse's station is just inside. They can give you any other information you might need."

Tim thanked her, and followed her directions. Arriving at the nurses station, he identified himself as "a family member" and was directed into Patterson's room.

When Tim entered, he truly hoped the old man would look the way he always had. But this time it was different. Laying on the bed, perhaps sleeping, there was a clear plastic oxygen mask covering his nose and his mouth, and he was being given something intravenously into his arm. When Tim came in, Patterson opened his eyes and removed the mask. "Tim," he asked, sounding weak. "What the hell are you doing here?"

"Oh, I heard you were ducking your responsibilities again, and thought I'd come down and see how you were wasting your time."

Tim dropped the side rail on Patterson's bed, and sat down on the edge. "Seriously Ron," he asked. "How are they treating you?"

"Oh," the old man replied. "I'm okay. I just feel so damned tired, anymore. I guess my 'wild ways' are catching up with me." Patterson closed his eyes and seemed to drift off, then he reopened them again and completed his thought. "But I've had a good time." And he smiled.

Tim didn't have any idea of how much of Patterson's condition was due to his heart problem, or to the medication that the doctors had given him to combat it. As he sat there on the edge of the bed, though, Tim did have something that he wanted the old man to know. "You know Ron, you've made a huge difference in the way my life has panned out." he began. "And I don't know if I ever really thanked you for doing it."

The old man shook his head and closed his eyes, rejecting the whole notion.

"But there's something that I've never asked you about." Tim continued. "That night in Longstown, how did you know I wouldn't shoot Adams?"

"I didn't know." Patterson laughed, then coughed. Then he returned the oxygen mask to cover his mouth and nose. After a few deep breaths, he raised the mask just off his face, to a point where it would be somewhat effective, but where he could still be understood. "You were standing there with that damned gun in your hand, and you could have blown his head off. But you didn't. You stopped yourself. And stopping yourself wasn't easy, it took a good deal of courage and self control."

Tim remained seated, and Patterson relaxed again, adjusting the mask back into its correct position. After a few minutes, the old man took Tim's hand and he held it, saying: "Son, I was very proud of you that night, maybe for the first time. But, for what it's worth, I've also been proud of you ever since."

At nine fifty-seven that night, Ron Patterson died. According to his medical records, he had been ninety-eight years young, and Tim had seen to it that he was calm and relaxed when his time came. He patted his hand gently, but Tim could not bring himself to feel bad. Patterson had lived a good long time, and he had enjoyed the time he'd been given. In addition, he had done the world some good. On a side table, on a tray, was Patterson's watch, wallet and personal items. Tim slipped a green tipped key from a key ring, into his pocket. Turning to Patterson once more, and touching his hand again, he whispered "Good bye, my friend" and left the room.

Printed in the USA
CPSIA information can be obtained
at www.ICGtesting.com
LVHW091619291123
764808LV00066B/2369